Echoes
of
Darkness

The Síoraí Legacy

by

Victoria Noxon

This is a work of fiction. Names, characters, places, and incidents are either the product of the author's imagination or are used fictitiously, and any resemblance to actual persons living or dead, business establishments, events, or locales, is entirely coincidental.

Echoes of Darkness: The Síoraí Legacy

Cover Art by *Rae Monet, Inc. Design*

The Wild Rose Press
PO Box 706
Adams Basin, NY 14410-0706
Visit us at www.thewildrosepress.com

Publishing History
First Black Rose Edition, 2011
Print ISBN 1-60154-922-9

Published in the United States of America

His lips traveled from hers, leaving her mouth burning with fire. Trailing across her cheek, he stopped at her ear where he suckled the tender lobe. She felt his uneven breathing on her cheek before his lips traveled to nuzzle her neck.

Blood pounded in her brain and leapt to her heart. Her knees quivered.

She gasped at the sudden sharp pain that flared in her neck. Strangely stimulated by the act, electricity flowed through her veins.

She took pleasure in his touch until a stream of moisture trickled down her neck.

What the...?

Opening her eyes, she came back to reality, an even more terrifying realization washing over her.

Oh god. Did he just bite her? Was that blood?

Liz brought her hands up to his chest. It took everything she possessed, mentally and physically, to push him away.

She looked at his face, horrified to see slivers of blood, *her* blood, trickle from the corners of his mouth. His tongue licked the remnant traces of fluid from his lips, and she shivered.

His lips curved in a half-hearted smile, not the kind she anticipated. Where she expected to see a smirk of possession, she saw an awkward, more of an "oops" type of grin, and she recognized an imperceptible note of pleading in his eyes.

"Who are you?" she whispered, catching her lower lip between her teeth. "What are you?"

Praise for Victoria Noxon

Dedication

To my husband, my children, and my parents...
thank you for believing in me.
To my wonderful critique partners
who took time to point out my flaws.
Without all of you, this wouldn't have been possible.

The Prophecy

Alba — Neolithic Scotland
500 B.C.

"Do not underestimate her."

Gods and goddesses of the Tuatha Dé Danann, their faces pale and pinched, surrounded the sacrificial altar atop the fire temple at Skara Brae. The flicker of flaming torches animated grave faces as lights and shadows danced across majestic copper skin.

They listened, in silence, to his warning. As Oracle for this divine race and a source of wise council, the Tuatha often sought his precognition skills and prophetic opinions.

On this day, the omen he delivered rife with uncertainty for the future of the human race.

"For a millennium, there will be peace." He shook his head and continued, "You must consider this time a short reprieve." A chill whispered across his skin at the visions that materialized in his psyche. Disgust rose in him and threatened to buckle his composure. "There will be those who follow the creature's practice of drinking human blood. Others will mutate over time. Wolves walk on two legs. Demons alter form." His eyes shifted around the circle. "They are all blasphemous creatures and must be destroyed."

The forest converged on the meadow that bordered the shrine. Tall trees and dense undergrowth presented a jet-black background that

1

ascended upward to the lighter shades of the skies where the sun began its slow climb over the mountains in the east.

In contrast to the total silence of the crowd, the woodland overflowed with sounds. The soft, whistled peeps of ringed plovers mingled with the high-pitched ensemble of crickets and the melody of croaking frogs.

A solitary wail dominated above nature's noise. A howling rise and fall radiated from beneath the surface of the land. The owner of the melancholy voice did not pause for breath, the echo constant, unnerving.

The deities ignored the offensive female tone.

"She is imprisoned here, in this soil, but she will not rise from this place. The exact moment and location of her resurrection is not within my vision. But know this—" he paused, drawing a deep breath. "She will rise again, sparing no one in her quest for vengeance. The passage of time no barrier to the memory of what has transpired this night. The evil one will seek to release the Fomorian, enemy of the Tuatha Dé, Ághmach, from the underworld and recreate her assemblage of the Camarilla." A deep, regrettable sigh passed his lips, his shoulders slumped. "I can see no further."

The mystic white glaze that covered his eyes cleared. His gaze passed over the audience surrounding him. "From the essences of babes, seek your guardians. Prepare them for her return."

Below the temple, fires burned low. Dark acrid smoke billowed into the brightening skies. The dawn chorus reached its crescendo, rumbling through the hillside as the woodland animals heralded the dawn of a new day.

The wailing ceased.

"She sleeps."

"From Falias came hither the Lia Fáil, which shouted under the kings of Ireland..."
~The Yellow Book of Lecan

Prologue

Scotland, 15th century

"Release me, ye bloody bastards!"
Fallon O'Callaghan twisted his shoulders attempting to free his arms from the two men who held him captive. The more he struggled, the tighter their grips became.

Identical in statue and appearance, his captors wore black robes that hung to their knees, tied at the waist by taupe-colored burlap. Their faces, swathed in a day's growth of facial hair, lay cloaked by black curls that skimmed their shoulders.

As if coming to a silent agreement, both men yanked Fallon's wrists, twisted his arms at the elbows, and wrenched them high behind his back. He grimaced as the bite of their fingers ripped into his flesh. A sharp pain seared across his shoulders extending down the length of his spine.

Fallon's anger soared to a blazing fury. He jerked his head up and shot the man to his right a look of pure loathing. The man's lips curved into a cynical smile, his eyebrow raised in amused contempt before he yanked his hands up to give Fallon's arm another sharp twist.

Fallon's initial instinct to spit in the man's face turned into an overwhelming need to survive. No matter how angry they made him, how badly he wanted to beat them to a bloody pound of flesh, he couldn't react. He drew a deep calming breath and forced his tense muscles to relax.

Already in a great deal of trouble for invading the Druid camp, it wouldn't be wise to antagonize them further. He'd trespassed, his punishment inevitable.

The humidity, thick and brutal, suffocated the night. Out of the corner of his eye, a flash of lightning streaked beyond the treetops to the west, followed by the distant rolling rumble of thunder. Signs indicating a violent storm headed this way.

Tucked into the folds of the Grampian Hills of Scotland, the Druid camp lay shielded from the incoming tempest by mountains to the north and east. To the south and west, a thick canopy of leaves protected the site from high winds blowing across the valley floor.

He'd be safe from the storm. At least for a while, until the Druids discovered his reason for being there and kicked him out on his arse. And they would, but not until he received a well-deserved thrashing.

It was edict. Outsiders were forbidden to enter a Druid sanctuary. The Matriarch herself decided penalties for such an offense. Fallon heard stories of broken fingers and toes, of fingernails agonizingly ripped out one by one, but never death. The Druids were philosophers, scientists, lore-masters and teachers, never murderers.

Subject to whatever punishment the Matriarch dispensed, Fallon wasn't afraid. Resigned to his fate, he refused to leave until he'd spoken with Rhiannon. He needed to tell her what a fool he'd been and beg her forgiveness.

"Why are you here?"

Fallon recognized the voice and cringed at the piercing tone that always grated on his nerves like nails across a slate board.

His captors forced him to his knees, and he muttered a curse as his shinbone smashed into a sharp rock.

Bloody hell! That was going to leave a mark.

Gritting his teeth against the burning sting racing down his leg, he waited for the Matriarch to emerge from the shadows.

The crowd separated, bowing their heads as she stepped into the light of the campfire. Movements hindered by more than eighty years, Morfesa still represented an imposing figure with cobwebs of silvery hair and eyes the color of a starless night sky, dark and fathomless.

"Morfesa." He spoke in a low, composed voice, his gaze steady as he acknowledged the elder with a brief nod. "Ye know why I've come. Where is she?"

For a moment, he dared to hold her gaze. The resentment in her eyes forced him to look away. He expected anger, but what he saw in her expression was greater than he'd anticipated.

Ill at ease, he asked again, "Where is she?" When she didn't answer, Fallon glanced up. His voice choked with emotion, he implored, "Please, Morfesa, I just want to speak with her."

Once again, he met glaring, reproachful eyes. An icy sensation formed in his toes and slithered up his backside where it seeped into his spine.

Without preamble, Morfesa said, "She no longer lives." She spoke in an odd, yet gentle tone, but Fallon detected a quiet emphasis beneath its softness.

He stared at her in confusion until the implication of her words registered. Overwhelmed by a raw and primitive grief, he closed his eyes as pain speared his heart.

For a brief time, shock held him immobile.

Fallon swallowed hard and opened his eyes. Shaking his head in denial, he attempted to speak, but a suffocating sensation tightened his throat, cutting off his words.

As though permitting him time to digest the shocking news, Morfesa held her silence. She studied him, her eyes intently watching his expression.

After a few moments, she released a long, drawn out sigh.

"Go home, Lord O'Callaghan. There is nothing for you here."

"Ye lie," he said in a voice thick and unsteady.

Morfesa's eyes flashed with contempt, her expression cold and unyielding.

"And you, Milord, would use accusations to deny the role you, yourself, played in her death." Her voice was stern, no trace of sympathy in its hardness. "You used my innocent Rhiannon for your pleasures then tossed her away like a piece of old baggage. Did you ever consider the consequences of your actions?"

"Nay, it canna be true. I never meant…" Fallon's voice broke. "How?"

"It does not matter how." Morfesa's voice faltered, her attention drawn to his chest.

His tunic, torn in his earlier struggles with her guards, lay open, exposing his bare flesh.

Her eyes widened.

Supported by her walking stick, she shuffled closer, rustling the leaves on the ground beneath her feet. With her free hand, she brushed the remnants of the tattered rags from his shoulders.

"The Mark of Danu," she whispered, her words hushed.

If not for the low murmur of the crowd circling them, Fallon might have believed no one heard but him.

Intense astonishment touched her pale face, and she jumped backward, a task not easily, nor gracefully accomplished for a woman of her advanced age. Her elderly frame staggered into the supporting arms of her kinsmen.

"You have been twice marked."

Fallon stiffened, uncertain why he felt insulted by her remark. His gaze shot to his shoulder. "Mere paintings of the flesh," he replied in a grudging voice.

"They are more than mere paintings. Do you remember when you received them?"

"Why do ye care?"

Her mouth thinned with displeasure, and she swallowed visibly. "I don't. You might say I'm inquisitive."

"Och, I see. If that be the case, I woke up with them after a night of too much ale," he answered indulgently. When her eyebrows rose in question, he asked, "What? Does my confession reaffirm yer convictions I'm the bastard ye always believed me to be? Is that what ye wanted to hear, Morfesa? I got so langered, someone branded me and I dinna even feel the needles pierce my flesh."

"It is of no matter when or how you received them."

A bitter chuckle escaped him. "Then why the hell did ye ask?"

"As I said before, I am curious by nature." She smiled briefly, although the small gesture never reached her eyes. "They hold special meaning for you. In fact, those marks are a gift. Your soul shall be guided by them."

Lovely, sweet Rhiannon no longer lived. A flash of agony ripped through him. "I no longer possess a soul, Morfesa. The one person who made me truly alive is gone."

"Your soul is vibrant and strong. It is why you have been selected for this distinction. You are unlike the others of your lineage."

His uncle's face, bitter and full of rage, flashed in Fallon's mind. His gut twisted. "Thank the gods for small favors," he muttered.

A glimmer of a smile crossed Morfesa's face, and she nodded. "In time, you will. You are destined for greater things."

"Destined?"

"Aye, you will become one of the defenders chosen to protect the world against the return of a great evil."

Speechless, Fallon scrutinized her for lucidity. "Defender against evil? What the hell are ye babbling about, woman?"

"The gods chose you for your strong internal fire, for your desires, both qualities obvious at the time of your conception." She hesitated, her expression thoughtful. "Rhiannon must have recognized these traits in you. It is why she fell in love with you." She shook her head and continued, "It is also the reason she has been taken from this world. There is no room in your life for love. Not yet."

Fallon saw the shimmer of tears in the elder's eyes and understood her pain. He'd lost the love of his life while Morfesa lost her only granddaughter.

Before he had the opportunity to offer his sympathy, she masked her sadness. "You have been chosen to become a protector of all that is Tuatha Dé Danann."

"Tuatha Dé Danann? The People of the Goddess Danu? The Celtic Gods?" At her nod, he continued, "Ye're daft, ole woman. The Tuatha Dé Danann doona exist. Those stories are the progeny of men who have nothing better to do with their days."

"The Tuatha Dé Danann does exist. From behind the magic of the Otherworld, they watch and wait."

"For what?" He stared at her, baffled.

"The coming of an ancient prophecy."

"I doona believe in foolish notions of prophecies," he responded in a low, composed voice.

"You must believe. It will come to pass as surely

as the sun rises in the morn."

Fallon frowned at the subtle challenge in her tone.

He gazed at her thoughtfully for a moment then asked, "If the gods are already protected, why do they need me?"

"You will not need to shield the gods from this evil for they will sense it long before its appearance. You will be a protector of innocence, those naïve to evil. People blind to the danger it represents. The powers gifted to you will—"

"Powers? Do ye speak of magical powers?" When she nodded, a spiteful chuckle escaped him. "I have no such powers."

"You will. The loss of Rhiannon has secured those rites. Fear not, Milord, others will join you in this war."

"Others?"

"Aye, immortal guardians selected to destroy demons before they ravage the land."

"Immortal? Demons?"

"Demon spawns of Ághmach and his succubus, Deidra Sidhe. It is foretold their offspring will evolve into half-breeds, their blood no longer as pure as their parents."

"Whose blood ever is?" Fallon asked bitterly.

Ignoring his sarcastic query, Morfesa continued, "That makes them no less dangerous. Ancient prophecies warn of Deidra's escape from her realm of unconsciousness. She will attempt to release Ághmach from the Underworld."

"Once again, ye speak of myths, false stories spread by storytellers," he drawled with distinct mockery.

Movement to his left drew Fallon's sidelong glance just as the guard raised his foot and landed a swift kick to his thigh. He cringed in pain and pressed his lips shut so no sound escaped.

"The Bards have been empowered by the gods to warn people of what is to come. Heed their words, Milord."

He remained motionless for a moment until the ache eased in his leg, then leaned forward.

"If what ye say is true, then mayhap ye'd be good enough to tell me if they're recruiting members. I might be persuaded to join their ranks." He spoke to all, but gazed only at her.

"You cannot! You must destroy them."

"I wilna do yer bidding," he replied in reckless anger.

"It is not mine, but the will of the gods." Her voice hardened.

"The gods? I owe them even less. Yer so-called gods have done enough for me. I wilna thank them nor help them for it," he retorted, his voice heavy with cold contempt.

"You cannot change destiny."

"To hell with destiny!"

Fury choked him, and he tensed. His muscles bunched and grew rigid. With a surge of energy he didn't know he possessed, he burst to his feet and raised his arms. The guards who held him flew to the ground.

Fallon straightened his shoulders and faced the Matriarch as her hands rose, extending out in front of her. A blinding white light shot from her fingertips and rolled toward him.

Paralyzed by an invisible force, Fallon's arms were bound to his sides. A translucent ring of bright light wrapped around his midsection. It tightened, constricting his breathing.

Without warning, his feet left the ground. He struggled to steady himself, his arms rigid. His stomach muscles clenched as the distance between his feet and the damp ground furthered.

"Your powers are weak, but I sense they shall

grow in time. With the news you have received this day, the cycle has begun. You were chosen for this important feat before your birth. You cannot escape it."

He sent her a black-layered look. "Pardon me if I seem less than honored."

With a deliberate, casual motion, Morfesa left the circular light of the campfire.

She returned moments later holding a dark blue container in her wrinkled hands. When she stood in front of him, she stared at him with an intensity he felt in every fiber of his being.

"Do ye seek to curse me, Morfesa? Ye doona need to waste yer petty potions. My life has always been cursed."

Without acknowledging his words, she removed the age-blackened lid and placed two fingers into the opening.

"Fallon O'Callaghan—"

A light sprinkle of rain fell. The campfire crackled, and dark smoke billowed into the skies, blending with the black clouds that now congregated above them.

Water trickled down Fallon's face, distorting his vision. The acrid smell of smoldering logs burned his nostrils and throat. He choked in reflex.

A deep, malevolent laughter rumbled and rose from him as she spoke. "You have been chosen, and because you have been twice marked, your destiny is twice folded. Throughout eternity, the powers granted to you by the gods will grow. Use them. With your mind, see them. With your ears, hear them. And with your heart, feel them. Seek forgiveness, for only then will you find release from your pain."

She withdrew her fingers from the jar and brought them to her lips. With one puff, she blew beads of sparkling powder into his face.

Fallon inhaled and coughed as the shiny particles entered his lungs. His limbs weakened. The light holding him faded and disappeared. His stomach lurched as he fell, powerless to stop himself from crashing into the hard ground. The air left his lungs in a loud *whoosh*.

A sharp, loud crack of thunder splintered the air, the clamor so close Fallon swore the ground rattled with its fury. The wispy shower of rain turned into hard, driving pelts that stung his skin.

The storm had arrived.

As though reading his mind, Morfesa leaned over him. "You will battle many storms in your immortal lifetime."

"To hell with ye, Morfesa." His words slurred.

His vision blurred, growing black as darkness descended.

Before he lost consciousness, Morfesa slipped a roped piece of twine over his head.

"The definition of Síoraí is eternal. The legacy of the Síoraí belongs to you. Embrace it."

Chapter One

Manistique, Michigan
Present Day

From somewhere above her shallow grave, human laughter, insistent yet tantalizing, urged Deidra Sidhe to awaken. She forced herself to move, drawing herself from a deep coma.

A slight shift in the sandbank, followed by a sudden burst of sand, sprang from the ground to form a twirling cyclone. It raced across the dunes that lined the wide expanse of beach. From inside the whirlwind, Deidra emerged as a twisted contortion of granules, a swirl with no definable shape.

In a flash of brilliant colors and sounds, she visualized walking beneath a mystic moon. The time and place were vaguely familiar, and she delved further into her mind.

And then, an image slammed to the forefront of her thoughts.

Syria, High Priestess of the Camarilla, stood beside a sacrificial altar.

A male human lay naked upon the marble stone, his hands and feet bound by barbed twine. As she strolled alongside the altar, Deidra traced a slim finger along his thigh. He cringed at her touch, and she smiled, glorying at the fear in his expression.

His eyes bulged when Syria, a primordial chant on her lips, raised her hands above her head, a knife clutched between her palms. The man opened his mouth to scream, but only a strangled gurgle escaped. His tongue had been cut out before he'd awakened from his drug-induced state of unconsciousness.

In a quick downward thrust, Syria embedded the blade deep into the man's chest. Blood spilled from the wound and poured into the carved channels that creased the perimeter of the altar. The nectar flowed through the straits, meeting at the V near his feet and then disappeared over the edge.

After the initial blood splattered to the dirt, Syria seized the skull chalice from beneath the platform. She placed it on the ground at the foot of the altar to catch the man's unsullied, intimate life's blood. When the red liquid reached the cup's rim, Syria held it out in offering.

Ah, yes, now she remembered.

The place of her life's blood, and the home she shared with her beloved Àghmach, her life mate. Together, they created the Crimson Empire, a safe haven for the cabinet leaders of the Camarilla.

In a flash, the day of its destruction surged from her memories. A growing torrent of resentment coursed through her veins, followed by a rage so powerful, the ground shook.

With feverish joy, she created herself. Even in her weakened state, she drew on long dormant powers and grew, taking solid form from the elements around her. She stretched her arms above her head, hearing the joints snap and crack as they settled and fashioned her shape.

Fully formed, she scanned the waterfront from her position high on the oversized mound. The moon shimmered off waves as the tide rolled in.

In the distance, a light flickered.

She smiled in anticipation at the figures silhouetted in the shadows around a large fire. The sound of their blood surging through their veins reached her ears. Flowing swiftly like a raging river, and the smell...gloriously sweet. Copper and metal filled her nostrils with a hint of rust and salt.

Her tongue darted out and caressed the long, pointed eyeteeth that protruded past her lips.

She was ravenous.

Deidra's eyes narrowed at the breeze that crossed her face. With it came a fragrance that sent chills across her newly formed skin.

She gazed toward the skies. A dark blemish blanketed the moon. How ironic she should awaken on the night of an eclipse. Beneath the darkened surface, she read the warning from the gods. They were already aware of her awakening. Had been since the first rustling of sand.

And yet, a new invigorating aroma drifted through the air. When she recognized it, triumph flooded through her, and she gloried in its scent.

Fear.

Beneath the gods' unspoken threat, their apprehension filled her with a warm glow.

And then another scent, familiar, yet foreign, permeated the air. She laughed aloud, certain the Tuatha Dé hadn't counted on an awakening that brought her to one of the objects she desired the most. The *Lia Fáil*, magical stone, was close. With the precious talisman, she could return Aghmach to her embrace and guarantee them long reign in this world.

Her head snapped up at the whispered voices of her children who welcomed her home. Her lips twisted, and she mentally propelled her commands to them.

Their responses pleased her. Until she regained her strength, they would search for the *Lia Fáil*.

With graceful movements, she wandered down the sandy bank toward the central circle of partiers. It was time to take possession of her new kingdom.

As she strolled through the crowd, she swerved around the fire, avoiding hot embers and sparkling ash that shot from the flames.

Forced to abandon years of non-existence, she lived, now motivated by the powerful need for revenge swelling inside her.

She was Deidra, Vampryss of Camarilla, and she was alive.

Once she reclaimed her powers, she would create her new minions in this world. With the powers of the stone, she would release her love, Aghmach, from his prison in the Underworld.

Together, they would call to their army, seal her immortal existence and reconstitute the Camarilla.

But in this moment, under the spell of darkness, she craved sustenance.

It was time to feed.

Chapter Two

Bloody hell!
Vampires, shape shifters, werewolves…every fucking one of them.

Fallon O'Callaghan raked an agitated hand through his hair and scowled as he stalked into the alley.

As one of four Síoraí Guardians, and the progeny of the Tuatha Dé Danann, he was honor bound to destroy the demon bastards hunting mankind. With the exception of the first thirty years of his life, he'd been a guardian for the past five long centuries, and, most likely, he'd be one for all eternity.

Immortality reassured him of that.

To him, living was nothing more than an empty existence that came with a huge price tag.

His scowl deepened.

About a hundred years ago, he'd grown weary of the fighting and tried to withdraw from the war he didn't start. Determined to find a place to call home, he bought a small cabin and property in the hills outside Rapid Rivers, Michigan and settled down to be alone. That was all he ever wanted.

To. Be. Alone.

But even in this small, isolated corner of the world, demons existed. There was no escape. As much as he ached for solitude, he couldn't stand aside and let innocent people die.

Protect. That's what they told him he'd been born to do. Not that he listened to the gods. He didn't care what they wanted or needed. He followed his own dictates. Always would.

The echo of voices reached his ears, and he shot into the shadows a second before four demons rounded the corner. They passed, and he cringed at the tainted smell of blood that lingered on their flesh, infusing his nostrils.

He slipped from the corner.

Before he had time to attack, the demons twirled around. Vampires, bloodsuckers, dead men on legs. Revulsion ripped through Fallon at their translucent blue skin. A fine network of veins lined their ashen flesh. Their eyes flamed scarlet, swirling around black pupils.

Feral snarls erupted in the alley.

Fallon grinned and raised his hands, "Ye caught me."

With low growls, they rushed him.

From behind, a hand clamped down on his shoulders.

Damn it! The bloody bastards set up an ambush.

They seized him. Sharp, long fingernails tore into the soft tissue beneath his arms. He grimaced. Ignoring the pain, he fought to break free, but their grips only strengthened.

He smothered a groan when his feet left the pavement. His stomach churned as he flew across the alley into the brick wall. The impact so great, the mortar holding the bricks together severed and sprayed gray dust to the asphalt.

Stunned by the attack, Fallon regained his balance. He grabbed the closest vampire by the throat, swung him around and shoved him into the dumpster. The thick metal creased and buckled under the assault.

"What are you?" the vampire croaked, shaking his head.

Without replying, Fallon sprinted forward and

sent his gloved fist, adorned with sharp silver blades, into his heart. The bloodsucker burst into flames and disintegrated into a cloud of ash.

Fallon turned to greet the next red-eyed parasite who stalked toward him, clawed fist raised to strike. He deflected the blow and delivered a staggering punch to the dead man's chin, snapping his head up. The vampire staggered backward. Fallon followed, his fists punching his chest repeatedly, compelling him back another step, then another.

While the vampire stumbled from the blows, Fallon pulled a large dagger from the pocket inside his black leather coat. The bloodsucker regained his footing and advanced, fangs exposed. A roar rumbled in his throat.

In a flash, Fallon dropped to the ground, swung out a leg and swept his feet out from underneath him. Fallon allowed no time for him to recover and sent the dagger through his heart.

Through a mist of vampire residue, a black blur soared from the rooftop of the building and flew over his head. It hit the ground with such force, the sound of splintering concrete echoed in the alley.

Fallon swung around sharply and met a black panther with fluorescent yellow eyes. "Ye're fighting a battle ye wilna win," he warned the shape shifter, in a low, sinister tone.

Suddenly, the alley spiraled into darkness.

In the next instant, his strength waned. The dagger he held in his hand dropped to the pavement with a loud *clink*. His muscles grew limp and legs bowed beneath him, refusing to support his weight. He staggered back in confusion.

What the fuck was happening to him? Why did he feel so weak?

The panther stood on its hind legs and swiped at Fallon's face. Pain pierced his jaw, snapping his head sideways. The coppery taste of his own blood filled his mouth.

And then his legs gave out and he collapsed. He landed on his arse, his back pressed against the cool concrete of the building behind him. His chin settled on his chest.

The snarl of the cat changed to a man's deep, mocking laughter. Fallon attempted to lift his head but even the muscles in his neck cramped at the effort. Heaviness settled in his limbs and compressed his chest. The weight so intense, he gasped for breath.

Hit by the sudden realization he carried the talisman, he mentally called what little power he had left to send the amulet to safety. No longer able to draw upon its magical forces, Fallon sank blessedly into the darkness that called his name.

The sound of approaching sirens rent the air, but he was past the point of caring.

About time someone put him out of his misery.

****

Elizabeth Forrester clutched the goose down pillow over her head and groaned against the persistent, shrill chime of the telephone.

Five rings…six…it appeared the caller had no intentions of giving up until she answered.

"Damn it!" She tossed the pillow aside and stretched her hand toward the phone, prepared to lambaste the insensitive numbskull for calling and disturbing people in the middle of the night. She stopped mid-reach when she recognized the Manistique chief of police's number on her caller id.

The clock near the phone flashed twelve fifteen.

Cursing again, she grabbed the receiver and brought it to her ear. "Murray, can't this wait until tomorrow?"

"Ah, darlin', not even a hello?"

Liz tensed, cringing at the humor in his voice.

In spite of her reserve, a tinge of exasperation crept into her voice. "It is after midnight. What did you expect? Sweet talk? Or maybe you were hoping for a bit of phone sex?"

He chuckled. "Now that you mention it, sweet talk is nice, but I think I'd go with the phone sex. It has a much better ring to it. Don't you think?"

"Go home and get some sleep. Maybe you'll dream the impossible."

"Tsk! Tsk! You're such a spoilsport, Liz. The way you get my hopes up then dash them. You're breaking my heart."

"I'm sure you will survive." She suppressed a yawn. "Now, why don't you tell me why you're calling me in the middle of the night?"

"There is a man on his way to the morgue. He's tall, dark, and unexplainably dead."

"Are you trying to set me up on a date? Thanks, but no thanks. My life is already complicated enough without adding a man to the mix."

"Liz."

Liz discerned the light warning in his tone and mumbled an apologetic, "Sorry." She sat up, settling against the headboard. "Well at least tell me…is he handsome? It wouldn't make much sense to give up my beauty sleep for a bow wow."

She heard a muffled groan and suppressed a giggle at the police chief's obvious frustration.

"I called Gloria and Dale, but neither answered their phones."

"I'm not surprised." Liz knew her two assistants probably recognized Murray's number on their own caller ids and chose to ignore his call. Too bad she wasn't as smart.

"I need you on this one. You're the best I've got."

Liz released a deep sigh. "Admit it, Murray. At the moment, I'm the only one you've got."

"Well, yeah, you can say that too."

"I just did." She spoke with as reasonable a voice as she could manage. "Look, I don't suspect the man is going anywhere. Can't it wait? I'm scheduled to work the morning shift. I'll be there, then."

"They want the report first thing in the morning, Liz."

"It sucks to be them."

She heard a muttered groan. "Why do you got to be like that?"

"Look, Murray, I don't give a rat's ass what they want, especially not..." She glanced at the clock. "...at twelve twenty in the a.m., I might add."

"Is that what this is all about? The time? Liz, you need to put the past behind you."

Reluctant to enter into this particular conversation with the man again, she murmured under her breath, "That's what you think." Releasing a deep sigh, she said aloud, "Let it go, Murray."

"Liz."

The frustration in his voice implied Murray didn't plan on giving up until he got what he wanted. Typical male...moron. She sighed and squeezed tired eyes between her forefinger and thumb. How the hell did she get out of this now?

"Are you still there?"

She swallowed past the lump in her throat. "I'm here."

"Can I count on you?"

"Murray—"

"Please," he begged, and Liz imagined his beseeching brown eyes.

Damn it!

She shoved aside the panic swelling in her chest. Mustering her bravest voice, she conceded, "All right, you win. I'll be there, but I'm telling you, this is the last time I'll do it in the middle of the night."

He chuckled. "That's my girl. Rapid Rivers is sending the body over to the morgue. He'll be there by the time you arrive. I don't know why they chose Manistique's morgue and not their own, but who am I to question? Anyways, I'll expect the report on my desk in the morning."

She opened her mouth to reply, but the sharp click followed by the dial tone signified she'd been cut off.

"Not even a goodbye," she grumbled as she dropped the receiver into the cradle.

Liz pushed aside the silk comforter and stumbled from bed, gasping as her bare feet touched the cold, wooden floor.

She dressed quickly, throwing on a bra, T-shirt and a pair of jeans. After slipping on her sneakers, she pulled her hair into a ponytail, deciding against makeup. Who did she think she would impress? A corpse? Not a chance. Beside, with her luck, she'd probably put an eye out with the mascara brush.

On her way through the foyer, she grabbed her windbreaker. Swinging her handbag over her shoulder, she stepped out the front door onto the porch.

The late summer breeze sent a cold blast of air against her face. She shivered and pulled the collar of her jacket closer around her neck. Goosebumps formed on her skin beneath her pants. Perhaps she should consider moving someplace warmer. She shook her head at the notion. Moving to California would only guarantee an earthquake registering ten point ten on the Richter scale. Such was her life.

Closing the door behind her, she stepped into the night, and froze. A chill etched down her back like frost on a windowpane as she stared out into a black void of darkness.

She clamped down hard on the stirring of emotion within her. A bubble of apprehension swelled in her chest, pressing against her lungs until it became difficult to breath.

Stop it, Liz!

She swallowed hard, released her breath in a quick exhale and inched off the concrete steps, waiting to experience the crunch of gravel beneath her feet.

As she walked to her car, she looked up, disoriented. No moon, no stars. She experienced a gamut of perplexing emotions until she remembered the lunar eclipse forecasted tonight. That might explain the dark skies but not what happened to the solar lights that usually lit up her walk.

She shrugged the unsettling feeling away and rushed to her black Pontiac, which blended nicely with the night.

Chapter Three

An eerie silence met Liz as she pushed through the swinging doors of the morgue. Inside, she headed in the direction of her office, sliding her handbag from her shoulder as she went.

Darkness swamped the room. She spun around. Her bag slid from her fingers to the floor with a loud *thud*. Panic swelled through her with each rapid contraction of her heart.

Why did she let Murray talk her into this?

It'd been almost a year since she'd been in this place during the graveyard hours, and the memory of Mel Jones' vicious attack slammed into her.

Liz hugged her arms around herself and swallowed. Relief overwhelmed her when she realized the door swinging shut had obscured the light from the hallway.

"Get a grip, Liz," she murmured, her voice echoing in the sterile room. She clenched her hands together in an attempt to halt their trembling.

She remained motionless for a moment while she regained control of her emotions.

When her heartbeat steadied, she stretched out a hand and staggered toward the wall until her fingertips made contact with the cool concrete. Her palm flush against the stone blocks, she walked through the darkness feeling for the switch. When her fingers touched the lever, she flicked it upward. The fluorescent bulbs in the ceiling sprang to life, illuminating the room.

Turning, her eyes took in the four white walls,

tiled floor, and the equipment table set against the wall. Everything was exactly where she'd left it yesterday afternoon, nothing out of the ordinary.

Liz retrieved her bag, stepped across the threshold of her small office, and tossed her purse onto the chair. Leaning across the desk, she switched on the table lamp. Mounds of paperwork littered her desktop, and she groaned, tempted to turn the light off to block the image. Instead, she looked away. She'd deal with that another day, but tonight, she'd do whatever necessary and get the hell out of here.

She stripped off her windbreaker and exchanged it for her laboratory jacket from the hook on the wall. As she strolled across the room, her sneakers squeaked against the floor. She reached into her pocket to withdraw her safety glasses, settling them across the bridge of her nose.

Grabbing the metal handle of the instrument table, she wheeled it beside the examination table where her guest waited, covered by a white sheet. At least the Rapid Rivers' police removed the body from the bag, a minor detail the Manistique police always failed to do. Most times, it left her in the position of calling in her assistant.

Liz hated to admit it, but a little company wouldn't hurt. Her nerves were stretched taut with tension, and that awareness alone gnawed at her confidence.

She took a deep breath and relaxed, attempting to convince herself she could do this without help. She was quite certain Dale and Gloria would avoid her call just as quickly as they had Murray's.

Liz picked up the clipboard accompanying the body and flicked through the pages. Her eyes skimmed over the hastily scrawled words.

White male, 6 ft, 185 lbs., approximately 30 years of age.

He was just a few years older than she was.

She brushed the thought away and continued reading.

Identifying marks: various tattoos noted across the deceased's chest and shoulders.

Body discovered at the corner of Western Avenue and 5th Street in Downtown Rapid Rivers. A pedestrian assumed the man slept and tried to wake him up. When he didn't awaken, police were called to the scene.

Victim naked. No identification found on or near the body.

Autopsy requested to determine exact cause of death. John Doe pronounced dead at 11:12 p.m. by Rapid River's Coroner, Jack Stannard.

Setting the clipboard aside, she murmured, "No help there." On occasion, a review of the crime scene provided medical examiners the opportunity to collect information that might otherwise have been overlooked by the coroner.

But then again, they were talking about Jack Stannard, weren't they?

She shuddered at the thought of the coroner. She'd met Jack a few times at social engagements. The peculiar man stood five foot three. Even if he lost a few pounds and purchased a bottle of Rogaine, Liz doubted his looks would improve all that much. Not only did his outward appearance make her cringe; he had a way of undressing her, and every other woman, with his eyes. Straight up, he gave her the creeps, and she avoided him at every opportunity.

Liz knelt to grab a pair of latex gloves from the bottom shelf of the cart. Pulling them free of the box, she slipped them onto her hands with a loud snap.

"Well, Johnny, my dear, let's get acquainted, shall we?"

Liz clutched at the corners of the sheet, which

she lowered and folded evenly across his waist.

Her attention returned to his face.

Stunned, she faltered in indecision, mesmerized by the sight. She released a slow, appreciative breath as a tantalizing shock ran through her.

This man possessed a rare masculine charisma only a few, lucky women ever saw, and, even in death, he radiated of it.

Fluorescent lights glimmered over a ruggedly handsome face. Long jet-black hair framed aristocratic features, a jaw strong and distinct. High cheekbones, shadowed by a faint dusting of facial hair, accentuated full, sensual lips.

She trailed her gaze over his body, admiring his tall, handsome and beautifully proportioned male physique. Wisps of dark hair covered his massive chest, trailing across a firmly muscled stomach to disappear beneath the sheet.

Liz forced her attention away from his magnetism and continued her visual assessment. Cause of death undeterminable at this point, but a simple point of fact remained. This man could be considered perfect in every way, with one exception.

He was dead, for god's sake.

An unexplainable sense of loss overcame her. It was as if she'd been deprived of something priceless. The admission caught her off guard, dredged from a place totally beyond the logic or reasoning she'd always relied upon.

Colossal shoulders hung off the sides of the table. His right shoulder modeled a tattoo of the moon, approximately two and a half inches in diameter, different than the majority of tattoos she'd ever seen.

It appeared charred, as if burned into his flesh. She cringed at how excruciating the procedure must have been.

Simple by nature, it visualized the moonlight

shimmering through the creeping limbs of a willow tree. Stars littered the darkened background.

Less than an inch above that tattoo rested another marking, similar to the larger one, except the tree was gone. Smaller than the first moon, she recognized something distinct. The vague imprint of a woman's face marked the center of the celestial body.

A lost love, perhaps?

A shadow of annoyance filled her, and she mentally berated herself. Why should it matter if he'd been pining away for some other woman?

His left shoulder sported a tattoo remarkably different than the willow. The artist had quite an imagination when he designed and painted the brass colored, large-winged, scaly serpent with a crested head and huge claws.

The dragon's visage, squared tightly to the man's bulging muscles, bore a long snout flaring in anger. Large fangs burst from the beast's mouth. The dragon's body covered the man's chest and shoulder. A pointed tail swept across his abdomen to circle his belly button.

Transfixed by the dragon's brilliant yellow eyes, she leaned closer. A flash of emerald sparkled from their depths. Her eyes widened, and she jumped away from the table, unable to control her gasp of surprise.

Oh, Sh...ugar!

She took a quick sharp breath, squashing her wild imagination. Those eyes *did not* just twinkle at her, did they? Leaning forward, she squinted at the image. When nothing happened, she stepped back and shook her head. It was just the lighting.

A light touch brushed against her cheek, and she swung around.

Her eyes darted around the room, but she saw nothing.

Someone stroked her cheek.

She brought her hand to her face.

"Touch him," a voice whispered.

Liz choked on a startled cry, her stomach twisted. What the hell was wrong with her? She should be used to the ethereal voices by now. After all, they'd been with her for almost a year now.

Even as she denied the voice, it compelled her, encouraged her, and she unconsciously lowered her hand over his chest.

"Yes," the whisper prompted in Liz's ear, sending a shiver down her spine. Her heart pounded an erratic rhythm, and she breathed in shallow, quick gasps. A cold knot formed in her stomach threatening to overwhelm her. Bile rose in her throat, and she swallowed.

She shook her head. "No," she shouted adamantly to the voice prodding her. "Why the hell don't you just go away and leave me alone. You're dead already, or don't you get that?"

Chapter Four

"Touch him," smooth, but insistent, the voice, accompanied by a gentle shove, whispered again.

Liz shook her head in defiance.

This whole spiritual fiasco started last year after her aunt's death. Her reaction to a painful experience, she was sure, but she was over all that...sort of. Why wouldn't the voice leave her alone?

For fifteen years, Reaghan D'Arde, her surrogate parent, sheltered and raised her. She treated Liz as her own daughter after the deaths of her parents in an automobile accident. Liz had been fourteen years old when tragedy struck her young life...the first time.

Aunt Rea, as Liz called her, was an eccentric old Druid whose far-fetched beliefs made Liz often question the old woman's sanity. And yet, despite those idiosyncrasies, she adored the woman who'd nurtured her.

Although traumatic, Aunt Rea's death faded in comparison to the unusual events now taking place in her life. Liz had always relied upon science for answers, but that knowledge didn't explain the voices of dead people that zipped through her mind or the visions of ghostly bodies when they materialized. She shivered, the lines between fantasy and reality fading, and she had to wonder how she managed to retain common sense.

The memory of her last meeting with a spiritual body brought a cynical, twisted smile to her face.

She swallowed hard, tears choking her.

"Embrace him." The odd voice pulled her from the past into the present. She glanced around the empty room, the backside of one hand covering her open mouth.

"Do it now," the voice demanded, more urgent this time.

Liz squeezed her hands into fists at her side, her nails biting into her palms. She prickled with the need to scream at the unseen spirit to leave.

Instead, her chest swelled with an uneasy mix of excitement and fear, drawn to the dead man's strength and power. Lifting her hand, she settled it across his taut abdomen. When her skin touched the hard, lean muscle, her body trembled.

He wasn't cold.

Her body stiffened in shock. A soft gasp escaped her lips, and her gaze zoomed to his face.

An uneasy feeling uncoiled in her stomach.

Why wasn't he cold?

And then, scorching heat rippled through her hand. Intense pain shot across the tender flesh of her palm. She whipped her hand away and waved it wildly through the air. Shaken, she turned her hand over, expecting to discover blisters. There weren't any, the skin not even red.

Liz shook her head and muttered, "Stop this nonsense, and get the job done." Looking around the room, she whispered to the voice, "Shut up. I don't need your help."

At her words, the spirit faded away. She turned to the corpse where she performed her preliminary exam.

First, she needed to assure herself the man was truly dead. For obvious reasons, his warm body gave her cause for alarm, and she placed two fingers on his neck, feeling his carotid artery. No pulse.

With her ear to his nose, she watched his chest

for movement. No rush of air brushed her ear, and she saw no rise or fall of his breast.

Second confirmation complete.

Lastly, she grabbed her stethoscope from the table. After placing the earpieces in her ears, she settled the sensor against his chest.

Silence.

Yep, the man was definitely dead, meeting the one requirement a body needed for her to do her job.

"What a shame," she murmured before resuming her autopsy.

A small puncture wound on the backside of his shoulder appeared fresh, but not significant enough to be ruled the cause of death. She found no other exterior wounds or injuries, except for the pink scar that ran from the corner of his forehead across his temple downward where it ended just below his ear. The hint of pink and swelling surrounding the injury suggested it happened recently. She shook her head, wondering what this man could have done to deserve such a wound.

Liz reached for the scalpel. She gripped the cold, silver handle between the tips of her thumb and index finger, and lowered the sharp point to the man's sternum.

Terrible regret assailed her, remorse at the thought she would mar this gorgeous body. For the first time in her career as a medical examiner, her hands shook. She settled the slanted edge of the instrument against his chest and applied slight pressure, enough to pierce the outer layer of skin.

She swallowed the nauseating bile rising in her throat.

Sh...ugar!

Before she changed her mind, she applied a little more pressure. A drop of blood spilled from the wound, and she hesitated.

At that moment, a strong, muscular hand

reached up and grabbed hers, pushing the knife away from his body.

Sheer black terror swept through her.

She jerked back a step, her gaze darting to his face.

Her breath solidified in her throat to find the man staring up lazily through half-closed lids. A dazed expression lingered on his face, but when his eyes focused on the scalpel, they dilated in a way that appeared sinister. Chills traveled the length of her spine.

"Now, why would ye want to do that, lass?" He glanced at her, one dark eyebrow quirked in question.

Speechless, she stared into his eyes as they searched her face. In contrast to the black of his hair, they were light, a unique shade of yellow that reminded her of daffodils and sunshine. The bright color smoldered in golden-flecked eyes.

"Do ye always fondle men while they sleep?" The beginning of a smile tipped the corners of his mouth, and his grip tightened on her hand.

She jerked free. The scalpel dropped to the floor with a loud *clink!*

Taking a deep, unsteady breath, she stepped away. Her hand covered her mouth. No, this couldn't be happening! She paused to catch her breath as old feelings resurfaced. A splinter of ice shivered along her spine creating a rash of goose bumps on her skin.

"But...you're...you're dead!" she stuttered, a faint thread of hysteria in her voice. Hearing dead people talk, perceiving their spirits, all second nature to her, but witnessing them actually rise from the dead, well, that always made her legs tremble. It took everything in her power to keep her knees from buckling.

His expression darkened with an unreadable

emotion, hidden when he sat up and swung long legs over the side of the table. His feet hovered an inch over the floor.

The sheet covering his legs slid from his body and landed in a heap on the tiles near his feet.

A soft breeze blew across Liz's face. With it came the fragrance of Aunt Rea's lavender perfume. Liz turned. Aunt Rea? A feather-like touch to Liz's cheek reminded her of Aunt Rea's goodnight kisses, and then her aunt's voice whispered in her ear, "You are stronger than the fear, Liz. Release it and live again. Find your happiness in the man in front of you."

Liz took a quick breath of utter astonishment as the shock of realization hit her full force. With the newfound knowledge that her aunt guided her, how could she possibly fear being alone? New and unexpected warmth surged through her as she stared at the man sitting naked on her table, the man who, moments ago played at being a corpse.

His nearness gave her strength.

The broad swell of his bare chest played havoc with her senses.

She struggled to breathe. Her heart beat furiously against her breast at the sight of his sheer magnificence.

Good Heavens! She couldn't turn her eyes away.

His mouth twitched in amusement. "Do ye see something ye like, lass?"

He spoke with such a foreign drawl, the deep tone reminded her of thunder on a glorious summer day. Oh Lord, it was so incredibly sexy. It shot through her with a disconcerting effect striking a vibrant cord inside her.

As the meaning of his words sank in, her blood pounded, and her face grew hot with humiliation.

She hesitated, torn by conflicting emotions.

A long pause bridged the gap between them.

In the silence, her insides squirmed in

frightened delight. She wiped her damp palms on her jeans and inhaled, fighting for control. "You are not alive. You can't be. The coroner pronounced you dead. I checked you myself." When his brows rose in humorous surprise, she sighed, forced to admit defeat. "Hey, look, I'm really glad you're not dead and all, but you have to understand this situation has created an unwelcome complication in my life at the moment."

Unaffected by her announcement, he jumped from the table and stretched. "If it makes you feel any better, I've been told I sleep like the dead."

At a loss for words, her mouth fell open.

The man now stood facing her sinfully naked.

Realizing she stared, she muttered, "Oh my...Sh...ugar!"

And yet, she still didn't turn away.

Chapter Five

An unexpected draft swept across his body. Fallon glanced down then lifted his face to stare at the woman who stood in the corner. He raised an eyebrow. "Dead, eh? And I suppose ye're going to tell me ye were attempting to revive me. Perhaps a wee bit longer, ye might have been successful." He peered around the cramped room. "Where are my clothes?"

She gave a choked, desperate laugh. "What makes you think I have them?"

"Lass, if ye doona have them, who the hell does?"

"I didn't steal your clothes. I don't know where they went. You arrived here exactly as you stand, without a stitch of cloth covering your person."

He grunted, turning his attention to his surroundings. "Where is here?"

"Manistique City Morgue."

"Morgue? What am I doing at the morgue?"

"The Rapid Rivers police sent you here..." she paused, peeking at his face from beneath long lashes. "...in a hearse. You were next in line for an autopsy." His confusion must have been apparent for she asked, "You really don't remember what happened to you?"

Fallon frowned. Autopsy? What the hell happened?

A fuzzy image intruded into his thoughts.

He'd been fighting demons. There'd been four of them. After destroying two, a black cat jumped into the alley, but what happened next was unclear.

The cat changed. Shape shifter. At first, he'd thought they were all vampires. How could he have been wrong?

Three escaped. Two vamps, one shifter. Bloody interesting. Those bastards were a thorn in his side, every fucking one of them.

He released his breath in a quick exhale and rubbed the back of his neck. His fingers met bare skin, not the usual twine cord that supported the Talisman. An uneasy feeling uncoiled in his stomach before a brief flash of memory filled his mind. He'd sent the magical amulet to the safety of his cabin before his world turned black.

Clenching his teeth, he seethed with anger and humiliation.

He never lost!

He swept another look toward the woman. Every curve of her body spoke defiance, and he smiled, pleased that she no longer feared him.

His eyes roamed over her features. Beautiful. Almond—shaped eyes, the color of lavender blue, accentuated a perfectly heart-shaped face. A light sprinkle of freckles complimented an exquisitely dainty nose and full, sensual lips that captivated him, begging to be kissed. He ached to oblige. His body burned with desire.

A tap on his shoulder and a gentle push had Fallon peering over his shoulder at the vacant room. Confused, he turned back to the young woman.

Another shove forced him to take a step forward, and he spun around. Empty. Who the hell keeps pushing him?

"Do you feel them, too?"

Her words were soft, yet he heard. Turning to the woman, he asked, "Who?"

A faint blush stained her cheeks. She faced away and murmured, "Dead people."

"What?" He gave her a sidelong glance of utter disbelief.

Another tap. This time, he allowed the invisible force to push him toward her. When he stood at her back, he caught the faint fragrance of flowers. Forgetting the presence behind him, his fingers captured a lock of her hair. It was as soft as it looked.

Fallon leaned close and whispered, "Och, lass, ye're a mighty fine beauty."

It had been so long since he last touched a woman, longer since he had tasted one. Hell, since he'd been this close to one.

She turned to face him. Her eyes widened, surprised to find him close. He removed the spectacles from her face and tossed them to the floor.

She flinched but didn't move away.

Fallon couldn't control himself, her soft fragrance filling his senses as his head descended to hers. His lips pressed against hers to gently cover her mouth where his tongue traced the soft fullness of her lips until they parted to allow him entrance. He growled at the sugary peppermint taste of her as he explored the sweet recesses of her mouth.

His body roared to life.

It had been so long.

Intoxicating.

A hot ache swelled in his throat, and strange twinges radiated through his limbs.

The thudding of his heart hammered in his ears. Incited by fervor, he took her mouth with savage intensity, his tongue tangling and mating with hers. His hands explored her soft curves as they molded to the contours of him, drew her closer against him.

Not now! His subconscious argued. He pulled away, burying his face in her neck where he pressed his lips to the pulsing hollow at the base of her throat.

The soft scent of lilacs filled his senses, drugging him with euphoria.

His face tingled, and his gums burned. The beast took control and twisted inside him, begging release. His fangs took shape and filled his mouth. The need to taste her grew stronger until he lost the power to control his own actions.

****

Liz's response to this man shocked her. A delightful shiver of desire ran through her. Her heart pounded an erratic rhythm, fluttering against her breast. The soft caress of his lips on hers set her on fire and launched the pit of her stomach into a swirl. When he traced her lips with his tongue, her lips opened to him and his deepening kiss.

She whimpered at the explosive currents racing through her body at the taste of his mouth on hers.

Lost. Defenseless to resist.

She had never known anything like the power and hunger of this man's kiss. His masculinity was like an aphrodisiac, and she abandoned all thoughts and surrendered to her carnal needs. Her body burned and ached for more.

His arms flexed around her, drawing her closer as his lips ravaged her mouth. She kissed him with an urgency she never knew she possessed.

Every inch of her body sizzled, and she wanted him with hot, wrenching hunger. The sweetly intoxicating musk of his body overwhelmed her and her pulse leapt with excitement.

A delicious shudder heated her body sending a quiver through her veins.

Common sense returned in slow degrees. Her mind urged her to push him away. Even as her conscious argued with her raging desires, she wrapped her arms across his broad shoulder, her palms flat against his back. Her hands traveled the strong outline of his back journeying downward where they stopped at the firm, taunt cheeks of his buttocks.

Good Heavens!

Liz wanted to tear off her clothes, reach between them, and guide him straight into that part of her vibrating with demanding need.

The need he created.

Every inch of him pressed intimately against her. She became aware his arms weren't the only part of his body rock hard and solid. Certainly not dead, but stiff, and the affliction had nothing to do with rigor mortis.

His lips traveled from hers, leaving her mouth burning with fire. Trailing across her cheek, he stopped at her ear where he suckled the tender lobe. She felt his uneven breathing on her cheek before his lips traveled to nuzzle her neck.

Blood pounded in her brain and leapt to her heart. Her knees quivered.

She gasped at the sudden sharp pain that flared in her neck. Strangely stimulated by the act, electricity flowed through her veins.

She took pleasure in his touch until a stream of moisture trickled down her neck.

What the...?

Opening her eyes, she came back to reality, an even more terrifying realization washing over her.

Oh god. Did he just bite her? Was that blood?

Liz brought her hands up to his chest. It took everything she possessed, mentally and physically, to push him away.

She looked at his face, horrified to see slivers of blood, *her* blood, trickle from the corners of his mouth. His tongue licked the remnant traces of fluid from his lips, and she shivered.

His lips curved in a half-hearted smile, not the kind she anticipated. Where she expected to see a smirk of possession, she saw an awkward, more of an "oops" type of grin, and she recognized an imperceptible note of pleading in his eyes.

"Who are you?" she whispered, catching her lower lip between her teeth. "What are you?"

Chapter Six

By the gods, she was a beauty!

The pensive shimmer in her eyes dimmed as she spun away. She strolled to the table, grabbed a tissue, and swiped at the blood smearing her neck.

Fallon closed his eyes and reached out with his thoughts, using them as he would his hand to caress her cheek. He needed to see inside her intellect.

The instant he made contact, he almost pulled away and severed the link. The powers and forces surging inside her puzzled him. He sensed tenderness and love, not the fear or terror he usually experienced.

Who are ye, lassie? What are ye?

She turned on him sharply. Her eyes flashed in anger.

"Stop that!"

Alarmed, Fallon recoiled against the solid brick wall she'd slapped up in her mind.

"Stop what?" He struggled to keep the surprise out of his voice.

"Stay out of my head."

He froze, stunned. She couldn't have known, could she? No one knew when he read their minds. How was it possible…? For lack of anything better to say, Fallon shrugged and agreed. "Okay."

Her gaze shifted over his body. A flash of desire crossed her features, quickly masked behind a look of pure resolve.

She grabbed the sheet from the floor, tossed it at him, and said, "And for god's sake, cover up!"

This woman was unlike any he'd ever known. Fallon threw back his head and roared with laughter. At her confused look, his laughter stilled, an easy smile playing at the corners of his mouth. Delighted, he'd forgotten how good it felt to laugh.

But a nagging in his mind refused to be silenced. For the first time since he set out on this odyssey, many centuries ago, he was forced to face reality.

As an immortal, an eternity of loneliness loomed in his future. A mere human, this woman, didn't belong in his world nor did she belong in his life. No woman did.

He wrapped the sheet around his waist and asked, "Repeat the question."

"Well, for one, let's start with your name. What is it, and what are you?"

Fallon held his silence. Could she handle the truth? How would she react to the news she stood facing an immortal guardian forged with the characteristics of a vampire by the Tuatha Dé Danann?

Yeah, right! After five hundred years, it even sounded outlandish to him.

And then, to his amazement, Fallon realized he didn't want to lie to this woman. He wanted to be honest with her, to share his innermost feelings. And yet, deep inside, he was forced to acknowledge that no matter how strong she appeared, he couldn't reveal the truth of his life.

"Where did ye learn to count, lass? That's two."

She lifted her chin and met his gaze straight on. "Don't be a smart-ass. Just answer the questions."

"Have ye ever been told ye're a feisty wee thing for someone so tiny?" Fallon snickered as she folded her arms below her breasts and tapped her foot. "The name's Fallon O'Callaghan, and ye are?"

"Elizabeth Forrester."

"Lizzie." His gaze traveled the length of her body

before returning to her face. "Aye, a fitting name."

"Most people call me Liz," she corrected.

"I'm no' like most people. Besides, I prefer Lizzie."

She shrugged, lowering thick, black lashes, her tone cool when she replied, "Whatever. I'll never see you again after tonight, so what the hell. Now, the other question, what are you?"

Fallon lifted an eyebrow. "Ye mean, ye doona know?" Her eyes narrowed, and he sighed with overstated exasperation. "I'm just a man, lass."

"Well, duh."

"Duh? What the hell does 'duh' mean?" Other than the notorious curse words he'd grown quite fond of, Fallon would never get used to the slang words of the changing times.

She shot him a withering glance. "Obviously, you're a man, but there's more to you than that. I've never known a man who has fangs for teeth, not to mention one who bites people on the neck and does it oh so skillfully."

Fallon smiled, amused by her apparent frustration. "Skillfully, eh? I like that. I havena gotten a compliment in a long time. Thank ye."

"Mr. O'Callaghan."

"Fallon, if ye please."

"And if I don't?"

"Lizzie." He took a deep breath as a jolt of adrenaline surged through him. His stomach twisted, and his heart pumped hard. Every nerve in his body screamed out in awareness.

Demons had entered the building.

The moment they crossed the threshold, Fallon identified their essence. The overbearing presence of evil radiated from their bodies, pinging against his senses.

Fallon was able to discern their location in an instant, the two floors separating them no barrier.

The evilness skittered across his skin, but he refused to yield to their sinister forces, drawing on his inner strength.

"What's the matter?" Fallon heard the bewilderment in Lizzie's voice and rushed to her side.

He placed his hand over her mouth. "Shhh," he whispered in her ear. "We've got company."

Fallon cursed. He needed to get out of here now. Without the protection of the Talisman, his powers waned, leaving him vulnerable in the small confines of the room.

It was too late to cloak them. The demons would be conscious of his essence just as quickly as he perceived theirs.

What the hell had he been thinking? He should have left when he'd awakened, knowing they'd track him. Because of his stupidity, they now had the perfect tracking device. His blood.

Fallon glanced at Lizzie and grimaced. By the gods! He'd bitten her, leaving his mark and his scent on her skin. If he left her behind, they'd torture her looking for information. To them, they wouldn't care she didn't know anything. They'd kill her for the sheer pleasure of it and bleed her dry.

He'd always fought this war alone, but now, he'd drawn an innocent woman into the middle. He couldn't leave her. To do so would mean certain death for her.

Fallon needed to get them both out of there and quickly.

"We have got to leave. Now. Is there another way out?" He kept his voice low but urgent.

"Only the front door."

"Bloody hell!"

"Who is it?" Her voice trembled. "Fallon, you're scaring me."

The heavy lashes that shadowed her cheeks flew

up. Her vibrant blue eyes widened in fear.

He clasped her hands in his and whispered, "I'm sorry. I dinna mean to drag ye into this."

"What is it? Who are they?"

"The men who put me here. They'd like to see me dead. If they find ye—" He left the sentence hanging, but his meaning was clear.

"Oh my god. What are we going to do?" She took a deep breath punctuated with several even gasps.

"Can we go to yer house?" He couldn't enter her home without her permission, and he urgently needed that now.

"I don't understand how we're going to get out of here."

"Let me worry about that. Where do ye live?"

"Fallon—"

She looked up at him in confusion and he rushed out again, "Lizzie, what's yer address?"

"Forty-three Bay Shore Drive, but…"

She shook under his touch, her fear evident, but with very little time left until the demons made it to this room; he pressed her for a reply. "Please, Lizzie. Can we go there?"

She looked into his eyes and nodded.

Panic filled her expression. He wished he had time to explain, but there wasn't any.

He looked down at the sheer terror etched on her face. "It's going to be all right. Trust me. Close your eyes, lass."

She stiffened but did as instructed. He pulled her against his chest and wrapped his arms around her.

Fallon's heart contracted and swelled. Blood flowed from one chamber to the other, revitalized with infinite energy. Awakened and alive, he'd never been more attuned to his body and to the body of the woman he held in his arms.

He imagined her home and willed it to happen.

Time stood still.

He pulled her to him, crushed her breasts against his chest, his mouth covering hers hungrily. His tongue explored the sweet recesses of her mouth.

When their kiss ended, the echo of their ragged breathing filled the air. Raising his mouth from hers, he gazed into the face of the most beautiful woman he'd ever seen.

Exquisite.

How was it possible for Lizzie to ignite his carnal urges to such unbearable heights? No one ever managed to achieve that at first meeting, no one except...

He shook his head, refusing to think of Rhiannon. Not now, not in the arms of this woman.

Liz's heart continued to beat its rhythm, strong and true beneath his palm, and he intended to keep it that way. He pressed his lips to the top of her head, breathing in the mellow soft fragrance of the sweetest lilac tree.

Forcing himself to step away, he raised his hand and caressed her cheek, her skin smooth as velvet beneath his fingertips. He released a sigh, looked around and commented, "Nice place."

Lizzie opened her eyes. When she did, he witnessed her stunned surprise as she took in her surroundings.

She gasped, "How?"

He shrugged. "I told ye I would take care of it."

She shook her head, her face paled, and she stumbled. Fallon rushed to her side and caught her as she collapsed.

With her in his arms, he walked toward the sofa that decorated Lizzie's living room.

Chapter Seven

The doors of the morgue swung open and slammed against the wall with a force that shook the contents of the room. The sound echoed with a resounding *thud*.

Dressed in black jeans, T-shirt and favorite leather coat, Dorian drifted through the open doorway, his body inches from the floor. He removed dark sunglasses and waved his arms to his two companions, Gyres and Triton.

"Find him," he commanded, and watched as they moved from his side.

Each man took a corner of the room. Their feet never touched the tiles as they traveled around the room, checking the office, under the metal table, anywhere their quarry might find to hide.

They found no one. The room was vacant.

"Where the hell did he go?" Dorian barked, his loud voice ricocheting off the walls.

Gyres and Triton returned to Dorian's side, their expressions cautious.

"He must have regained his powers, my liege," Gyres commented, his voice anxious.

He shot him a withering stare and Gyres took a step backward. Dorian frowned at the telling action.

It was no secret that whenever angered, Dorian favored taking his ire out on those who dared to stand the closest. Most often Gyres was that target, but Dorian deemed the man an idiot. Retreating would not spare him.

With hands clenched into fists, he turned to

Triton. "We delayed too long. We should have gotten here before his awakening."

"We had no choice but to wait for his essence to reappear before we tracked him," Triton defended.

"That is no excuse." His brows furrowed as he looked at Gyres. "If the dolt there hadn't lost track of the coroner's vehicle, we would have arrived in time."

"But he wasn't wearing the Talisman when we attacked him in the alley," Triton said.

"You are a fool! Obviously, he sent it away so we wouldn't locate it," Dorian growled. "We need him. If we find him, I'm sure we can persuade him to hand it over."

"Do you really believe he will hand it over to us without a fight? I don't think so," Triton said, his voice thick and unsteady.

"He may be unwilling at first, but there is only so much pain one can endure. Even for one of the god's precious guardians," Dorian commented, his anger flaring at Triton's obvious defiance. No one dared to challenge him.

"He is Síoraí. Trained by the gods to withstand all pain. He will not break without difficulty. He is a strong one, too. Did you see how quick he killed Sean and Yeoman? They didn't have a chance against him."

"They were weak and deserved what they got."

"What makes you so sure we can—?"

"Do you have so little faith in my abilities?" Dorian raged. His mouth twisted when both men flinched.

"No...No...No, my liege," Triton stuttered.

Dorian rubbed his chin. "With the Queen's return, we must gain her favor. The Talisman will guarantee us grace. Her call has promised great rewards to anyone who brings the stone to her. We must be the first to find it."

"We will be the ones to reap the benefit, but I beg of you, we must not rush into a confrontation with him. This one is legendary for his ability to travel through space. We have his blood. Have faith in the knowledge that he has eluded us only for the moment," Triton said then hesitated, his gaze on his leader.

Dorian sniffed the air, his senses strong in the sterile room.

"He is not alone," he said, his voice steady and low. "It appears the Síoraí has chosen. A female, a mate. His blood has mingled with hers."

The implication of Dorian's words sparked a smile on the faces of all three men.

Two scents were better than one.

If they found the girl, chances were they would find the guardian and then, the stone.

"We must speak with the Queen," Dorian muttered.

"Do you think that wise? You are part animal. Without the Talisman, she may destroy you."

Dorian shot Triton a look of disgust. "She must be warned of the existence of the Síoraí. We have the guardian's scent. She will see us for that reason alone."

With a snap of his fingers, the three men faded from the room.

Chapter Eight

Fallon swept Lizzie into his arms. He groaned aloud and closed his eyes at the sudden rush of raging desire that surged over him. Heat coursed through his veins, and his skin tingled where their bodies touched.

He drew a deep, agonizing breath and opened his eyes. With movements slow and gentle, he walked toward the chaise lounge on the opposite side of the room. He needed to put her down, but a reluctance to let her go swept over him.

After pressing a soft kiss to her forehead, he lowered her to the sofa keeping a hand beneath her neck for support. With his free hand, he reached across the couch to grab a chocolate-colored throw pillow, which he slipped beneath her head.

Once settled, he sat beside her and lifted a hand to her face where he traced the arc of her jawbone. His fingertip sketched upward across the soft skin of her cheek. Fallon marveled at the innocent beauty on her face.

Elizabeth Forrester was lethal to his senses. He barely knew her, but his want for her burned hotter than Hades inside him.

Over the years, he'd bedded his fair share of women, but it had always been easy to walk away. Lizzie was different. The stirring within him and his need to protect her led him to believe she would never be a mere trophy.

He stared at her, and then massaged the back of his neck. "Bloody hell," he whispered, sliding his hand over the back of his head. A cynical inner voice cut though his thoughts and issued a warning. Somehow, this wee lass had slipped past his defenses and chipped a hole in the barrier he placed around his heart and, in that moment, he knew he wanted more than sex from her.

He frowned. What did he want?

How long since he allowed himself to enjoy the company of anyone, especially a woman? Always a loner, he kept his distance from the human population, preferring his solitude. But now, Lizzie awakened him to sensations he hadn't enjoyed in years.

He shook his head in utter bewilderment.

This couldn't be happening. A tumble of confused thoughts engulfed him. He lived a complicated life. At least, what little life he allowed himself to have. Being an immortal protector for the gods of the Tuatha Dé Danann was not an advertisement to post on a billboard for the world to see.

He'd no more chosen immortality than he'd chosen this lonely existence. The gods, in their infinite wisdom, bled him dry, made him a freak, proclaimed him perfection, but never once asked him what he wanted.

Fallon vowed never to forget the devastation, the heart wrenching grief he'd been forced to endure at their hands, nor would he allow himself to ever experience such agony again. He'd kept his emotions concealed, hidden beneath the dark pretense of rebel with a "curse them all" attitude.

This same pretense had always worked for him, until tonight...until Lizzie.

Sweet Jesus!

He closed his eyes and ran a weary hand across his face.

What in the world possessed him to bite her? To

taste her blood?

Opening his eyes, he leaned forward, resting his forearms on his thighs. A muscle in his cheek jumped with the clenching of his jaw.

His hand crossed the distance between them, and once again, he caressed Lizzie's cheek. *A woman such as Lizzie would never trust ye with her heart*, his conscious mocked. *Have ye lost your mind as well as yer soul to even consider such a thing?*

What would his life be like if he found both?

He dropped his head to his hands, raking his fingers through his hair, blowing out the deep breath he hadn't realized he held. Fallon tensed under the sudden attack of guilt. His mind blazed with pain. A fire raged inside him, and he fought against it. To feel again meant they won, and he refused to let the gods win.

With one last look at Lizzie, he stood.

Staring down, his mouth curved into a self-mocking grin at the sheet from the morgue draped around his body. Maybe when Liz woke, if she was up to it, she would go to the mall and buy him some clothes. It might take her mind off their situation.

For the moment, they were safe. The mental shield he'd placed around the house would prevent the demons from tracking him, at least for a little while.

Making certain Lizzie remained unconscious, his eyebrow cocked at the opportunity to nose around and find out more about the beauty who captured his sleeping heart.

Near the front door, a small foyer led into the living room by way of one step down. Lizzie's purse sat on a Merlot foyer table that rested against the wall. Beside the black handbag, a porcelain bowl held a set of keys. A pair of fur-lined black boots leaned against the wall near the door.

Various sizes and shaped tan rugs scattered

floors custom-made with natural wooden planks. Modern-style furniture, upholstered in the same colored fabrics decorated the room.

He wandered around the living room, nodding with admiration at the paintings, books and wildlife knickknacks adorning both walls and shelves. He traced a finger along the book spines, reading the many William Shakespearean titles. Among them some of his favorites, *Comedy of Errors, Hamlet, Julius Caesar* and *King Lear*.

Good taste. And she tasted so blessed good. Shaking his head at the comparison, he continued his inspection of Lizzie's small abode.

Broad panels framed a fireplace, made of solid oak. Bordered by a tiny balustrade, the mantelpiece stood wide and sturdy. More wildlife knick-knacks lined a shelf constructed six inches wide. Fallon picked up the miniature statue of a white wolf. Whoever made it did so with loving hands, the carving intricate, the details flawless down to the rounded green eyes and intricate layers of fur.

Fallon admired the sculpture.

Simply striking.

He set the figurine on the shelf and glanced up. Tacked to the wall above the ledge, a fine beveled mirror with brass candle scones hung on each side.

Not exactly his favorite décor, mirrors were a constant reminder of the man he no longer was. Fashioned after demons, Fallon bore no reflection, and he'd long since failed to recall what he looked like. Judging by Lizzie's reaction to him, he rest assured he sparked her interest.

In the corner of the room sat a mahogany desk, a flat screen computer monitor in the middle. Opened envelopes and papers littered the keyboard.

Skylights embellished a high-arched ceiling, and Fallon caught sight of the moon. Shit, he hated skylights, especially during the day when the sun was high.

When the gods granted him immortality, they condemned him to walk in darkness. In doing so, they secluded him from the rest of the world.

As a Síoraí, Fallon annihilated the demons that walked the night. He tracked and destroyed those bastards as they preyed on innocent people. According to the Tuatha Dé Danann, his sole purpose was to save the world. He attempted to accomplish this feat, at least in his corner of it, but he didn't follow their dictate. He did it to atone for his guilt over Rhiannon's death.

Fallon swiped a hand across his mouth. Most people never saw his fangs, but he knew they existed. In fact, they lay dormant except on occasions when he experienced an adrenalin rush. During battle and extremely hot arousal, the latter of which he'd only just discovered for himself.

He glanced over at the woman lying on the couch. And now, Lizzie, the only woman who'd ever brought them to the surface, knew. Not only did they pierce her skin, she'd caught a glimpse of them when he wiped her blood from his lips.

He walked to the veranda doors where he pushed the russet-colored draperies to the side.

Fallon's breath caught at the stunning lake-front view.

He glanced over his shoulder where Lizzie remained unaware. Quietly, he unlocked the door and pushed it open.

With his sheet tucked around his waist, he stepped onto the porch. An array of semi-budding plants rested along the railing. Barren flowerbeds lined the steps leading to the beach.

Fallon strode to the rail where he leaned over. His gaze wandered up and down the coast. For miles, darkness bathed the area, an indication that either everyone was asleep or there were no homes for miles.

A breathtaking sight, built of a pale, grey marble and cedar, Liz's home lay situated against an assortment of large-leafed maple trees.

Absolutely stunning, just like its owner.

And he'd leave at first opportunity.

Back inside, he searched for a phone. Locating it on the desk beside the monitor, he picked up the receiver and dialed, his fingers flying over the digits.

A muffled "hello" answered on the third ring.

"Hey, Seth, it's me."

"Fallon, where the hell have you been? I've been calling your cell all night but kept getting your voicemail. Don't you ever listen to your messages?" The sleepy tone immediately vanished, replaced by concern.

"I would have if I hadna lost my cell."

"Lost your cell? Where?"

"I ran into some friends. It must have slipped out of my pocket during the fight."

"And you're still alive?" Seth's voice rose in amazement.

"What the hell is that supposed to mean?"

"Where are you?"

"Manistique."

"Manistique?"

"Yeah, it's a long story. Right now, I need ye to go to my place, get the Talisman and my extra cell. They're both in the top drawer of my writing table."

Fallon heard the disbelief in Seth's voice, and imagined the other man's stunned expression when he asked, "You aren't wearing the stone?"

"No' at the moment. Fucking demons set up an ambush. I had to release it for its own protection."

"Are you okay?"

"Aye, ye know me. I always land on my feet."

"Glad to hear. How did they manage to get that close without you sensing them?"

"I doona know. I'd just destroyed two of them. A shape shifter jumped from the rooftop, and my limbs suddenly failed me. I was as weak as a babe. I must be getting on in my old age."

"Well, you are more than five hundred years old. Not exactly the spry chick anymore."

"So you keep reminding me, *old* friend," Fallon replied, placing some emphasis on the word old. After all, Seth was a few hundred years old himself, so he really had no room to talk about Fallon's age.

Seth chuckled. "Of course. What kind of ally would I be if I didn't? You forgot, didn't you?" His tone grew serious.

"What did I forgot?"

"The Lunar Eclipse forecasted for tonight."

Bloody fucking hell!

Fallon cursed himself for forgetting something so vitally important. That memory lapse could very well have cost him his life since the Síoraí drew their powers from the moon and the goddess who coveted it. Whenever any event, natural or unnatural shadowed the moon's powers, his powers weakened, making him fair game to demons, especially those who knew of this weakness.

"By the gods, I forgot about that. At least I know I'm no' getting weak, and why I dinna sense them before they jumped me."

"I bet you won't forget again."

Fallon snorted.

"What happened to you tonight, and how did you get to Manistique?"

"I dinna start out in Manistique. After my legs weakened, I collapsed. I vaguely remember hearing police sirens minutes before I passed out. The next thing I knew a knife rested on my chest about to slice me open from neck to cock."

"Knife? What the hell are you saying?"

"The Rapid Rivers police thought I was a dead

man and sent my body to the morgue here in Manistique for an autopsy."

"Autopsy? You're kidding me." Fallon heard humor in Seth's voice.

"Strike me down if I'm no' telling ye the truth."

"That's a new one."

Fallon peered toward to the couch where Lizzie rested. "Ye have no idea."

"Fallon—"

"Doona say it, Seth. When ye have the Talisman, I need ye to come to—" he rattled off Liz's address. "Ye have to look after someone for me."

"Look after someone? Who?"

"I'll explain later."

"Okay, man, but—"

"Later, Seth."

"Okay, okay, I'm out the door. I'll try to get there ahead of the sun, but if I don't..." Seth left the sentence hanging.

"I know the drill."

Fallon hung up the phone, knowing Seth would have to move fast if he were to arrive within the next three hours. If he didn't, Fallon would be stuck here until dark. Without the Talisman, he hoped his mental powers were enough to keep them safe.

It seemed so long ago that a trail of demons led him to Rapid Rivers, Michigan. He'd destroyed them all, but before he'd been able to head down the road, the Talisman drew him to Seth's doorstep. As he prepared to strike the vampire down, Seth informed him that unlike the other demons Fallon sought and destroyed, he possessed a soul. He refused to kill innocent people to secure his own survival, his meals coming from the local butcher.

They'd formed a friendship, a partnership of sorts. Fallon got into trouble; Seth bailed him out. Fallon forgot to do something; Seth reminded him. Seth was one of the reasons he decided to stay.

Between the two of them, they vanquished more than a hundred of those demon bastards, but the numbers continued to grow.

Long ago, Morfesa promised him a never-ending battle, and Fallon had been forced to accept that the woman didn't mince her prophecies.

He raked a hand through his hair and blew out a deep breath. Eyes narrowed, he watched the moonlight shimmer across the water.

What the hell should he do now?

Chapter Nine

A faint mist floated across the lake.

The beaches were empty, the sand drenched by rains from an earlier storm. Tranquility settled across the sky, but on land, the violence of the squall could still be seen in the churning white caps that exploded onto shore.

High on a hilltop overlooking the water stood a battered building, its concrete walls pitted by time and weather. The Bradford Institution was at one time a well-renowned hospital providing treatment to patients who suffered from mental disorders. It was condemned in the early 1960s after fire burned through the third and fourth floors. Since that time, the building stood in a sinister shadow of emptiness believed cursed by the souls of those who died within its walls.

Tonight, it wasn't deserted.

The occupants inside didn't need light, their vision twenty-twenty in the darkness.

Deidra's feast on the beach had boosted her powers enough to send out an invitation to her descendants existing in this time. She called them to this place.

At least thirty arrived on her doorstep, and she fully expected in another two days time, the numbers would rise to near a hundred. They would be cramped in the small cellar, but the foundation provided them safety and protection from the devastating sunlight.

Soon it would be time, and they'd leave this

place.

"My Queen."

Deidra peered at the one called Dorian through narrowed eyes as he knelt on one knee in front of her. His head bowed.

She sniffed the air above his head.

"You are not such as us. I sense..." she hesitated, sniffing again. "...animal in you."

"I am cat." Dorian glanced up at her, and his eyes sparkled, the luminosity of yellow-green color.

Deidra rose from her seat as if propelled by an explosive force, her jaw clenched and eyes narrowed. "Tainted blood. I should kill you for invading my sanctuary."

"I kneel at your feet, my Queen. My services are yours to command."

She lowered her lashes slightly as her gaze swept over the animal. One corner of her mouth tilted, and she struggled to control her anger. She had little use for creatures covered in fur.

"And you are a fool. What makes you think I would need or even want your services?"

"I can lead you to the *Lia Fáil* and the man who protects it."

Deidra's breath burned in her throat and she looked at him, pinning him with a steady gaze.

As if sensing her doubt, he nodded. "I assure you I speak the truth."

Her heart pounded with an uneasy mix of annoyance and anticipation. She licked her lower lip. For the moment, she needed him, but only until she possessed the *Lia Fáil*.

"Who protects it? I will destroy him." Her voice low, taut with irritation.

"While you slept, the gods created guardians, known as the Síoraí, in preparation for your return. The gods fear you. While they waited for your rebirth, these guardians have hunted and destroyed many of us. Not just vampires, all demons."

"They will not destroy me."

"My Queen, they have been granted immortality and superior powers."

"Bah! I do not fear them." She waved her hand in a gesture of dismissal. "You have said you know where the Talisman is. Tell me where to find it."

"As is foretold, it has been placed for safe-keeping with a guardian. He protects it."

"Where?"

"He uses it to boost his powers, to keep his chosen mate safe from me, but that will not last long."

"Chosen?"

Dorian parted his lips to speak, but wavered.

Her eyebrows rose at his hesitation.

He cleared his throat and explained, "For centuries, the guardians have walked the earth alone. It has been written that each will find a mate. Once the guardian has drawn the mate's blood, they are bonded for eternity in all ways...spiritually, physically, magically."

"Where would I find this mate?"

Despite her complacent tone, Dorian lowered his head.

"Answer me!" Deidra's voice bounced off the walls with a thunderous crack.

Tension saturated the room. Out of the corner of her eye, she saw her followers slink into the shadows. She scowled at the significant act.

"I do not know where they have gone, but I have tasted the guardian's blood. I will know where to find both of them in little time."

Deidra leaned over him, and he cowered backward, expecting her to attack. He breathed a quick sigh of relief when she sniffed the air above him again.

Her eyes brightened. "Ah, yes, an added bonus."

"My Queen?" Dorian asked in curiosity.

She lifted her chin and met his gaze with an icy, commanding look.

"It is of no concern of yours. Your time is limited, cat. Bring me the stone, and I'll consider sparing your miserable life. If you do not, you will suffer a torture as no other." She inclined her head toward the door and pointed her finger. "Now remove yourself from my sight."

After the mangy creature left, Deidra grimaced in disgust. Her pure bloodline had evolved into monsters. Appalling, she abhorred these creatures. How had it happened? She pondered who might have traveled outside their lineage and mated with an ill one. There would be hell to pay when she discovered their identity.

Her stride deliberately slow, she walked across the room and stepped up on a large concrete slab. A couple more footsteps brought her in front of a red high winged back chair where she swung around and sat. Her gaze rounded the room, and she shook her head at the demons huddling in to the corners.

Cowards! They were all damn cowards!

She shifted once in the seat and settled back. Uncomfortable it may be, but this throne symbolized her power.

Deidra closed her eyes and a picture of a petite, young woman flashed into her mind. Ah ha, there she is. *The Princess of Light*, the added insurance she needed in her plan to bring Åghmach back to her arms. The young girl lay motionless, her head propped up by a pillow.

The gods' precious guardians didn't concern her. In fact, they'd done her a favor. When the possessor of the stone sunk his teeth into the Princess, his mark released her inner essence and sent it floating through the air...to her.

Deidra focused on the scent, drawing a picture

of the woman in her mind. Her exact location unknown blocked by a white aura that prevented Deidra's entrance into her mind.

Undeterred, she strived to get inside her head but found this effort blocked as well.

Strong willed.

Deidra vowed to be stronger.

"Already finding ways to keep me out, are you, little one?" She laughed, elated by her new objectivity. "But it will not last forever. I will find a way inside and when I do, you will no longer fight me. You'll be at my side."

Chapter Ten

A deep, monotone voice crept into Liz's subconscious. She opened her eyes and searched for the origin of the voice, squinting in an attempt to adjust to the morning light.

Wow, she must have been exhausted. She rarely, if ever, fell asleep on the couch, and never with the television droning on.

Her eyes shut, unable to stay open. On the other hand, her ears worked perfectly, and she listened intently to Jeremy Banks, anchor at KYPX.

"A late evening beach party turned into an early morning horror show. A man walking his dog along the Manistique Park Beach stumbled upon a grizzly scene. When local authorities arrived on the scene, they discovered what appeared to be remains of an undisclosed number of bodies. According to an inside source, distinguishing one body from another proved impossible. Autopsies are scheduled to begin today where officials will use dental records for identification. Police are asking if anyone has any information concerning this incident to contact the Manistique Police Department at the number listed on your screen."

Liz shivered at the grotesque picture painted by the newscaster. Her stomach knotted when she realized the murders happened less than five miles from where she lived, a little too close for her liking. Then, an even more mind-blowing thought rushed over her. For the first time in nearly three years, her morgue would be the happening place to be today.

Liz stretched and whimpered at the excruciating pain that shot through her temples. She sat up, leaned her head against the couch and massaged her temples.

"Ow," she groaned and closed her eyes.

Wait a minute!

How the hell did she get here? Did she really fall asleep on the couch last night?

The last thing she remembered...the morgue, and, oh yeah, Mr. Hot and Sexy.

Her eyes shot open. She grimaced, but glanced around the room to discover it peacefully empty, the only noise coming from the television.

It must have been a dream.

"Bummer," she murmured.

Liz leaned back, her arm shielding her eyes. She needed to take some painkillers to soothe this killer headache.

"What does bummer mean, lass?"

Liz shot upright on the seat at the sound of the deep voice behind her. She grasped her head at the shooting pain, which flashed behind her eyes.

"Ow," she cried again.

When she found her bearings, she squinted up and saw her dream guy standing over her, his expression one of remorse.

"What are you doing in my house? And how did we get here?" she sputtered.

"Ye doona remember?"

"I wouldn't have asked if I remembered." Even the mere hum of her own voice made her head hurt. She lowered her voice to a whisper. "What did you do to me?"

"I'm sorry, lass. Most people doona handle my nature of travel well, but I dinna have a choice at the time."

"Your travel?"

"The hop, skip, and jump that brought us here. I

like to call it a shift."

"Shift? What the hell is that? Oh my god, are you from outer space?" Forgetting her headache, her voice had raised a fraction. She scooted her butt across the cushions, stopping when she reached the arm of the couch and couldn't go any further.

Fallon chuckled. "Nay, I'm no' from outer space." He scrutinized her. A devilish grin lit up his features as he added, "But ye might be able to persuade me to be yer favorite Martian."

"Mr.—?" Ah, Sh…ugar. She forgot his name.

"The name's Fallon. That's one of the side effects, too. Sorry." He must have recognized her confusion because he twirled a hand around his head. "The motion scrambles the brains a wee bit."

"Mr. Fallon—"

"Just Fallon. No Mr."

"Look, I don't know what's happening, but I think it might be best if you left now."

Fallon shook his head. "Sorry, Lizzie, I'm no' going anywhere. I canna take the risk of leaving ye alone."

"Why not?"

He shrugged.

"Look, I'm a big girl and can take care of myself. I've been doing a good job for quite some time now."

She struggled from her position on the couch, using the coffee table to draw herself to a standing position.

As she stood, her knees buckled.

Not good, Liz.

He reached out a hand to steady her.

"Don't." She brushed his hand away. "Please don't touch me."

Although he didn't frighten her, Liz wanted him to leave. If a phone call to the police accomplished that, then so be it. Her gaze shifted to the phone on the desk and then moved back to his face.

With an eyebrow raised in curiosity, he commented, "Lizzie, I'm no' going to hurt ye, lass. I give ye my word. Ye doona need to call anyone to come to yer rescue."

"And I'm to believe you? I don't even know you."

He smiled. "Ye know me well enough. As I said before, the memories will come to ye. Trust me."

It came as no surprise to realize she did trust him. She shook her head, turned, and staggered to the kitchen, amazed she managed to stay on her feet and not fall on her ass.

She reached into the cabinet over the sink and pulled out a bottle of painkillers. Grabbing a glass from the dish strainer, she turned on the faucet and waited for the water to chill. Even the light noise of rushing water made her head throb.

The pounding intensified, and her hands shook as she twisted the top off the bottle. Her stomach churned, and she swallowed the nauseating bile that rose in her throat. Just as she removed the lid, she lost her grip on the container. Pills flew in every direction, spilling on the countertop and in the basin.

"Sh...ugar!" She grabbed up three of the tablets and popped them into her mouth. Taking a sip of water, she tilted her head and waited while they slid down her throat with minor effort.

After setting the glass down, she rested her hands on the sides of the stainless steel sink and looked at the blue tablets scattered around.

She shook her head, released a sigh and collected the remaining wayward pills, put them back into the container, and returned the bottle to the cabinet.

"What the hell is going on around here?"

Realizing she'd spoken the words aloud, she clamped her lips shut. Her gaze shot to the door.

Great, now he probably thinks she's crazy, too.

She leaned up against the sink and closed her eyes waiting for the medication to kick in. A flash of light behind her eyelids brought her standing up straight as memories of the morgue suddenly, and without warning, swirled through her like scenes from a Twilight Zone flashback.

"Oh. My. God," she whispered. "This can't be good. Not good at all. What have I gotten myself into?"

****

Fallon stood to the side of the kitchen doorway, hidden from her sight. He'd followed her to make sure she remained on her feet.

Lizzie Forrester surprised him.

She handled the shift surprisingly well. It didn't happen often, but the last human he'd shifted remained cataleptic for days. When the woman regained consciousness, her memory was scattered and fragmented. She didn't remember Fallon, which turned out to be a good thing. It gave him the opportunity to disappear without having to say good-bye.

Fallon jumped away from the doorway, startled when something black ran past him. A furry, energetic creature, a blend of living bones and tissue ran across the living room and disappeared through the doorway on the opposite side of the room.

Blast and damnation! He hated cats. They gave him the creeps.

The scent of lilacs drifted up his nose and he turned. Lizzie leaned against the doorframe. Her brows creased with worry, highlighting her colorless complexion. He rushed forward. "Lizzie, are ye all right, lass?"

She held up a hand, stopping his advance, and stumbled past him, holding her head. At the couch, she lowered herself down slowly. "I'm fine."

He held his silence, giving her a few moments to

reflect on the events of the evening. She'd gone to work to do her job. Instead, she "made out" with a resurrected corpse, transported from the morgue to her house and ended up with a mind-blowing migraine.

Her eyes bloodshot, he saw her pain and wished he could make it better for her, but his powers were limited in that arena.

If he couldn't take her pain away, perhaps he could distract her from thinking of it.

"Lizzie?"

"What?"

"I know yer head hurts, but do ye think ye're up for a shopping trip to the store?"

"Shopping? Huh?" Her voice sounded tired, but he had to try.

He studied her expression as he dropped the sheet he wore. Her eyes widened, and despite the pain in their blue depths, Fallon swore he saw the sudden flash of desire.

"I seem to be missing my trews," he declared, spreading his arms wide.

Chapter Eleven

Liz's heart fluttered. Open mouthed, she stared at his bronzed, very masculine form. She'd already seen the magnificence of his broad chest and shoulders, knew his appeal, but the flawlessness of God's work drew all the breath from her lungs. His hard, grooved stomach drew her gaze downward to his strong thighs and powerfully built calves.

She tried to deny the pulsing knot, which formed in her stomach. Filled with a strange inner excitement, a lump rose in her throat. The warmth searing between her legs intense, stronger than anything she'd ever experience, all with a single look.

Sh...ugar!

Her heart raced, and blood heated until she damn near exploded. Anxious to escape his enticing presence, she looked away and closed her eyes.

Working in the morgue, Liz had seen all sizes and shapes of the male anatomy, but none of them compared to the man who stood in front of her.

At the morgue, his lifeless body radiated masculinity. Now, sexual magnetism literally gushed from every pore.

She opened her eyes.

"You don't play fair." She cleared her throat and lifted her gaze to his.

"Lizzie—"

Liz lifted her index finger, the other four clenched tight in a fist. She waved her finger then pressed it to her lips. He must have understood the signal because he kept his mouth shut. Smart man. With a semblance of ease, she pushed herself to her feet and left the room.

****

Fallon started to follow but hesitated, afraid he might push her over the edge. She didn't look well. A pale shade of gray lined her face. He'd also seen the bewildered look in her eyes.

Bloody hell!

Why should he care? After all these centuries of keeping his emotions buried deep inside, why now? How could that have happened?

Bastard! An uncontrollable anger surged through his gut.

What possessed him to bite her?

Still a man, Fallon suffered the same maladies as any other chap, craving a release only a woman's body could provide. And women happily obliged his needs. He cast his mind back to the last filly that had lain in his bed some five years ago. He did his thing and left, taking the lass's memory with him. If he remembered correctly, the sex wasn't anything to boast about.

With Lizzie, it took one touch of her soft lips, and he lost all common sense.

To bite meant to choose.

Gut instinct told him to get away from her. Her life depended on it. By the gods, why did he succumb to temptation and claim her as his own?

Through the veranda doors, Fallon observed the sun rising. With the realization Seth wouldn't make it in time, he fought the urge to curse again. Muttering under his breath, he pulled the drapes shut, carefully avoiding the slivers of light slipping through the folds.

If sunlight touched him, Fallon would burn and lose control of the mental shield he'd placed around her home. There would be nothing to stop the

73

demons from honing in on his position.

"Do you think it's wise to stand in front of the window with no clothes on?"

He turned at her voice and gave her his most charming smile. Shrugging, he said, "I closed the shades."

She walked into the room with a pile of men's clothing in her hands.

Fallon grimaced. He assumed she lived alone, never thinking to ask if a husband or boyfriend were in the picture. A raw and primitive jealousy overwhelmed him, twisting his gut.

This couldn't be good.

She dropped them on the coffee table.

"They belong to my friend's brother, James. He's almost your size, although not as..." She cleared her throat. "Well, anyway, he's away in the Navy, but keeps a spare change of clothes here in case he needs them when he comes to town."

"Are ye and this James—?" Fallon let his question hang unfinished.

As though understanding, Liz shook her head. "Christine and I have been friends ever since I came to live here in the fifth grade. We grew up together. Best friends forever and all that. And then, she went off to nursing school, met the illustrious Dr. Mark Sterling, got married and relocated to New York City. He received a great job offer as Medical Director at St. Vincent's Hospital in Manhattan. Their parents moved to Florida last summer. They finally gave up the cold for the warmth." She shrugged her shoulders and wrinkled her nose. "Anyways, James travels a lot but still maintains ties to this area. He visits whenever he's in the area." Fallon grinned at her ramblings. She must have sensed his humor for, in the next moment, her lips snapped shut, and her cheeks turned a vivid scarlet.

She shot him a withering glance before she shrugged and finished in a low voice. "He's a good friend, and I help him out. That's all."

Fallon almost laughed aloud at her mortified expression.

Instead, he smiled, while mentally, he released a sigh of relief. It would be hard to explain to a significant other they had to get the hell out of his way. A blood bond takes precedence above anything else.

"Thank ye, Lizzie."

"Look, Fallon, it doesn't seem like you're in any hurry to leave, and, at this point, I don't care. My head is killing me. There's a shower down the hall, last door on the right. I'm going to take a nap." She studied him. "We'll talk when I get up."

"I'll be here." He nodded toward the window. "The sun is coming up. I wilna be able to leave until it gets dark outside."

"Oh, Sh…ugar, you really are—" Her voice trailed off, and she rolled her eyes. Spinning on her heels, she turned and disappeared into her bedroom.

The door closed with a click behind her.

After his shower, Fallon dressed in the green T-shirt and blue jeans Liz provided. The jeans were a wee snugger than he liked, but they were workable.

Fallon left the bathroom, stopping outside Liz's door. He turned the doorknob, pushed it open a crack and peered inside.

Gold and earth tone colors of the carpet matched the shade of the comforter covering the bed. Lying on her stomach, Liz's hand dangled over the side of the double bed. She'd taken the tie from her hair and strands of honey blond curls fell across her face.

Her deep, even breathing told him she slept.

The black cat curled at her feet. When the door opened, it lifted its head but snuggled into the comforter as if unconcerned by his presence.

Fallon closed the door and moved to the couch where he lay down, his feet hanging over the end. He placed his hands behind his head and stared at the ceiling.

Cold bastard, that's what he was. When he brought Lizzie into this, he put her life in danger. As his chosen mate, she would develop powers and strengths similar to his. They would consume her until they possessed her completely.

With one foot tottering on the edge of a huge chasm, Fallon visualized untamed, crimson eyes staring up at him from the black hole. He heard the laughter mocking him.

He needed to figure out a way to put an end to this.

His gaze traveled to Liz's computer desk sitting in the corner.

The power of the Internet.

Fallon opened the cabinet door and flicked on the switch. He leaned against the wooden backing of the chair and waited for the computer to power up.

Necessity forced Fallon to learn to adapt to the changing times. When the Internet first surfaced in the nineteen eighties, he'd scoffed at the information he'd found. It reminded him of the old storytellers, all make believe. It hadn't taken him long to realize any information provided a foundation on which theories were formed.

As the Internet grew, the legends and fables found on the pages substantiated his life, or, at least, parts of it. Fallon viewed the newest technologies as a necessity, a resource of information. Analyzing the data required delicate care.

When the computer finally booted, he leaned forward and began his search.

Several hours later, he stood and stretched. Frustrated, he ran a hand through his hair and released a long held breath.

Bloody hell!

It appeared that the solution to his quandary was a well-guarded secret. Many websites were unable to provide information on how to break the Síoraí Guardian blood union.

Over the years, Fallon had developed online relationships with ancient scholars, and he'd even sought their help. Their advice, usually reliable, didn't give him the answers he wanted to hear. Killing one of the mates was the only way to sever a blood bond.

He refused to have Lizzie's blood on his hands.

Unwilling to draw her into his violent world, Fallon knew he would never allow any harm to befall her. He vowed to do everything in his power to keep her safe, although that task appeared no small feat.

The bond they shared drew them together and tugged at their senses. Fallon needed to keep his sanity and ignore the powerful magnetism he knew would come.

He stretched out on the couch and closed his eyes, imagining her reaction to the news he planned to stick around for a while. Bobbing his feet back and forth, he couldn't help but smile.

He looked forward to her reaction.

Blasted woman.

Chapter Twelve

They knelt in the center of a bed...her bed.

She marveled at his naked chest, bronzed, muscular, and incredibly sexy.

His hands seized the front of her blouse and gripped the fabric. With a firm tug, the buttons popped and flew across the bed. He slid the satin material off her shoulders and tossed it to the floor. With one hand, he unsnapped the front clasp of her bra. It joined her shirt on the carpet.

He leaned back far enough for his gaze to travel over her face where he searched her eyes. The fire that raged around the periphery edges of the bed was no match for the flames of desire this man created inside her.

They didn't touch; content to stare into each other's faces. Her heart danced with excitement at the scorching glow she saw in the golden depths of his eyes.

Passion filled her, mounting inside her like the hottest fire, clouding her brain. Her body ached for his touch. The sweetly intoxicating musk of his body drew her like a magnet, and she buried her face against the corded muscles of his chest. He radiated virility.

His hand settled under her chin, pulling her face upward.

"Lizzie," he said, in a hoarse whisper.

She tingled in anticipation. "Yes," she murmured.

In one fluid motion, his arms encircled her, and

he drew her against his broad chest, smothering her lips with demanding mastery. He tasted of cinnamon spice.

She returned his kiss with a reckless abandonment fueled by her own explosive hunger. His lips traveled from hers to trail across her jaw until he reached her earlobe where he began to sensuously nibble on the fleshy tissue. She shivered with pleasure.

Her lips burned in the aftermath of his fiery possession. Filled with a burning desire to taste his mouth once again, she whimpered and attempted to recapture his mouth. His teeth nipped her ear, and she moaned. Her body craved his touch as waves of desire pulsated through her.

Fallon lifted his mouth from her ear. His gaze slid downward, raking over her. He traced a path from her shoulder and down across her breast with one long-tapered finger. Her flesh surged at the intimacy of his touch as he teased the taut pink nipple with his fingertip.

Her body shuddered at the electricity of his touch, and she drifted toward him, driven by her own passion.

He wrapped his arms around her and jerked her to him. She gasped in delight when they fell to the bed, her curves molded to the contours of his body. He leaned over her, his breath warm and moist against her face. Liz saw the longing in his eyes before he lay beside her and drew her against him.

Reclaiming her lips, he crushed her to him. He licked, nipped, tasted, and suckled her lower lip. Her body melted against his, and her world filled with only him.

His hand caressed her breasts, her hips, and her thighs. His kisses, long, deep, and slow changed to hard, fast, and punishing.

"Fallon! Please!" She arched her back, needing to

be even closer to him, drawn to a height of passion pounding through her heart, chest and head.

Fallon rolled her onto her back. He loomed above her, his body a silhouette of darkness. Liz searched his eyes exhilarated by the power she saw in their depths.

"What do ye want, Lizzie?" he challenged her, his voice raspy.

"Only you." Her breathing ragged, her voice breathless, she raised her fists to beat on his chest. "I want you."

He caught her hands and pressed them against the bed.

A heartbeat passed, then another as they stared into each other's eyes. Gripping both of her hands in one of his, he held her in place. His free hand slid over her.

"Fallon!" Her body throbbed. She needed him. A moan of ecstasy escaped her lips.

He nuzzled her neck, his hand sliding across her stomach to the swell of her hips, his voice soft against her hair. "What, lass? Tell me."

Liz's skin tingled from the sensuality of his tone.

"Make love to me. Make us one," she gasped.

He nudged her thighs apart with his knee and settled against her moist heat. He thrust his hips forward, pushing against her, but didn't enter her.

She groaned in frustration and grasped his hips, pulling him toward her. "I want you, Fallon."

He teased her, his hand exploring her thigh before moving up to fondle one small globe, its pink nipple marble hard.

"Wanting me isna enough, Lizzie. Ye must feel like ye canna breathe without me. Tell me ye canna live without me. No matter what the cost."

She looked into his face, acceptance on her lips.

Liz jerked awake with a violent start. Her breath escaped in short, ragged gasps, her body so intensely stimulated she trembled from head to toe.

She gripped the bedspread with clenched fist. Her legs moved restlessly against the sheets, tangling her nightgown around her hips.

****

Fallon shot up from his horizontal position on the couch.

He raked a hand through his hair and drew an agonizing breath. His body ached with throbbing passion.

For those few minutes, his thoughts and body merged with Lizzie's. They were one.

Fallon chewed his lip in indecision, stunned at his own actions. His emotions took on a mind of their own, demanding Lizzie accept him, all of him, including what he was.

Reality forced him to break the link that connected them. He'd seen the acceptance in her eyes and needed to stop before she uttered the word. If she'd consented, he wouldn't have been able to stop.

As much as he wanted to take her, to make love to her, Fallon couldn't consecrate their union. To do so would cement the loosely threaded link that connected them. He would be powerless to stop her from crossing the threshold that separated his solitary world of violence and darkness from hers.

Once a Síoraí has chosen, the bond must be complete before the new mate received the same powers as the guardian. Lizzie was human, one wee lass. He wasn't sure if she could control that much energy.

What would it do to her?

A muscle twitched in his jaw.

By the gods! Fallon blocked the thought from his mind.

His ears caught the sound of a click as a door opened.

81

He glanced over his shoulder. Lizzie leaned against the doorframe of her bedroom. Her hair curled wildly around her face with a natural loveliness that reminded Fallon of a wood nymph, beautiful and sexy.

He stood up and pushed his hands deep into his pockets.

She caught her bottom lip with her teeth and released it slowly, an inexplicable look of withdrawal on her face.

"Are ye feeling better?"

She blinked. A probing query entered her eyes. Her mouth opened as if to speak. Instead, she clamped her lips shut, turned, and padded down the hall, disappearing from sight.

****

The soap slipped from Liz's hand and fell to the bottom of the tub. She left it there while she closed her eyes and tilted her head to let the hot water from the shower spray across her face.

Tired images formed behind her lids, and she was surprised to realize that none of them had the power to scare her anymore. Life had taken her so far past that point.

She swiped the water from her face, wondering how she could be so accepting of this whole situation. How was it possible she shared a deep connection with this man? This stranger? Why did he seem so familiar? What happened in the morgue? Had their connection been forged the moment he'd bit her?

So many questions, but no answers.

She ran her hand across neck feeling for the wound. Would there be marks there? She switched off the shower, grabbed a towel, and stepped from the bathtub.

She raced to the mirror, her hand wiping the residual mist of steam from its surface.

What she saw in the mirror didn't surprise her.

No monster with huge fangs and chalky skin. The face of Elizabeth Marie Forrester, her face, stared back.

Liz rested her forehead against the glass, drawing in a deep breath. She raised a hand to her neck. Tiny indentations swelled beneath her fingertips. Tilting her head to the side, she examined them in the smudged mirror. The four puncture marks now white little pinpricks against her light skin. They looked so innocent, but what had they done to her? What had *he* done to her?

Enough!

The time had come to find out how Fallon O'Callaghan ended up in her life, in her dreams, and more specifically, in her bed.

Victoria Noxon

Chapter Thirteen

A door shut, and the sound echoed down the hall. Moments later, the shower flared to life.

Was the water freezing? Icy? Enough to cool her heated skin? After their erotic mind play in her bedroom, he could use a cold one himself.

The thought only reinforced his need to get as far away from Lizzie Forrester, away from the temptation, as soon as possible. Fallon looked at the clock and sighed. Only two o'clock. A long afternoon loomed in his near future.

The phone rang.

Fallon looked at it warily but didn't rise to answer it.

A recorded likeness of Lizzie's voice told the caller she was unavailable and to leave a message after the beep.

"Hey, Liz, it's Murray. That report wasn't on my desk this morning. Rapid Rivers is breathing down my neck. They're looking for answers. Also, I'm not sure if you saw the news this morning, but the police picked up a mess on the beach. The morgue is going to be pretty busy. I know you were up until the early hours of the morning, but I'm sure they'd appreciate your assistance. Give me a call as soon as you get this message. You've got the number."

Click.

Instinct warned him the report this Murray waited for had been his autopsy. He wondered how she planned to deal with that one.

A movement drew his attention to the hall.

84

Lizzie wrapped in a pale, pink robe, leaned against the wall just inside the living room. Fallon's imagination ran rampant, curious to know what she wore, or didn't wear, underneath the fuzzy housecoat.

He squelched his thoughts and desires while searching her face.

She avoided his gaze, vigorously rubbing her wet hair with the towel.

"Who was on the phone?"

"Murray. He left ye a message."

She stiffened. "Sh...ugar." Lowering the towel, her brows curved into a frown as she looked toward the answering machine. She wrapped the towel around her neck and muttered, "What the heck am I going to tell him?"

"The report he wants is mine, eh?"

She looked toward him, eyes narrowed. "I suppose, but hey, let's stop and think about that for a sec. You're here with me. You're talking, walking and breathing. That tells me I couldn't legally do an autopsy on you." She lifted her hands and dropped them on her thighs with a loud slap. "Uh oh, imagine that. No dead guy, no autopsy...there is no *damn* report to give to the man."

Fallon enjoyed her tirade. The fire in her eyes lit up her features, her cheeks rosy. Gorgeous. "I doona imagine there is. Is there anything I can do to help?"

She regarded him with a speculative gaze. "Would it be too much to ask...yeah, I suppose it might be—" She stopped, and then giggled before wagging her head. "Nah. I couldn't ask that of you."

Fallon chuckled, leaned back against the couch, and spread his arms wide in invitation. "Go ahead. Ask. I'm yours to command."

A small enchanting smile touched her lips.

She glanced down, the vision gone, and she stepped into the room where she lowered herself into the chair opposite him. After pulling up her legs, she tucked them inside her robe and wrapped her arms around her knees.

He followed her gaze to the computer screen. Her eyes widened, and she looked at him in question.

Fallon shrugged. "Research."

"Research, huh?"

"Aye, it's amazing the amount of information available on the net."

Liz dropped her feet to the floor and clenched her hands in her lap.

"What do ye have on yer mind, lass?"

Her blue eyes turned to an amazing shade of lavender, and she chewed on her bottom lip.

"Lizzie?"

"It appears you've been on my mind, and in my bed, and I would like to know how that's possible."

****

Fallon's heart skipped a beat. He was surprised she would think their encounter anything other than a dream. Keeping a straight face, he said, "Excuse me?"

"You heard me."

He rubbed his jaw, inhaling a profound breath. "Yeah, I heard, but I doona understand what ye're saying."

"Fallon." Her voice held a warning note, and from the look of determination on her face, he figured she wouldn't let him off the hook that easily.

He shook his head. "Lizzie, this isna a good time."

"Now is the perfect time." Liz opened her mouth and then shut it with a snap. After a moment, she seemed to change her mind and shrugged. "I don't usually talk about myself. Most people wouldn't understand, but I sense you're different, unusual in some way."

He chuckled. "I'll take that as a compliment."

"Can I?"

"Can ye what?"

"Can I talk to you?"

"Of course." Puzzled, Fallon watched the play of emotions on her face: first, bewilderment followed by indecision, and finally, resolve.

She nodded.

"About a year ago, I was working the midnight shift when they brought in the body of a twelve-year-old boy. His parents claimed he had fallen down the stairs."

"Where's this headed, lass?"

She raised her fine, arched eyebrows. "I thought you said I could talk?"

Fallon nodded. "Sorry," he said apologetically, his voice barely above a whisper.

"Family court authorities weren't entirely convinced his death was an accident. Apparently, there had been a history of domestic violence in the family, and they wanted to rule out abuse."

Tears formed in her eyes and glistened onto her lashes. He ached to comfort her but stayed put, sensing she needed to talk.

"Last night, with you, it was like I was reliving it all over again."

"What?"

"At the same time, I began his autopsy, Adam Jones started talking." She shook her head. "He told me his father's beatings were a ritual in their house. That night, Adam lost his balance at the top of the stairs when his father slapped him. He was afraid if he didn't say anything, the same thing would happen to his sister." At that moment, Lizzie looked him and smiled. It held a touch of sadness. "You don't seem surprised by my gifts."

Fallon shook his head, not quite sure what she needed to hear. To him, spiritualists existed everywhere, but it did explain her reaction. Instead, he changed the subject. "Did they hang the bloody bastard?"

"They issued an all point's bulletin and posted pictures on the news."

Fallon sat upright. "Do ye mean to tell me he's still out there walking around a free man?"

She shook her head. "They finally caught up with him, but not before he nearly killed the person he blamed for destroying his family."

"Who?" Fallon asked, yet the harder he tried to ignore the obvious, the more it persisted. Her next words confirmed his suspicions.

"I spent three weeks in the hospital."

Fury choked him, and he jumped to his feet. "I'm going to kill the fucking bastard." He glowered at her. "Where is he?"

Lizzie shook her head. "It doesn't matter. They put him away for a very long time."

"Why tell me this now?" His voice, although quiet, held an ominous quality.

"Because, like me, you're different. I see the dead and hear them talk." She paused, visually swallowing hard. "Every time I get near someone, their lives, their memories become mine. The dead who experience tragic deaths are the worst."

As she spoke, Fallon watched her, his heart pounded. Her confession explained so much about the strong mental bond they shared.

With special powers of her own, Lizzie's telepathy attracted his powers as a Síoraí, pulling them together. It explained why he couldn't stay away from her, why she appeared to be the most logical choice for a mate. His own instincts must have known, even when his mind denied it.

"Ye've chosen an unusual profession, lass. I canna imagine it's a pleasant one, especially if yer cadaver led an unsavory life."

"I didn't always have this gift. It started a little over a year ago." A spark of sadness fluttered across her face. Her fingers twirled the sash of her robe. "I've been a Medical Examiner longer than I've lived with this power. I used to love what I did, the investigative nature of uncovering the evidence needed to solve a crime." A crooked smile curved her lips. "I hate my career now."

"What caused these gifts to blossom? Or did they just appear one day?"

"I lost someone very special in my life. Shortly after, these bizarre abilities started. I've needed to adjust and work through it. God knows, it hasn't been easy."

Fallon couldn't help it. He needed to know who could have had such a powerful effect over her life. "I'm sorry. Boyfriend? Husband?"

Liz smiled sadly. "Oh, neither. I've never been married. My Aunt Rea and I were very close. She was the only family I had in the world."

Fallon relaxed. "Why do ye continue to do it then?" At her questioning expression, he explained, "Be a Medical Examiner."

"I won't deny this power scares me, but I've discovered that, with it, I can help people. You know, right the injustices of the world. The voices shock the hell out of me, rising dead bodies even more so, but the end result makes me feel like I accomplish something good with my pitiful existence."

Fallon stood and stretched, turning his back to her. He sensed Liz's gaze follow him as he walked across the room to stand in front of the mantel. His finger traced the wolf figurine.

"Fallon?"

What should he do? Didn't she have a right to know about him? It affected her, too.

A suffocating awareness filled his throat.

He didn't sense her leave the couch, nor did he

feel her until she stood behind him and placed her hand on his arm.

"Fallon, talk to me. When I saw you come alive on my table, I recognized something distinctive. There is something special in you."

"Lass, I was sleeping," he defended. "As I've said before I'm just a man."

She gave him a disbelieving look but made no comment. "There's a power inside you that you keep hidden in darkness. You're fighting something dark and evil. Why do you deny it?"

She didn't have any idea how hard it was for him to remain coherent when she stood so close. Her courage and determination were like a rock inside her, holding her steadfast and true to her path. She didn't know how much it shook his restraint.

No, he wouldn't, he couldn't let her get inside his head or his heart.

Fallon yanked away, ripping her hand from his arm. He took a few steps away, threw back his head and laughed, hoarsely and bitterly.

He turned to face her again, his expression grave. "Ye have no idea what I'm about, lass."

"Then tell me," she demanded. "Tell me I'm not losing my mind. I deserve at least that much, don't I?"

****

Liz noted his set mouth. When he raised his face to the ceiling, his Adam's apple bobbed, and a cynical smile crossed his expression.

Without looking at her, he shook his head and said, "Ye arena ready for an explanation."

The heat of anger flared within her. She jerked his arm forcing him to look at her.

"How dare you, Fallon O'Callaghan? How dare you disrupt my life and think you don't owe me anything in return?"

A muscle flicked in his jaw. When he lifted his

eyes to hers, she barely controlled her gasp of surprise. His eyes had turned an ominous shade of black, amber fire shooting from the pupils outward.

Liz's legs trembled in the face of his anger. Yet, she refused to cower in front of him.

"Can ye no' see it, lass?" His expression darkened. His brows drew together into a tight ball that wrinkled his forehead, giving him a sinister appearance. The corner of his lip rose revealing a razor sharp fang.

But it was his eyes that scared her the most. No longer human, they blazed demonic amber. "I'm hell on earth."

Chapter Fourteen

Liz recoiled at the cynicism in his voice. A wave of nervousness swept over her, and to her annoyance, her hands shook. To still the shaking, she clenched them into fists at her side. Her defenses weakened in the face of his anger.

Strengthening her resolve not to give into his tantrum, she masked her inner turmoil with deceptive calmness. She swallowed hard, lifted her chin, and met his gaze, pinning him in a steady glare. She might be trembling, but she had not and would not buckle.

She opened her mouth to ask him what the hell he meant, but a low knock at the front door interrupted her. A warning whispered in her head followed by an odd prickling sensation at the base of her neck. "Are you expecting someone?"

He frowned, twin furrows digging into the skin between his brows. Measuring her with a cool appraising look, he dared her to defy him. "Is there a problem?"

"You didn't think to ask before you invited friends over?"

A muscle ticked in his cheek at the clenching of his jaw. "I dinna believe it necessary," he replied, his baritone voice edged with control.

She bit her lip to contain her angry outburst.

The nerve of the man!

"And Lizzie, be sure to ask who's there before ye open the door."

"Do I look like a child to you?"

Fallon shrugged, fueling her anger. "Open the door, Lizzie. Doona keep our guest waiting."

She cast him a look to let him know they weren't done discussing this issue, and with a huff, she turned on her heels and strode to the foyer.

When she reached the door, she looked back at Fallon who nodded. He held her gaze, unflinching for a moment before a slight grin curved his lips.

When she didn't immediately move to the door, he crossed his arms over his chest and quirked his eyebrow in question.

She seethed with mounting fury.

How dare he?

She glared at him with burning, reproachful eyes. "You're a butt munch!" She threw the words at him like stones, her voice low, taut with anger.

A swift shadow of rage swept across his face, and Liz nodded, satisfied. At least he knew an insult when he heard one.

Turning to the door, she leaned against it, and asked, "Who's there?"

Muffled by the obstacle, the voice low and quiet, but she heard, "Seth MacLean."

Liz flicked the switch on the wall beside the door, sending soft light flooding over the porch. She opened the door a crack and glanced outside.

Behind her, Fallon called, "It's okay, Lizzie. Let him in."

She swung the door a little wider to see a man with the bluest eyes she'd ever seen, startling against fair skin and light hair. Although quite handsome, he didn't radiate sexual charisma like Fallon.

He smiled. His lips parted in a dazzling display of straight teeth that sparkled white against the shadows of darkness behind him.

Strong features held a gentle friendliness.

"Is Fallon here?" The warmth of his tone echoed

in his voice.

Liz let the door sway open. She followed the man's gaze to where Fallon stood in front of the glass doors, his back to them.

Fallon didn't turn around, but he said in a distant voice, "He canna come in unless ye invite him in, lass."

She turned to Seth. An easy smile played at the corner of his mouth while he waited her response. "You too, huh? It would seem everyone's gone a little bit wacky these days."

The man shrugged, and smiled without malice, almost repentantly.

"Well, golly gee, Miss Polly, come on in and make yourself at home. Mi casa es su casa. What the hell? All of Fallon's friends are welcome here."

Seth's brows rose at her sarcasm. Thankfully, he made no comment as he stepped through the open doorway and into the living room.

Fallon met him as he entered, holding out his hand to Seth who clasped it with his own.

"It's about time ye made it."

Seth shrugged. "An accident on the highway tied traffic up for over an hour last night. By the time I made it to your place, the sun peeked. I had to spend the day there."

"I hope ye dinna make a mess, and if ye did, ye cleaned up after yerself."

"There's not much damage one can do when they're sleeping."

Fallon laughed and slapped Seth on the shoulder. "Mi casa es su casa," he repeated Liz's earlier adage.

Liz had followed Seth into the room. When Fallon turned to her, she flinched at his dark, angry expression.

He frowned at her reaction.

In the next instant, her rebellious nature took

over, and she shot him a cold look.

"Seth, this is Elizabeth. Lizzie, this is Seth."

Liz acknowledged Seth with a brief nod. "Hi, Seth. Most people call me Liz, and I apologize for my behavior. I wish I could say I was expecting company, but I wasn't." She glared at Fallon who completely ignored her.

"Hi, Liz. I understand. Fallon tends to be a bit high strung at times."

Seth handed an object to Fallon who slipped it over his head. Electric lightning shot from his body. She blinked and shook her head to clear the image, keeping her expression under stern restraint.

After a few moments of uncomfortable silence, Liz cleared her throat. "Well, I'll leave the two of you alone. If you need anything, I'll be in the other room. Just give me a holler."

Liz headed to her room. Before she shut the door, she heard Seth ask, "What the hell have you gotten yourself into here, Fallon?"

"That's what I'd like to know," she mumbled.

In her dresser, she found a white T-shirt and a pair of jeans. She tossed them on her bed and slammed the drawer shut. Mumbling under her breath, she jerked her blue Levis on and tugged the T-shirt over her head.

That man infuriated her.

Deep baritone voices echoed into her room from the living room. Muffled by the plastered walls, she couldn't hear what they were saying.

She lay on the bed, and let the events of the past twenty-four hours replay in her mind.

Who *was* Fallon O'Callaghan? And how did he end up on her table at the morgue? Or in her bed? Only one person could answer those questions, and he refused to explain himself.

She had avoided a confrontation with Murray simply by not returning his call. A short-lived reprieve she knew she'd pay dearly for.

She'd called the morgue around seven o'clock and spoke with one of her assistants, Dale. Like Gloria, Liz relied on him although Dale could be a bit scatter-brained at times. True to his nature, he'd panicked when Liz told him she wouldn't be in. It took ten minutes for Liz to reassure him everything would be fine. She'd be there first thing in the morning. Familiar with Liz's history, neither one of her assistants ever questioned her reluctance to work at night.

An hour passed. The front door creaked opened and then closed with enough force to shake the walls of her room.

Liz stepped into the living room to find Seth sprawled on the couch, his eyes glued to the television.

He looked up and smiled. "Hey, there."

Liz searched the room. "Where's Fallon?"

"He went out to take care of some business."

"What business?"

Seth shrugged. "He doesn't always tell me what he's up to."

"Oh." She started to turn away, but stopped, looking back. "Why are you still here?"

"He wanted me to hang out and make sure you're okay."

She frowned. "I'm not a child. It's been fifteen years since I've needed a nanny."

Seth's eyes glowed with amusement, and his lip curved. "Funny you should say that because it's been three hundred since I've been one."

A quick breath of utter astonishment filled her chest. "Three hundred? You don't say?"

"I do." He grinned with no trace of animosity. In the next second his attention returned to the television.

Liz viewed his action as a simple gesture of

dismissal.

She was going to kill Fallon when he returned, or at least cause him bodily harm for taking off and leaving without a word. She flinched at the nagging voice whispering in her head and wondered why she even cared if he came back or not.

Chapter Fifteen

The exit from the highway came sooner than Fallon expected. He downshifted and hit the brakes at the same time he swerved onto the off ramp. At the top of the exit, a green highway sign indicated Rapid Rivers 10 miles north of his current location. Just short of the city limits, he veered to the right and followed the bright red arrows onto a small road barely wide enough for Seth's Pontiac.

Damn, he missed his Harley.

Illegally parked four blocks from where he'd been attacked, the Rapid River's police placed it in impound. Seth would take care of it and make the necessary arrangements to have it delivered to his house where Fallon agreed to pick it up later.

The halogen headlights sliced through the dark woodlands shining off the chain link fence that lay parallel to the road. Every quarter mile, Fallon posted black and white *No Trespassing* signs. He'd hung them when he first purchased the several hundred acres of land more than ninety years ago. The fence ended below his small log cabin.

Fallon switched off the headlights having no difficultly seeing the silhouette of his cabin against the blackened hillside. He drove into the driveway, turned off the engine, and left the car.

The thought of leaving Lizzie gnawed at him, but he needed to get away. The images of her in his arms, their bodies intertwined as they made love didn't allow him to concentrate on anything but her.

Fallon didn't tell Seth about the connection he

and Lizzie shared. He didn't need to know about that. Not yet.

Of course, Seth pitched a fit about having to babysit, but when he saw the television, his couch potato nature took over, and he settled down to watch *I Love Lucy*. Fallon often warned the vamp he would fry his brain watching the crap they played on that contraption, but it hadn't made any difference to Seth.

Fallon had no need for any of the frivolous extras people enjoyed these days. Everything he required lay right here in this small cabin.

Visions of Lizzie's face flashed in his thoughts. A war of contrasting emotions raged within him and his head swirled with doubts.

Did he truly have all he wanted?

He pushed the disturbing question away as he flew up the porch steps and through the door. Although not quite as elegant as Lizzie's house, this was his home.

Over the years, he received many offers to sell the place but never took any of them seriously. He'd purchased this land legally and for next to nothing. It was the only thing he would ever likely own, and he had no intentions of giving it up.

He glanced around at his meager furnishings, which consisted of a desk, two chairs and a laptop that set in the center of a table. Behind the closet wall lay a hidden room where he slept beside his armory of weapons.

He let out a long, audible breath. It wouldn't be safe to bring Lizzie here. Surrounded by trees, his small home would be an easy target.

No, it was safer to stay at her house.

The borrowed jeans he wore were tight enough to castrate a man. He changed into his own clothing, a black turtleneck, black jeans and sharp-toed cowboy boots. He breathed a deep sigh of relief as blood surged back into his groin. Lizzie may have torn his heart in two, but at least his jewels remained intact.

The Talisman nestled against his bare chest, concealed beneath his turtleneck. Fallon remembered the electrifying charge as his powers strengthened. He smiled. The magical stone always had that effect on him.

He grabbed his leather jacket and tucked a few wooden stakes alongside a spare cell phone.

Personal belongings in hand, he scanned the empty cabin. He didn't feel sorry about leaving the sanctuary it gave him. In fact, he looked forward to Lizzie's company. At least until he destroyed the demons that tracked him. Then, he'd get the hell out of her life.

Tossing his possessions into the back seat of the car, he jumped behind the wheel.

Time to go hunting.

Less than an hour later, Fallon flicked off the headlights and drove into the alley behind The Station, a bar and grill where demons liked to visit. They hung out in the shadows and waited for patrons to leave the tavern. Demons weren't selective in their choice of meals, but some preferred alcohol tainted blood. The alcohol heightened their senses.

Considered taboo to cross the lines that distinguished the covens, demons kept to their own breeds. But in the past hundred years or so, things changed. Vampires made packs with werewolves and shape shifters and vice versa. They'd come to some kind of peaceful co-existence, hunting in packs, and enjoying the bounty of their kills together.

To Fallon, it didn't matter what breed they were or what group they traveled in. If they killed, they could be killed, and he planned to do it.

"Fallon! Hey man, what are ye doing in this

neck of the woods?"

Fallon's defenses sharpened. His shoulder tensed. He swung around at the voice, whipping the knife from his belt.

He relaxed when Devlin McNeil, the eldest of the four Síoraí Guardians, sauntered through the alley toward him.

Devlin raised his hands in the air. "There's no need for that. I'm on yer side, or have ye forgotten about us?"

Where Fallon was the gods' least favorite; Devlin was their pet. Fallon didn't give a damn. More power to the man. Created more than five hundred years before Fallon left his mother's womb, Devlin's origin remained a closely-guarded secret.

"Dev, what brings ye to Rapid Rivers?"

"The gods called us to the vicinity to check out a surge of power in the area. Cara and Cameron are walking the beaches."

Fallon tensed. It must have been one hell of a surge for four guardians to be in the place at the same time.

"Funny, I dinna hear anything."

Devlin shrugged. "Perhaps ye werena listening."

Fallon snorted. After all, he had been busy over the past twenty-four hours, and, mayhap, just dinna hear the call.

"They believe something big is coming."

"Believe? They doona know?"

"No' yet. That's why they sent us here."

"Some gods, eh? I thought they knew everything."

"Watch it, Fallon. Ye have been granted leniency, which, I might add, I fail to see why, but I doona have to listen to yer lips talking trash about them."

Fallon raised his hand in surrender. "Hey, man, I doona have any issues with ye."

Devlin inclined his head in acceptance. "Good, if ye chose to pick one with me, ye'd lose."

Fallon let out a grunt at Devlin's presumption.

Devlin smiled, his expression changing to one of curiosity as he looked at Fallon. "Ye know, Fallon, I doona understand ye."

"What's to understand?"

"Ye chase and kill demons like ye were born to it."

"I've been told that's why I exist."

"Aye, well, we all were, but ye're different than the rest of us. Cara, she's a Síoraí through and through. She can smell a half-breed a mile away, and its scent stays with her until she's destroyed it. Cameron is still a newbie."

In spite of himself, Fallon chuckled. "Newbie? He's two hundred and fifty years old. I'd hardly call him a newbie."

Devlin grinned and shrugged. "Aye, but he's still learning the ropes. He's accepted being a Síoraí and the value that comes with it, but he strives too hard. He fights with a passion I'm afraid might get him killed. But ye, ye have accepted the powers. Ye play the part, but ye havena embraced the destiny the gods granted ye."

Fallon laughed without humor. "Let me explain. They're pissed off because I'm the only one of ye who refuses to be a puppet on their strings. I wilna crawl to them on hands and bended knees, and praise them for doing this wonderful, grand endowment for me. Answer me a question, will ye, Dev?" he asked softly, his tone sarcastic. "Doesna it piss ye off to know ye were created by them for use in their personal wars? No' to mention, in order to receive this grand privilege, they stripped away everything that made ye human. That's the only way anyone can become one of their precious immortal guardians."

"They dinna inflict the pain, nor did they strip anything away. That's what life is all about. The gods dinna set out to screw up my life nor did they set out to screw up yers. It happened, but they gave me something to look forward to. I prefer my life now. I'm sure ye would too, if ye gave them a chance."

"Look, Devlin, I know ye're trying to help, but do me a favor, leave it be. I've lived a long time the way I am, and I've grown accustomed to it. I like the asshole I am."

Devlin laughed, nodding. "Asshole, aye, but first and foremost, a guardian and a strong champion for these people."

Fallon gave a wry grin. "I do the best I can with what I've got."

Fallon stiffened as the distinct stench of death filled his nostrils. He knew Devlin picked up the scent too when the elder nodded. Demons hovered nearby.

Smiles of anticipation lit up their faces.

"Well, well, well, it looks as if it's our lucky day, boys."

Fallon and Devlin spun around at the same time to face the demon whose voice boomed from the shadows.

Devlin counted off the group as they came into the light from the streetlamp. "The three on the right are vamps. The other two shape shifters." He nodded to the male on the left. "See the fleas on that one? If I were to guess, I'd say cat. The other, hmmm, that long nose and fingernails would make him a bird."

"It doesna matter what the hell they are. They'll be dead verra shortly."

At his prediction, a low growl ricocheted through the group and bounced off the walls of the alley. A burst of adrenalin charged through Fallon's veins at the imminent fight, and his fangs took shape.

The demons rushed them. Fallon and Devlin each raised a hand to erect a luminous wall between them and their attackers.

Two of the vampires slammed into the force field. Their bodies jerked as white electric lightning encircled them. They spun around several times before the force released them, flinging them against the brick wall on the opposite side of the alley. They landed with a sold *thud* on their arses. Shaking their heads, they jumped to their feet, their faces murderous.

They charged again.

"Ah, I think we ticked them off," Devlin observed.

"Good, a ticked off demon is a dead demon."

Fallon raised his hand and mentally called for a piece of wood leaning against the dumpster. With a quick flick of his wrist, he sent the six-inch stake whizzing through the air where it struck the pale, blue-veined bloodsucker deep in the heart. The vampire disintegrated into a cloud of gray dust.

Devlin, a knife in hand, took a step forward just as the shape shifter altered into the form of a leopard. He raised his hand as the cat leapt through the air. The knife sliced through the fur and entered the soft underbelly of the animal. After a final twist, he flung the dead beasty to the side and focused his attention on the three remaining half-breeds.

Fallon hissed as a searing pain cut through his shoulder.

Sweet Mother of God!

While he fought a young, azure-skinned vampire, the other shape shifter altered into an eagle and attacked. He hissed as the bird clawed into his shoulder, slicing his flesh to pieces.

While the bird assaulted him, Fallon drew a sharp stick from the pocket of his jacket. Ignoring the wood slivers piercing his skin, he stabbed the vampire. *Poof.* Gray powder splattered the pavement as its body burst apart.

He whipped around and grabbed the eagle by its legs. The bird's wings thrashed about in frenzy, and its sharp beak slashed at his hand in an attempt to escape. Before it shifted back to its human form, Fallon twisted the eagle's neck until the bones snapped. He dropped the fowl to the concrete.

Fallon turned in time to see Devlin withdraw his stake from the last vampire. The body disintegrated.

Devlin turned to Fallon and grinned. "Now that's what I call fun."

"Aye," Fallon replied, breathless.

"Well, I best be moving on. Where are ye headed?"

A simple, innocent question, but it sent Fallon's nerves on edge.

"Devlin, why do I get the feeling yer no' here, in this part of town, by coincidence?"

Devlin's expression never wavered.

Fallon prickled with suspicion. "They sent ye here, dinna they?"

"So what if they did?"

"Are they having me tailed?"

Devlin shrugged, his eyes level under drawn brows. "I do as I'm told. Unlike ye, I follow orders."

"And what are yer orders?"

"Ye have been marked. The gods sent me in to protect ye and make sure ye remain unharmed."

Fallon chuckled. "Protect me? Ye're kidding, right?"

"Nay, I'm no'. When ye were attacked—" Devlin hesitated.

"How do ye know about that?" At Devlin's raised forehead, Fallon shook his head. "Never mind. Ye doona need to answer."

After all, the gods knew everything.

"The three demons that attacked ye got a nip of yer blood, Fallon. Once they catch our scents, they can easily find our trail. That's why it is so important they die before they get the chance to get away."

"I doona lose, Dev."

"So ye say, but they escaped."

"Only because I forgot about the eclipse," Fallon grudgingly admitted.

"I know, but ye canna use that as an excuse. There is none. The gods fear they will take ye and get possession of the Talisman. If ye lose—" his voice faltered.

Both men were aware of the consequences if that happened. As a great source of power, the Talisman would grant demons a huge advantage over the Síoraí and the gods.

"They have so little faith in me?" Fallon asked, uncertain why his stomach knotted in anticipation of the answer.

"Oh, come on, man, ye havena given them any reason to trust ye."

"Whether they want to admit it or no', they doona have a choice. Why is it, Devlin, of all the Síoraí Guardians, I am the one who wears the Talisman?"

Triumph flooded through him when Devlin winced at his words.

"Damned if I know, but the gods must have a reason. Ye do understand why they're concerned, doona ye?"

After a long pause, during which he fought for control, Fallon vowed, "I wilna allow those bastards to take the Talisman."

"They'll be able to track ye."

"I can handle them. I've developed this awesome mental shield," he said, with easy defiance.

"That will work for a while, but those three…"

"...have to die." Fallon finished for him.

Devlin nodded.

Fallon clasped him on the shoulder. "Nice to see ye again, Dev. We'll have to do this again sometime. It's been fun."

Again, the elder nodded. He reached into his coat pocket and withdrew a card. "Here's my cell number. If ye need any help, call, and we'll all be there for ye."

Fallon took the card. Without looking at it, he tucked it into the inside pocket of his jacket. "Thanks, I'll keep that in mind." He turned on his heels and began to gather his weapons.

"Fallon?"

Fallon glanced over his shoulder.

"Ye doona have to do this alone. There's safety in numbers." Devlin paused. A slight smile crossed his face. "Take care of yer lass. All isna as it seems."

"How—"

Before the question passed his lips, Devlin disappeared around the corner of the building. His whistling lyrics faded into the distance.

Devlin's words echoed in his mind.

Bloody hell!

Lizzie!

Chapter Sixteen

With a basket full of clothes perched on her hip, Liz flicked off the switch sending the laundry room into darkness. She crossed the threshold into the kitchen and cursed. She'd forgotten to turn on the other lights and had to stumble through the dark to the living room.

The ticking of the wall clock echoed in the silence. The green glow of the oven timer read one o'clock, the only light to infiltrate the darkness.

Fallon hadn't returned, and no matter how hard she tried, Liz couldn't draw Seth away from the television set. So instead, she got a jump-start on her chores. She pushed open the swinging doors leading into the living room, breathing a sigh of relief she'd made it through without stubbing a toe.

She tiptoed through the room, shaking her head at the idiotic smile on Seth's face as she passed the couch.

In her room, she dropped the basket on the bed and started to fold its contents. A dark shadow materialized over her hand. Startled, Liz dropped the shirt she'd been holding and screamed. She swung around, her hand balled into a fist; her arm back, her muscles tight.

An instant before her closed fist connected with its target, a hand caught her wrist, yanking her up against a rock hard chest. She inhaled his scent. Fallon. It was undeniably him, a blend of a forest at dawn combined with the heady scent of leather.

His warm breath stirred her hair. In a voice

thick and unsteady, he spoke. "It's me, Lizzie. I dinna mean to frighten ye."

Liz's heart pounded in her chest, and she breathed in shallow, quick gasps as she tried to control the spasmodic trembling inside.

She drew on the heat of the gentle arms around her, letting it seep into her body. Her shock faded beneath a heavy onslaught of fury.

What if she'd been naked?

"Get away from me!" She shot the words at him like stones and pushed herself from his arms. Her hands clenched at her sides. She turned away, anxious to hide the angry tears that threatened to spill down her cheeks.

Damn it, not now!

She swallowed hard, willing them to stop.

She drew in a couple of deep soothing breaths and counted to ten. "I wish you wouldn't do that," she whispered, a hand on her breast.

"Do what?"

She twisted around to face him and sighed in exasperation, her eyes narrowed. "Sneak up on me." Pleased at how blasé she sounded.

He had the nerve to smile. "Aye, ma'am."

"And don't call me ma'am. It makes me feel old."

"Aye, ma'—Lizzie."

Liz wanted to slap the smirk off his smug face and would have, but the door opened, drawing their attention.

"Are you okay, Liz? I thought I heard a scream," Seth asked anxiously.

Liz glared at Fallon. "I was fine until he popped out of thin air and gave me a frigging heart attack."

"I told ye I was sorry." His eyebrows rose in question. "Doesna that count for something?"

"At the moment, no!"

Liz glanced at the door to see Seth back out of the room. She heard him mutter something about faint-hearted women, spiders and mice.

Fallon raised a hand in protest. "I wanted to make sure ye were okay."

"Do you mean before or after you came flipping in here and grabbed me? You could have picked up the phone and called."

He smiled sheepishly, scratching his chin. "I would have, but I doona know yer number."

Liz choked on a cry, her heart jumping in her chest. She reached out and clutched his hand. "You're hurt."

Blood seeped from beneath his jacket and ran a trail down the back of his hand.

He jerked his hand from hers. "I'm fine."

"Let me see." She reached for his coat. Just as she was about to slip it from his shoulders, he grabbed her hand and stopped her. Electricity shot through her fingertips at his touch, and she gasped.

He didn't notice. "Later."

"It'll get infected if you don't clean it."

He smiled. "Nay, it wilna. Besides, it'll heal before ye get the chance to put a band-aid on it." He didn't give her the opportunity to say anything else as he turned and hollered, "Seth."

A moment later, Seth poked his head through the crack in the door. "Yeah?"

"Keep an eye on her. I have to go pick up yer car. I'll be back by sun up."

"No problem."

Turning to Liz, he studied her as though memorizing the contours of her face, and then he was gone.

Liz waved her hand through the air where he'd stood and squinted in stunned disbelief.

Nothing. Nada. Zip.

She looked over her shoulder at her babysitter who lounged casually against the doorframe. "How the hell does he do that?"

Seth smiled. "Magic."

****

Fallon gripped the steering wheel in both hands, knuckles white under the strain. He'd just left the highway and headed to Lizzie's house on an isolated back road.

No matter how hard he tried, he couldn't deny his attraction to Lizzie, and that knowledge twisted his gut. The moment he met her, he'd snapped and became a different man.

And this new him wasn't setting well with the old one.

When Devlin mentioned Lizzie, all thoughts of the hunt for his demon trackers fled. A cold knot formed in his stomach, and he'd rushed off. The urge to keep her safe caused him to do stupid things. Like popping in unannounced. The fact he'd frightened her came as no surprise, but he had to ensure she was safe. Bloody Hell. He'd never done anything like that before.

Then again, what if he did make Lizzie his?

If he consecrated their union, she'd claim his powers and strengths, and no longer need a protector. She'd be capable of defending herself. As an added bonus, he would never be alone again, his existence no longer dark and empty. Maybe, with Lizzie, he could, once again, experience the love and laughter he'd known briefly with Rhiannon.

Tempting, the idea held appeal.

Fallon held the image close and savored it, even though it would never happen.

Every night for the past five hundred years, he cursed the gods for this power, for his immortality and the centuries of loneliness he suffered at their hands. He could not selfishly bequeath such a horrible fate to another.

When he drew her blood, she became his mate, with no way to undo his transgression. He felt as if a

111

hand had closed around his neck cutting off his oxygen.

Icy fear twisted around his heart at the undeniable and dreadful facts. He may not have bed her, but that didn't mean he hadn't succeeded in drawing her into his world in a myriad of other ways, each an unseen connection that bound her to him.

He slammed his fist against the steering wheel.

Demons would hunt her as they hunted him. He needed to set her free.

He could only think of one way, but that meant breaking a promise he'd made to himself centuries ago.

Lizzie was worth it.

He cranked the wheel to the left and swerved to the shoulder of the road. He whipped the gear-shifter into park and jumped from the car, shouting to the empty space around him, "Dagda, show yerself!"

Except for the chirps of the night crickets, and a hoot of an owl in the distance, all remained silent. The atmosphere stilled.

"Dagda, I know ye hear me. I wish to speak to ye."

Again, silence.

"Ye bloody bastard, are ye such a coward? Do ye fear me that much? Come on!"

A voltage of electrical energy permeated the air, and the hair on his arms stood up. The cool stale air turned heavy.

An iridescent light appeared near the shoulder of the road. Fallon shielded his eyes from the glow. A column of light stretched high into the sky.

Dagda drifted through the spatial chamber. Over seven feet tall, he hadn't changed from the memory Fallon painted in his mind of the commander all those years ago. Illuminated by an incandescent white aura, his robe and shoulder length black hair blew against an unseen breeze. His face portrayed a mask of rage, and his eyes glowed of red amber as he floated toward Fallon, his feet five inches from the pavement.

Electricity crackled in the air. They stared at each other, the tension escalating each moment that passed.

"I should destroy you, Rebel." Dagda's tone low, yet edged with steel. His mouth twisted with the threat.

"Then do it." At least Lizzie would be set free.

Fallon waited, his stance challenging the god to go through with it.

A flash of humor crossed Dagda's face. "I don't think so." He lowered himself to the ground facing Fallon. "Your courage far outweighs your stupidity."

"I am no' one of yer guardians."

"You deny your destiny, yet you play the role you were born for."

"I doona do it for ye."

Dagda shrugged, dismissing Fallon's assertion. "The reasoning behind your actions is of no matter. It is enough that you do." With a gleam of interest in his eyes, he asked, "Why did you summon me?" His eyes turned a dark shade of burgundy with his next words. "And the next time you do in such a manner will be your last."

"Deal with it. I do."

The amused look left Dagda's eyes, and an agonized expression crossed the elder's face.

Dagda swiveled away and raised his hand. The conduit from this world to his returned, and he walked toward it.

As Dagda entered into the light, Fallon took a step forward. "Where are ye going?"

The god turned to face Fallon when he answered, "Back to the Otherworld. It is apparent you must seek your answers alone with whatever issue brings me here."

"How do ye release a blood mate?"

One corner of Dagda's mouth curved into a slight smile, and without malice, he replied, "There is only one way."

"How do I do it?"

"Death," he said with quiet emphasis.

The words, short and curt, confirmed Fallon's fear, and he flinched.

Dagda turned toward the chamber once again.

"There has to be another way. Tell me!" Fallon demanded.

Without facing Fallon, the god hesitated. Over his shoulder, he said, "All is not what it seems, Fallon. You have a precious gem in your care, and I do not speak of the Talisman. Keep them both safe, my son."

The light faded into blackness. Alone once again, Fallon turned and started walking toward Seth's car.

In the next instant, Dagda's voice echoed across the worlds that separated them. "If you fail in this, we all fail."

The finality of Dagda's words reverberated in his head.

Chapter Seventeen

The humans of this time were pathetic creatures! Weak and feeble, they were unfit to feed a high power Vampryss such as herself. Even their blood tasted different, and yet, without it, she would perish from undernourishment.

Deidra refused to grant the gods that satisfaction and vowed if she were to feed, she would find pleasure in the hunt. In truth, she welcomed the opportunity to put these sniveling cowards out of her misery and their own.

Her blood surged at the memory of the one she'd killed last night.

She'd been wandering and found herself in a cluster of trees on the outskirts of town. The sickly sweet fragrance of firs drifted thick across the light wind. Fallen pine needles blanketed the path she trudged. With sweeping footsteps, she avoided twigs and made a detour around a large branch that blocked her path.

She made the steep climb upward and emerged into a huge clearing at the top of the trail where her eyes met the vision of a dilapidated shack. Light shone from the windows signaling occupants inhabited the rustic building. A sharp wire fence surrounded the property. The strands of cable drooped from wobbly posts, the metal barbs rusted.

Deidra easily stepped over the sagging barrier.

The door of the building creaked open. A dark skinned man with cropped hair appeared in the doorway. He bolstered the door open with a cinder block and disappeared around the side of the building, reappearing a minute later with an armload of chopped wood.

She lifted her nose to the air and sniffed. Besides her own scent, only one other drifted across the breeze.

She smiled.

By the time he made a second trip and stepped across the threshold, Deidra waited inside.

His eyes widened when they took in her appearance. Sweat trickled down his forehead when she smiled and ran her tongue across her sharp fangs.

Oh, yes! Dinner was served.

He tossed the firewood at her. She easily sidestepped the flying timber, taking no notice of the loud *clunk* as it smashed against the wall behind her.

Instead, she tracked the man's progress as he ran out the door.

Unhurried, she followed, stalking him.

When he tripped and rolled down an embankment, she jumped into the crevice beside him.

She strolled closer. He kicked out, twisted and tried to crawl up the bank. She planted her foot in the center of his back, pushing his face in the dirt.

"No," he cried, his voice muffled, frantic.

Deidra removed her foot. He rolled over and with wide eyes looked at her face. "Please," he begged.

His fear pulsated through her, and she thrived on the exhilarating scent that invaded her nostrils. The smell urged her onward. Blood pounded through his veins and inundated her hearing.

"It would be my pleasure." Deidra slashed out, her long fingernails grazing across his stomach, leaving an oozing trail of blood in its wake. The wound seeped open. His innards slid from the crevice she created.

Somehow, he managed to stand, but swayed, his eyes bulging in pain. She grabbed him around the neck. His eyes rolled, and he mumbled his terror into the suffocating hand choking him. He attempted to bite her flesh with his black teeth. She squeezed tighter and drew him to her. Her fangs grew, and she sunk them into the vein pulsing in his neck.

The warmth and stickiness of his blood, although tainted with an acidic piquancy, filled her belly. She fed from him until the air hissed lazily from his lungs.

She basked in the knowledge of her power, and yet, all of her loneliness and confusion welded together in one upsurge of devouring yearning. She missed her Ághmach, and until he stood by her side, she would never be free.

Caged.

Imprisoned in this primitive world, everywhere she turned, invisible, impenetrable, walls blocked her escape. Everything stank of humans, but lately, another smell, an odor far less tangible, yet equally real, mingled with their stench. A mixture of frustration, anger, hate and desperation, the scent of rage, and they all radiated from her.

Soon, it would be time. Her powers grew stronger every time she fed. A little more patience and it would all be hers.

The demons here were different from those that existed under the Camarilla's rule. Poor creatures. How they must have suffered.

While they searched for the amulet, she sought the Princess. Many times over the past few days, she had attempted to lock onto the woman's spirit, but that one possessed a great supremacy that refused Deidra complete passage to the knowledge of her whereabouts. This unknown woman emitted her own light.

If only Deidra could locate its source.

She couldn't fail in this. She needed the Princess of Light and the Talisman for the ritual to succeed. To have her Ághmach at her side would make this place bearable.

Low, distant voices drew her back to the present. She smiled. Hidden from sight within a cave she'd found earlier in the evening, she stared outside. A couple headed in her direction. She grimaced at their clasped hands. Her stomach twisted and nauseous rose like acid into her throat at their sense of loyalty.

She trailed with cold purpose and stalked her prey on soundless feet. The scope of her vision narrowed as a bright light edged into her sight. She turned her head and sighed in loathing as a manmade beast sped across the beach toward her meal. The loud blast of a horn buzzed across the sand, and she cringed at the annoying hoot. The couple, startled, jumped and spun around.

When it came to a stop beside the humans, they hopped into the back seat.

The metal monster spun around and sent sand in her direction. Deidra spit as the tiny granules landed in her face and on her lips.

She cursed as her dinner disappeared from sight.

Chapter Eighteen

"No, Murray, I wouldn't joke about this."

Liz held the phone to her ear, listening to the irate Police Chief on the other end. She had been lucky enough to avoid Murray since that night. He'd been busy investigating the murders on the beach, and she certainly didn't go out of her way to pick up the phone and call him.

But he finally found the time to give her a buzz.

"Murray, there wasn't a body. After everything I've been through, I wanted to kill you. How could you? I didn't find it funny at all."

Liz held the receiver away from her ear as his voice rose in denial.

"Murray, calm down. Maybe Rapids River decided to keep the body. If not then I'm afraid your corpse got up and walked away prior to my arrival. Listen, I've got to go. I have to be at work in less than an hour. I don't know what you want me to say. Without a body, there is no report."

She hung up the receiver, praying for forgiveness at the lie, yet hoped she'd sounded convincing enough.

How could she explain to him or anyone else that the man delivered to her morgue wasn't dead? That he "woke up", they kissed, she almost ripped his clothes off, and they left the morgue by way of mojo magic before a bunch of demons tried to kill them? Even she didn't believe that story, and it happened to her.

"Did he believe ye?"

Liz jumped at Fallon's voice in her ear.

She spun around. "Would you stop sneaking—" her words caught in her throat. Fallon stood behind her. His breath brushed warm and moist against her face. The heat of his body rolled over her, and she resisted the urge to reach out and touch him.

He chuckled. "Sorry, Lizzie, I forgot."

Liz took a pace backward. She refused to allow herself to fall under his spell again.

To her surprise, he strolled forward, reached down, and cupped her face in his hands. Warm shivers coursed through her.

He leaned forward. Her heartbeat thudded against her breast at the brush of his breath on her cheek.

"Ye are so beautiful, Lizzie." He lowered his lips. He kissed the tip of her nose, then her eyes, and finally, his lips covered hers. The gentle massage sent currents of desire through her.

A short, passionate kiss, and when he pulled back, the smoldering flame in his eyes startled her.

Crushing her to him, his mouth swooped down to capture hers hungrily, forceful and scorching, plundering her mouth until her head roared with the sounds of the lake outside in the midst of a storm. His kiss was a demand, a command with arrogance that she return his affection. Her mind staggered, and she would have refused, yet her mouth met his challenge.

Suddenly, a cold blast of air blew over her when he stepped away.

****

Is this how it is supposed to happen when a Síoraí found their mate?

Fallon understood all too well what it was to want. Over the centuries, there had been many things he'd sought in his life, but because of his non-existent existence, he walked away. They weren't worth the risk.

Yearning for Lizzie could never be acceptable, not to him, and certainly not now.

He was transfixed, hypnotized by her splendor, or maybe he responded to the bond drawing them together? He couldn't be sure of anything anymore.

To crave her with such passion could prove to be more dangerous than fighting demons. He couldn't afford to seduce her, to take her to bed, and most of all he couldn't let himself think of her as anything other than an innocent who needed his protection. Why the hell did he kiss her?

Bloody idiocy!

Cupping her chin, he searched her upturned face. Her beauty rushed through him like an intoxicating wine in his blood, and he lowered his lips to hers.

When he drew away, his gaze skimmed over her. Blooming roses filled her cheeks, and a dangerous passion clouded her eyes.

And when he took a step back, she said nothing, her eyes dazed, unfocused.

Fallon turned on his heel and strode down the hallway. He needed to get away from her before she chanced to look in his face and see the sadness that resounded behind the color of his eyes.

Over his shoulder, he called, "Have a good day at work, lass."

Chapter Nineteen

A shrill buzz crept into Liz's subconscious. She groaned, rolled over and tapped the snooze button on the top of the alarm.

A few more minutes.

Liz snuggled under the warmth of her comforter. It would be so easy to allow herself the luxury of drifting back to sleep, considering she'd only dozed off a few hours ago.

Her slumber had been restless, her dreams dark. She stood outside, surrounded by an opaque blanket of gloom. Pitch black. No welcoming glow of the moon lit her way. Occasional flashes of light brightened the sky for mere seconds only to fade into darkness again. Stars fought to shine against the velvet background, obscured by thick clouds that spread across the heavens like ink stains on a blotter.

And then, the translucent vision of a woman appeared from the shadows. A chenille ebony gown draped her hourglass figure, and long ink-colored hair flowed around her waist. She brought up a ghostly hand and swept the loose tendrils from her face. Her countenance exquisite, yet pain haunted her eyes. Her hand stretched to Liz, and she begged, "Help me. Please help me!" Her voice distant, shaky.

Fallon emerged beside the woman. The expression on his face frantic, he shook his head and mouthed, "No!" over and over again.

Liz walked to Fallon and stretched out a hand. Just when their fingertips touched, something grabbed him from behind and whipped him away. She watched, in disbelief, as he faded and disappeared from sight, his arms still extended toward her.

Only a dream, and yet, even now her heart pounded at the memory. Her drowsiness vanished as the dream replayed in her mind.

She rolled onto her stomach, folded the pillow under her head, and opened one eye to peek at the clock. Liz moaned at the bright blue digits advising her she would be late if she didn't get her butt moving.

Fallon claimed he was hell on Earth, but Liz knew better. But now, hell appeared to have arrived here on Earth, especially if one counted the number of bodies in her morgue.

Too many, in fact, and the numbers continued to grow every day. Every time she turned on the television, another report of a murder somewhere in Manistique hit the news, and every time, that person died exactly the same way.

Brutally!

Only last week, she'd decided to investigate a crime scene in the hopes of uncovering any clues that might answer the question...what the hell was going on in Manistique?

What a big mistake that turned out to be!

Body parts literally scattered a half-acre area of Sable Park near the beach. She'd been unable to inspect the corpse thoroughly and had to wait while police pulled bits and pieces out of trees. Arm and legs literally ripped from the torso.

Thank goodness she skipped breakfast that morning, or she would have spilled her stomach's contents over the pavement.

She rapidly examined the remains amidst the rush of police officers. When she finished, their incessant chatter muted her ears while she stumbled to her car, desperately trying to make sense of the madness invading her life.

Needless to say, that had been the one and only time she went out in the field since this rash of murders began three weeks ago. Even now, the mere thought of the desecrated body sent bile rising in her throat.

She preferred to do her assessment in the morgue, but even that had become a grueling task. She'd never had to piece bodies back together before just to do her job.

Each day, when she stepped across the threshold into her exam room, queasiness attacked her stomach and burned a line up her esophagus to spill into her mouth. Her head ached and palms sweat like a raging river, making it difficult to hold, much less operate her instruments.

And if that weren't bad enough, the voices had returned. As each body crossed her table, the spirit of the deceased spoke. Their words too soft, fragmented for Liz to understand. If only they were louder, more pronounced, they could tell her what did this to them.

An odd prickling sensation formed at the base of her neck. Something wasn't right here, and she couldn't quite put her finger on it. The spirits never spoke during the day before, and this new pattern had her scratching her head in confusion.

Yesterday, what remained of a twenty-year old man arrived on her table. Whispered, muted mumblings roared into her ears. She'd closed the door hoping to discern his words, but his chopped sentences made no sense. She spent close to an hour attempting to decipher the clues she did understand...*blood, sharp, pain, woman,* and *Butch.*

Butch?

She'd later learned the man had a Rottweiler named Butch who'd been discovered running loose on the beach a few hours later.

But still, she had no concrete answers.

The fire codes restricted the number of bodies waiting for autopsies to five. In addition to her own room, her assistants, Gloria and Dale had their own, which left two bodies waiting in the hallway. Because the number of murders far exceeded five on any given day, they'd been forced to ship bodies to the Rapid Rivers' county morgue.

Manistique's mayor issued a curfew of seven o'clock. Anyone caught out past that time would be escorted home after receiving a hefty fine.

Seth still spent most of his nights on her couch. He watched television while Fallon went hunting. Hunting what, Liz decided she didn't want to know.

She'd given up trying to get the two men to leave her home.

Persistent little buggers.

"We canna leave ye unprotected, lass."

"Unprotected? From what?" she'd asked.

"Trust me, ye doona want to know."

In the next moment, he turned his back, successfully ending the conversation.

The annoying "buzz" sounded again.

This time, she stretched over and flicked the button off.

With a very unladylike groan, she sat up, flipped the comforter off and slid her feet over the side of the bed. After slipping on her robe, she tied the sash at her waist and stepped into the living room.

She strolled through the room into the kitchen, craving coffee. After grinding the beans, she tossed the fresh grounds into the pot, added water, and pushed the button.

Entering the living room, she stopped short, surprised to see Fallon stretched out on the couch. Strange. He'd been avoiding her, never came home until she'd left for work.

Why was he here now?

At the foot of the couch, she paused.

His eyes were closed, and she took a moment to observe. Muscular arms emerged from beneath a T-shirt that hugged his chest. Her gaze traveled down his body. Tight jeans accentuated strong thighs. She suppressed a giggle at the sight of his feet dangling over the couch arm.

Handsome and innocent and, oh yes, very, very sexy. The blood surged from her fingertips to her toes, and a hot ache formed in her throat.

Even while he slept, her body burned with desire for him.

Wrenching herself away from her preposterous obsession with his arresting face, she stepped back from the couch.

After a long shower, she swiped the mist from the mirror and grimaced at the dark circles marring the smooth skin under her eyes. She added a faint touch of makeup to hide the tell tale signs of her sleepless night. Slipping back into her robe, she left the bathroom and padded down the hall to her room.

She chose a light blue pant suit that, modest though it may be, accentuated her halfway decent figure, and emphasized her blue eyes.

Routine led her back to the kitchen for her morning coffee. After pouring a cup, she sat at the table, closed her eyes, and breathed the fresh hazelnut smell. The nutty scent rolled inside her lungs, waking the last remaining slumbering cells. Taking a sip, the flavor rolled across her tongue inflaming her taste buds.

Then it was time. Duty called. Finishing up the last of her coffee, she set the cup in the sink and headed for the door.

As she passed through the living room, she picked up her purse from the corner of the desk. At the door, she grabbed her jacket from the coat rack.

Just as her hand settled on the knob, Fallon's voice swept over her. "Where do ye think ye are off to, lass?"

She swung around.

Fallon's head popped over the top of the couch. His stare traveled over her. An appreciative glint lit up his eyes when they met hers. The heat of embarrassment fanned into her cheeks at the look of desire he shot her.

"Where do I usually go?"

Fallon sat up and ran a hand over his face. "Work, eh?"

"There's been a lot going on."

"Aye, I noticed. Why doona ye call in today? Ye havena taken a break in the past three weeks."

Her mouth dropped open, and she drew a breath of utter astonishment. "You're kidding, right?"

"Nay, I'm no'. No' in this."

"I can't. I have too much to do. Between the bodies and the paperwork, Dale and Gloria can't handle the workload by themselves. I need to be there."

"If ye have to go, be home before the sun goes down. Ye havena been getting home until almost dark. Ye need to be in the door by five." He issued the command before he returned to his relaxed position.

"Excuse me?"

His voice rang out over the couch as he repeated, "Is something wrong with yer hearing, lass? I told ye to be home by five o'clock."

That did it! This man had nerve.

Liz stormed across the room and stood at his feet, her hands planted on her hips. She gritted her teeth and waited, tapping her foot rapidly, for him to remove his arm from his eyes. He didn't budge, but she knew he heard her for his arm slid a quarter of an inch lower to hide the glimmer of a smile.

With a sweeping motion of her hand, Liz knocked his feet off the arm of the sofa. His body jerked as they slammed to the floor. This time, his arm did move, and Liz flinched, retreating back a step at the look of annoyance in his expression.

Damn it, she refused to back down from him. Not this time. She needed to stand up to him. This was her home, not his.

"You are not my father, Fallon. What right do you have to tell me what to do?"

He sat up, planting his feet on the floor, and turned away so she couldn't see his eyes. "Lizzie, it's for yer own safety. I canna protect ye if yer no' here."

"Would you look at me?"

He glanced up and studied her with curious intensity.

"You have been here for almost a month, and, not once, in all that time have I ever been in danger, nor have I ever needed your protection."

Fallon's brows dipped in a frown. "Liz, it is coming and when it arrives—" His words hung ominously between them.

"What's coming? You have yet to tell me what *it* is, Fallon? Does this have something to do with all the murders?"

"It could be. I'm no' sure."

"I don't understand you."

"Most people doona," he replied with a sad smile, then lay down and replaced his arm over his eyes.

"What makes you think I won't call the police on you?"

Again, he removed his arm, this time, an eyebrow quirked in response to her threat. "Oh, and who would ye call? Murray?"

Sh...ugar.

"Maybe I will. What will you do?"

Fallon lips curved into an unconcerned smile,

and he shrugged.

Fury choked her. She swallowed hard, biting back her anger. "I want you to leave my home, Fallon."

"I know you do, Lizzie." His expression was one of pained tolerance, and Lizzie wanted to stomp her feet.

"Don't sound so damn condescending. I expect you to be gone before I get home from work."

"Sorry, lass. I canna do that."

"Damn you to hell."

At her words, Fallon's eyes darkened, and his mouth twisted. His expression sent a chill up her spine.

"Stand in line, lass. Ye're no' the only one who wishes to see me burn in the hell's fires and, most likely, ye wilna be the last."

She didn't know how to respond to his claim so she did the next best thing and stomped away.

"I'll see ye this evening. Doona forget. Be home before five."

At the door, with her hand on the knob, she turned to look at him one more time. He'd already lain back down and couldn't see her. It was childish, but she stuck out her tongue anyway.

"I can think of better things to do with that, woman."

Heat crept into her cheeks. She tore open the door and slipped outside.

Before it closed behind her, the rich sound of laughter followed after her.

****

As the echo of Lizzie's car faded into the distance, Fallon stretched out against the couch, closed his eyes, and listened to the deafening silence.

Bloody Hell, it was too damn quiet.

In Lizzie's absence, this place always got lonesome. If it were possible, he would keep her here beside him, if only for her company. He'd even thought of using her safety as an excuse, but something told him that wouldn't be good enough reason.

Not for Lizzie.

He'd been a wee bit surprised when she asked him to leave. How could she not take his concerns seriously?

She brushed them away as though they were no more than a pesky bug sent to annoy the hell out of her. He feared her nonchalant attitude might get her killed.

In truth, during the day, Lizzie was safe enough. Most demons refused to walk in daylight. For some, the sun's rays fried them into crispy critters, so they'd hibernate. Others, the darkness at night hid their brutality and their presence.

Ever since their short kiss, Fallon avoided Lizzie, not an easy thing to accomplish when living in the same house. When she went to work, he slept. When she came home and the sun went down, he went hunting.

The hunt didn't ease the ache inside him. He wanted her, and as every day passed, the union holding them together grew. The voices continued to urge him to make her his.

A long time ago, he'd vowed he wouldn't be responsible for the death of anyone else he loved.

A warning voice jumped inside his head.

Love? Did he love Lizzie? No, he couldn't possibly love her. Their bond drew them together. That was it, wasn't it?

Fallon shot upward with an "*oomph*" as an object large and furry landed on his stomach. Yellow cat eyes met his. A faltering stab of recognition flashed through him, something strangely familiar. Overwhelmed by discomfort, Fallon attempted to brush the cat away.

"Scat cat."

Instead of leaving, the cat meowed and nuzzled against his hand. It paced back and forth on his chest, and purred, until the fur ball settled in the crook of his arm. Fallon ran his hand across the silky coat of the cat's head.

"It would appear it's just ye and me for the day, cat."

As though pleased by the thought, the cat purred louder.

"What are we going to do with yer master? She's a stubborn wee lassie who doesn't know what's good for her."

Meow!

"Ye noticed that, too, eh?"

Meow!

"Are ye understanding me, cat?"

Meow!

The cat's eyes fixed on his face, and the animal's ears perked up as if it comprehended every word he spoke.

Fallon laughed, wondering if Lizzie could talk to animals as well as ghosts.

"Now, wouldn't that just be bizarre?"

Meow!

Chapter Twenty

Overwhelmed by the events of the past few weeks, Liz muttered a curse and dropped back in the chair. Instinct warned her that this chaos was only beginning. The events would continue to plague her until she found the answers to some prominent questions.

What was killing the people of Manistique?

When will the viciousness cease?

What the hell was going to happen next?

The uncertainty of these questions took their toll on her. Exhausted, her nerves stretched and her body ached from the strain of taunt muscles.

She indulged herself in a huge self-pitying sigh and leaned forward intent on completing the mounds of paperwork scattered on her desk. After an hour of rifling through reports and photos, she gave up. Each medical record filled with vulgar pictures of mangled bodies. Horror at the victim's brutalizing pain, the humiliation and all the dark feelings they experienced at the time of their deaths propelled her stomach into a swirling mass of bile.

Goosebumps tickled her spine at the mutilated flesh pictured in the file on her desk. Based on the remains of the body her best estimate gauged the boy at approximately sixteen years of age. He had yet to experience life. What could have stripped his life away so violently?

No more!

She slapped the folder closed and shut her eyes against the sight, but the vision remained.

In her years as a Medical Examiner, she'd never seen anything like the recent carnage of the bodies that spewed across her table.

Liz's preliminary reports, at least those she'd written down on paper, concluded the cause of the deaths a direct result of an animal attack.

When the questions poured in…

What kind of animals could commit such savagery?

Here, in Manistique?

How many?

…she couldn't give the town council members the answers they sought.

In the next instant, her thoughts swerved in another direction, away from the council.

Fallon.

Hands clasped together, her index fingers formed the perfect steeple. She stared at their image.

Who was this stranger who'd walked into her life and changed it forever? Who *was* Fallon O'Callaghan? Everything that happened in Manistique began at the same time as his arrival on her exam table. Was it possible? Was he somehow involved with the killings?

Out of the corner of her eyes, she caught the flash of her computer screen. Struck by another thought, a surge of excitement raced through her.

The Internet? Hadn't Fallon said it was a wealth of information?

She dragged the keyboard and mouse closer. After starting her browser, she typed "Fallon O'Callaghan" in her favorite search engine and waited.

Her eyes widened. She couldn't believe it. There were more than a hundred thousand links claiming to have an accounting on the life of one Fallon O'Callaghan.

All these men...they all couldn't be about *her* Fallon. Could they?

A stifled chuckle escaped her lips. Her Fallon? If only.

Clicking the first entry, her eyes widened at the sight of his face. The caption beneath the black and white charcoaled drawing that read Lord Fallon O'Callaghan, fifteen twenty five, AD, Scotland, enthralled her.

Her eyes read and re-read the words.

"It couldn't be, could it?" asked a little voice inside her head. "Of course it was." That realization proved to be an awakening experience that left her reeling.

A soft breeze blew across her face. Aunt Rea's lavender perfume drifted around the room. A sense of calm invaded her. With eyes closed, she let her mind speak for her.

"Aunt Rea?" Aunt Rea's gentle eyes and encouraging smile flashed behind her eyelids.

The elder nodded. "Trust in yourself, Liz. Trust in him."

"You make it sound easy," Liz cried, her voice trembling.

"It will not be easy, but you are strong. You are his equal, child. Always remember that."

And with those words of advice, Liz's aunt faded away.

When she reopened her eyes, the computer screen flickered. Her gaze traveled back to the article, and Liz read the black and white words plastered on the screen.

Lord Fallon O'Callaghan.

The young Lord, born on August 7, 1500 in Elgin, a small village along the coast of Northern Scotland. His parents, Irish born Patrick O'Callaghan and Elaina (McNevin) O'Callaghan were killed in an accident when the boy was five. He was reared by his uncle, Fergus McNevin in Glasglow. There is no record of Fallon after 1532. No documentation of his death has ever been recorded.

Some say Fergus McNevin disowned his nephew when Fallon fell in love with a Druid Maiden, Rhiannon. Fergus considered the Druids dirty and wouldn't allow his bloodline to be tainted by a woman such as her. Fergus threatened to burn their camp to the ground if they didn't leave the area. Fallon knew nothing of his uncle's scheme. Risking reprisal from the Druid Matriarch, he tracked down the Druid Caravan to proclaim his love to Rhiannon. He was never given the opportunity, for it was said that Rhiannon died in 1530 of a broken heart while giving birth to a son fathered by Fallon.

She collapsed back in the chair and released the breath she didn't realize she'd held.

Good Heavens! With a life that hard, was it any wonder he'd become such a hard man?

"Lizzie."

She stood, the chair's legs scraping against the tiled floor. Unexpected heat pooled in her groin at the sound of his voice.

This couldn't be happening. Not now. She balled her hands into fists, swallowing the anger building in her throat. How dare he do this to her? And how could he do this to her body?

They were her personal thoughts. He had no right to infringe upon them.

"Fallon, I told you to—" she spoke aloud then looked around, alarmed. If found talking to herself, her colleagues would think she'd lost her mind.

Closing her eyes, she let her mind speak, her thoughts transferring to his. She didn't attempt to keep the frustration out of her tone. "Stay out of my head!"

Then, to Liz's surprise, warm and gentle hands caressed her face. A bright light appeared behind her eyelids, and his image focused in her mind. Gold-flecked eyes held her enthralled. Dark brows drew together in an agonized expression, and his hand stretched toward her.

"It will be dark soon. Ye need to come home." His voice roughened with anxiety.

When she didn't respond, be begged, "Lizzie, please!"

Wide, luminous eyes emphasized concern.

When he spoke again, his voice was tender, almost a murmur. "They will come for ye. I canna protect ye unless yer here with me."

"Who, Fallon?"

"Come home. Please, lass. I'm begging ye."

She faltered between the annoyance he exuded, and the reassurance he, in fact, cared what happened to her.

She chose the first.

"Get out of my head." She slapped up a wall closing her mind to him. A smile of satisfaction emerged as she imagined a groan as he hit his forehead against her imaginary barrier.

An even more terrifying realization washed over her. What if he were right? What if someone were coming for her?

Deciding to listen to his advice, she flicked off the computer and grabbed her handbag. As she ran through the hall, she passed Gloria's examination room and hollered, "I'll see you tomorrow, Gloria. Would you lock up for me? Thanks. Goodnight."

Not waiting for her assistant's reply, she ran up the stairs, through the building into the parking lot. A quick glance to the skies revealed the sun as it disappeared over the mountains. Her hands shook as she unlocked her car, slid behind the wheel, and stuck the key in the ignition.

Liz swung onto the freeway at breakneck speeds. Fallon's words urged her on, the fear she heard in his voice an emotion she couldn't ignore.

She left the highway and made a right onto a side street. Another five minutes, and Liz breathed a sigh of relief as she drove into the driveway. Opening the car door, she unfastened her seatbelt and rushed up the walk into the house.

The large oak door slammed shut behind her. She tossed her purse to the floor, and stormed into the living room where she found Fallon standing in front of the mantel, his arms crossed over his chest. She gave him a hostile stare. He answered her angry look with an impersonal nod as if to say, "It's about time."

She crossed the room in three steps. The sound of her palm slapping against his cheek cut through the silence.

Fallon rubbed his jaw, startled. "What the hell was that for?"

"Don't play innocent with me. You were in my head after I told you to stay out."

He stiffened. "Lass."

In no mood to listen to his explanations or excuses, she stated, "I told you I don't want you in my head. What part of that don't you understand?"

"And I told ye to be home before dark."

She curled her hands into fists at her sides. "Don't insult me. I am not a child who needs you to hold my hand and walk me across the street."

His eye brows quirked upward, and the corner of his mouth tipped into a half smirk. "And I suppose ye're trying to tell me ye doona have temper tantrums? Like the one ye're obviously *no'* having now."

She moved to slap him again, but he caught her wrist in his hand. "Ye doona want to do that, lass."

Fallon's features hardened.

Wrenching her arm away from him, she seethed, "I want you out of my home tonight."

When he failed to leave, Liz rushed around the room, scooping his meager belongings into her arms.

"What are ye doing?" he asked, a hand stretched out for his possessions.

She swiveled out of his reach and headed toward the door.

He rushed after her. "Lizzie, doona open the door!"

The cool breeze blew a burst of fresh air against her heated cheeks. Outside, the only sounds were the crashing waves of the water on shore.

"Lizzie, doona do it!"

She shrugged and threw his possessions out onto the lawn.

"Sweet Jesus, Lizzie, the Talisman was in my jacket pocket."

"Best go get it then," she snapped, holding the door wide. He rushed by. As he passed her, she said, "Get out of my head and out of my house."

Once he was outside, she slammed the door shut behind him, sliding the lock into place.

A second later, the handle rattled but didn't open. He banged on the door until it shook. The wood splintered, but it held fast. "Bloody hell, Lizzie, open the damn door."

"Go away, Fallon."

Her letterbox opened. Through the door, she heard Fallon's muttered curse, and smiled, brushing her hands together. "I've taken out the trash," she murmured in satisfaction.

She turned to walk away, but Fallon's voice reached her ears, halting her movement.

"Lizzie, please. Let me in."

She recognized the defeat in Fallon's voice but wasn't ready to surrender. Not yet. When the letterbox slot popped open, she attempted to slam the flap shut, but his fingers got in the way. "Move them or lose them," she warned, pushing the flap down with her foot.

His muted curse filtered through the heavy oak, but his fingers disappeared.

"Lass, ye doona know what danger ye're in. Ye have to let me in. I couldna stand it if ye were hurt."

The desperation in his voice frightened her, and a terrifying realization washed over her. What if he was right? What if nightmarish creatures did want her dead? Even more startling, could she go a day without him in her life?

Liz's forehead came to rest on the door. Through the wood, she murmured, "This is my house. My rules, Fallon. You will give me respect, or so help me I will make your life hell. Do you understand me?"

"Aye, lass. I understand."

She jumped, and her heart jolted at the sound of his voice behind her. Fury almost choked her as she swung around, raised her hand, and prepared to swing at him for a third time, but at the expression on his face, she wavered and lowered her arm.

Fallon's ashen face, ruffled hair, and eyes, filled with anguish, shook her foundation.

Nervously, she moistened her dry lips. "We need to talk,"

His eyes widened at her plea, and he nodded. "I give ye my word, lass. We will."

"But first, I want your promise. You will *never* intrude on my thoughts again."

"I'm sorry, but once the sun goes down, they come out. I canna keep ye safe when ye're so far away. It was the only way I could reach ye...to protect ye."

She took a breath to calm herself before she spoke again. "Protect me from what? I'm still waiting to hear what you think you are protecting me from. Who are you so worried about?"

He stood in front of her. His eyes virtually glowed in the light as he implored, "Lizzie, ye have got to trust me."

"You keep telling me that, but I don't even know you."

"Ye know me better than most."

"All I know is a few weeks ago, you were a corpse on my table. You were dead! And then, out of nowhere, you're jumping off the table very much alive."

She flushed at the memory of what occurred after.

"Finish it." His gaze remained steady as he looked at her with silent expectation.

The smoldering flame in his eyes startled her. What remained of her anger slipped away into the dark and sensual sensation building in her body. Her heart fluttered at his nearness.

She fought the crushing need to wrap her arms around his neck and yank his lips to hers. Lifting her hands in the air, she lowered them against her thighs with a loud slap. "I'm done."

She twisted away and headed toward her room. His hand, massive and strong, gripped her arm and spun her around to face him.

"How about how hot ye were for me," he said with quiet emphasis. "Admit it. Ye wanted me just as much as I wanted ye," he added in a lower, huskier tone.

He leaned toward her, the smile in his eyes containing a sexual flame. She wished he wouldn't look at her like that. It sent shivers over her and fired her blood.

****

Fallon fingered a loose tendril of her golden locks. Against his will, his hand slipped around her neck, and his fingers tangled in her hair. She smelled of fresh flowers, the fragrance intoxicating.

He pulled her toward him and dipped his head down to give her the whisper of a kiss, warm, soft and undemanding.

His tongue brushed inside and rubbed against hers. He took his time exploring her mouth until even that wasn't enough. He tightened his embrace and deepened the kiss. Her sweet mouth made him crave her more, his need savage.

By the gods, she drove him crazy. The realization ricocheted through his head.

A veritable prisoner of his own desires where Lizzie was concerned, Fallon knew the need to harness his power, to get a hold of himself for both their sakes.

His body snapped to rigid attention as thoughts of the price seeped into his consciousness. Caution had him back away. An empty hunger filled him.

Common sense was overrated.

A tremor touched her lips, her eyes void of emotion.

"Lizzie…"

When she didn't respond, he brushed a hand against her arm. "Lizzie, are ye ok?"

The desire faded from her eyes. "What?"

"I canna."

"Can't or won't?"

"Oh, lass, if ye only knew how much I want you, ye wouldna have to ask. If we make love, it'll change ye."

"Don't you think that's my decision to make? My choice?"

"Ye doona understand, lass. Ye'll be changed forever. There's no going back from that, and I'm afraid I wilna be able to protect ye like I want to, like I need to. I wilna let anything happen to ye."

"Like what happened to Rhiannon?"

Fallon's eyes narrowed and clouded with pain. His back went ramrod straight. He spun away, his agony apparent in the way he clenched and unclenched his hands at his sides.

She straightened her shoulders, cleared her throat, and walked up beside him. Resting her hand on his arm, she whispered, "Fallon?"

He jerked his arm away from her. "Doona touch me."

Liz froze, her lips parted in surprise. It was true. The article was about him!

Her mind and body trembled from the rage she heard in his tone.

The next minute, he turned on her, tall and angry with burning, reproachful eyes. A faint tremor quivered in his voice when he said, "Doona ever mention her name again, lass."

Liz swallowed hard, lifted her chin, and met his gaze. She flinched at the look of intense darkness in his eyes, suddenly anxious to escape his disturbing presence.

Taking a deep, unsteady breath, she took two steps away, turned and stalked toward her bedroom; aware his sharp gaze bore into her back.

Without turning around, she stopped and leaned against the doorframe, attempting to find the courage to look at him. After a few seconds, she managed to face him. When she raised her eyes, a flash of wild grief ripped through her at the look of tired sadness on his features.

If only he would let her into his heart, to console him, but Liz knew that wouldn't happen—not yet. He wasn't ready.

Reluctantly, she walked into her room and closed the door with a soft click. She flopped on her bed, grabbed a pillow, and hugged it close to her chest, tears trembling on her eyelashes.

****

Liz dreamed of darkness, a vast overshadowing obscurity that closed her off from the world. A flicker of uneasiness spiraled over her at the gloom surrounding her.

In the heart of the shadows, a woman with hair the color of midnight and eyes as dark as coal, emerged. Dressed in a black gown, a long translucent cloak billowed behind her in an unseen breeze. Her steps were slow, yet steady and confident like an animal stalking prey already trapped in a cage.

Mesmerized by the woman's eyes, Liz froze, her breath trapped in her chest. Those eyes seemed to capture her and look deep into her soul.

The woman wept. Tears, the color of blood, spilled down her cheeks.

"Who are you?" Liz asked, using only her mind to speak.

"My name is Deidra Sidhe. I am not of your world but have been trapped here." The anguish in her voice sent chills crawling over Liz's skin.

"What do you want from me?"

"I need your help. I miss my love, Ághmach. The gods have sent him to the Underworld. We have been apart for a long time, and I want him by my side. I miss his arms around me."

Liz shook her head in utter disbelief. This was too friggin' much! Gods, underworld...what next?

Although her insides churned, she maintained an air of nonchalance when she asked, "What does that have to do with me?"

"You can help bring him back to my side."

"What can I do?"

"The man who stays with you wears a token around his neck. With that, I can free Ághmach, and we can find the happiness we once shared. Help me get it and fulfill my dreams."

"I cannot." Despite the trickle of unease that rushed the course of her spine, she raised her chin with a cool stare.

"Please, it is the only thing that will ease my sorrow. If you cannot get it, bring the man to me, and I'll take it."

"No, I won't," Liz replied with easy defiance.

The woman leapt at her and screamed, "Bitch!"

Deidra's arms were like steel around Liz. She gathered her into the enveloping folds of her cloak. Eyes blazing an unholy light, she lowered her head and whispered in Liz's ear, "Do not defy me."

A sense of primal fear rose in Liz's throat, a muffled scream, her scream, jolted her awake. With a thick sheen of perspiration on her skin, her heart pounded against her breast. The beat so fast and hard she thought it would burst from her body.

She reached for her bedside lamp, and flicked the switch, illuminating the room. Her eyes shot around the room only to find it empty. She was alone.

With a trembling hand, she brushed the hair from her eyes and drew a deep breath.

"Just a dream," she spoke aloud. She leaned back and closed her eyes. "A delusional nightmare."

Chapter Twenty-One

Dark. Unfathomable. Forbidden.

In a foul mood, Fallon barely spoke to her over the past few days. Every time she looked at him, his eyes were mysterious, his thoughts hidden, forbidding her entrance into any part of his sphere of existence. Whenever he did speak, his tone came out callous, yet courteous, almost too perfectly polite.

Liz could only stare, too stunned by the irritation coiling through her veins to do anything more.

Only yesterday, he'd made an unnecessary comment about her choice of toothpaste. Who the hell cared if it was mint, not cinnamon? Clutching an apple in her hand, she'd almost whipped the piece of fruit at his head, but thoughts of cleaning up applesauce brought her up short.

Instead, she'd slammed the apple down and kept her distance but promised to pick up two more tubes of mint when she went to the store.

At night, she set her clocks to Seth's arrival. Nine o'clock on the dot, never a minute too early or too late. Shortly afterward, Fallon left without a word or look in her direction. She didn't know where he disappeared to, but she did know he would be back in the morning.

The nightmare she'd experienced remained a constant in her mind. She didn't dwell on the woman who invaded her dream, tucking the memory in the back of her mind, but the action neither erased the terror that speared through her nor answered her questions.

How did she know of Fallon? His Talisman?

More questions.

Seth proved to be quite the character. Not an overly talkative chap, he spent most of his nights with his eyes glued to the television. On several occasions, she found herself amused by his animated features, the raised eyebrows, cock-eyed smiles or the tip of tongue that hung from the corner of his mouth. And the deep-gutted laughter that radiated from the couch made her giggle. Once, a loud *thud* sent her running to the living room where she discovered him on the floor, gripping his stomach in hilarity.

Liz once asked him where Fallon disappeared at night but received a one-syllable answer. "Hunting."

"Hunting what?"

He looked at her with those bright blue, gorgeous eyes and shrugged. "Fallon hunts what's hunting him."

At his response, Liz swallowed hard, trying not to reveal her anger. She failed miserably for sarcasm spilled into her voice. "Seth, what the hell does that mean?"

His gaze had already returned to the television. "Liz, you need to talk to Fallon. He's the only one who can give you the answers you want to hear."

In other words, he wasn't saying a word.

Fury raged through her veins, and she clenched her teeth, gritting out. "No thanks. He's as worthless as you when it comes to knowing anything."

That got his attention, and his gaze shot to her face. "Hey, that's not fair."

"No one's talking, so I assume no one knows what they're talking about. Hence, the silence," she added with a slight smile of defiance before she turned and walked away.

His soft laughter followed her, and she thought

she heard a mumbled, "Touché."

****

Fallon leaned against a concrete barrier that marked the boundary of a deserted manufacturing plant. His arms crisscrossed his chest, the heel of his left foot raised, planted solid on the border behind him. His eyes wandered around the property. Wooden crates lined the exterior walls of the factory, and trash and garbage littered the grounds.

A loud *crash* drew his attention when a metal door flung open and smashed against the outside of the building. Four demons exited.

He smiled at the adrenalin rush. His fangs took shape.

He pulled himself up to his full height. Every muscle in his body tensed and knotted, and he stepped from the darkness releasing a low, evil laugh. He recognized the three on the left as the ones who attacked him and left him for dead in Rapid Rivers.

"It's about bloody time ye showed up. Where ye been hiding?"

As they drew closer, the fetid stench of feline burned his nose and made him gag. The one in the middle of the group, shape shifter, stood the tallest, around six-three. Much shorter by at least six inches, the others sported the translucent bluish skin of vampires. Their eyes, sunken pits, in pale faces glowed of fire, and dried blood colored their chins.

The man cat's gaze glinted in the darkness. His white teeth snapped together in belligerence; his incisors and canines grew sharp and lethal in his mouth. He glared at Fallon. "Ah, I thought I smelled you nearby. I'm glad you're here. You've saved me a lot of time and aggravation searching for you. Why don't you save me some more and hand the Talisman over?"

147

"Why no' come and get it?"

"Why not, indeed?"

They attacked.

Fallon wrapped his hand around the throat of the first vampire to reach him. He tightened his grip, and in one motion, lifted and slammed him against the wall. With a twist of his wrist, a wooden stake sprung from the sleeve of his jacket. He thrust his hand forward, stabbing the vampire in his bony chest. A moment later, the vampire exploded, cascading grayish-colored dust over him.

Angry snarls sounded behind him.

His hearing picked up slight movement to his right. He dropped to the ground, twisted his lower body, and kicked high, striking a vampire in its upper torso. The force behind the strike was so powerful the demon flew across the lane. He landed on a broken wooden stick perched upward from the ground, exploding into a zillion pieces of fine powder.

Scuffling behind him identified the third vamp's location. Fallon held his patience, waiting for the footsteps to draw nearer. They hesitated behind him; Fallon swerved, grabbed the demon, and flung him into the arms of the fourth demon.

Both vampire and shifter staggered and lost their balance. Fallon chuckled at the two demons that tripped over one another before they landed in a tangled heap on the concrete pavement.

Clumsy bastards.

He glanced down and caught sight of a piece of wood at his feet. While they struggled to stand, he stomped his foot down, catching the end of the stake. It shot up, and he caught it mid-air.

By this time, the two creatures had regained their footing. Without hesitation, Fallon tossed a wooden stake into the heart of the vampire, and watched, in satisfaction, as he exploded into a shower of gray powder that sprinkled the shifter whose lips twisted in disgust.

The shifter's eyes widened, a look of fear tingeing his face. Fallon snickered. "It looks like it's just the two of us now. Would ye care to go around? May the better man win?"

"This is not over, guardian. The name's Dorian. Remember it, for you haven't heard the last of me. I seek to please my Queen, and she wants the Talisman you carry. I have your blood and the blood of the one you have chosen. Mark my words," he said with a sneer. "We *will* meet again."

Fallon's heart skipped a beat. Sheer, black fright swept over him. This bastard knew of Lizzie and their bond.

Before Fallon could react, Dorian took the form of a black jaguar and leapt on the box crates lining the alley. Up and up he jumped until he reached the rooftop and vanished from sight under streaks of silver moonbeams.

"Not if I find ye first, shape shifter," Fallon muttered, staring into the empty blackness.

What was a shape shifter doing with a pack of vampires?

****

Fallon arrived at Lizzie's house before dusk. Seth remained on the couch, his hands tucked behind his head, as always, watching television.

Fallon tossed his jacket across the spindles at the back of a chair. "Doona ye get tired of watching that crap?"

"Not at all. I'm addicted. Do you think they have television watchers' anonymous?" He laughed as he sat up. When he looked up again, his face changed. His eyes darkened, and his expression became serious. "So, how did the hunting go?"

"Good. I dusted three tonight. Two of them were the ones that put me in the morgue.

"What happened to the third?"

149

"Well, turns out he's a shape shifter. Ever heard of the saying, leap higher than the tallest building?"

"A shape shifter with vampires? Damn, that means they're clustering again."

"It would seem. Do ye know of a shifter who goes by the name of Dorian?"

For a few seconds, Seth's expression turned thoughtful, and then his eyes widened. His mouth took on an unpleasant twist. "Yeah, I've heard of him. He's a bad ass who turned on his own kind to become some kind of mixed breed. Half vampire, half shifter. He's pissed off a lot of his own with the way he passes himself off as King of the Damned."

"Aye, well, he's pissed me off, too. He is one dead cat when I get my hands on him."

"Fallon, he's a sadistic bastard. Maybe you should call the others and ask for help."

"No," Fallon barked. "That bastard is mine."

Seth sighed. "He drew your blood and lived. That puts you in grave danger, and anyone else you've been close to."

"And that's why it's important I find him." Fallon nodded.

Seth was closer to the truth than he realized. When Fallon bit Lizzie, his blood blended with hers, making her as much a target as himself.

Interest lit Seth's eyes, and he tilted his head toward the door where Fallon knew Lizzie slept. "Can I ask how the little lady fits into this? You are my friend, Fallon, and I've watched out for her because you asked me to, but it's time I know. Why is she significant?"

One corner of his mouth twisted upward. "She was in the wrong place at the wrong time, and I sort of...well, kind of..." he hesitated, watching the look of astonishment cross Seth's face.

"You've chosen her as your mate." It wasn't a question, but a direct statement.

Fallon stiffened, his mind and body engulfed in tides of weariness and despair. He nodded, unable to speak the undeniable and dreadful facts aloud.

"Bloody hell." Seth's curse echoed throughout the room. "Your scent is in her blood? They'll hunt her as they hunt you."

"Aye."

"Have you sanctioned the union?"

Shaking his head, Fallon said, "No, I havena sanctioned the union. What manner of man do ye take me for?"

"That's just it, Fallon. Síoraí you may be, but you're still a man, a man with needs, and Liz is a magnificent woman. Will she accept you?"

"Seth, I doona want her to accept me. I wilna ask that of her."

"I like Liz. She's quite a woman. Whether you chose to admit it or not, she is your equal, and now, by your own choice, your life mate. I believe she's quite smitten with you, as well. Besides, you know the rules. Once a guardian has chosen, there is no way to break the bond. It will eat at you until you succumb to the power of the blood union."

"I doona deny she's special, but no matter how strong she is, I wilna draw her into this."

"Whether you want to believe it or not, you already have, my friend."

"What have I been drawn into?"

Both men spun around at the sound of Liz's voice. Fallon's heart skipped at the sight of her tousled hair and sleepy eyes.

"Nothing," Fallon replied, turning his back to her and settling on the couch.

Seth decided he wasn't going to get involved and headed for the door. "I'll see you tonight."

"Thanks for sticking around, Seth."

He nodded at Liz as he walked by.

"Good night, Liz."

The door closed with a soft click behind him.

Tired, Fallon lay on the couch and closed his eyes.

In the next instant, Lizzie's footsteps padded across the floor, growing louder with each step.

"Fallon, look at me," she demanded.

"No' now, Lizzie. I'm tired. Let me get a little shuteye, and then we'll talk."

His feet went flying off the bottom of the sofa, his ankle striking the table. Damn, that smarted. His eyes shot open, and he gritted his teeth against the stinging pain that flared in the bone.

Lizzie stood near the foot of the couch. Her hands rested on her hips, her brows high and rounded. She glared at him, her eyes full of fierce determination

He sat up, the beginnings of a smile tugging at the corners of his mouth. By the gods, she became a delightful sight when fired up. "Ye're starting to make a habit of that, lass."

"I wanted your attention."

Fallon raised an eyebrow. "Ye wanted my attention?"

"That's what I said. I'm tired of being ignored."

"Lizzie, believe me when I tell ye this. Ye already have more of my attention than ye should have."

Her cheeks colored rosy and pink. Charming.

Fallon hoped she'd rush off into her room in embarrassment, but instead, she bounced back with a perky response. "It would seem so, especially when I'm not even in the room. Look Fallon, I don't like it when people talk about me as though I don't exist. What the hell is going on between you and Seth?"

Fallon leaned back and crossed his arms across his chest. "Nothing."

"That's bullshit, and you know it."

He chose to ignore the exasperation in her voice.

Oh, how he would love to hear the sound of his name on her lips in the throes of passion. He wanted to make her breathless as he made slow, passionate love to her. He ached to see the desire for him, only for him, in her eyes as he took her.

The scent of lilacs spilled around him. His gaze dropped from her face to her shoulders to her breasts. Need pounded through him and his body swelled with craving. He curled his hands into tight fists at his side to keep from touching her.

And then she spoke, splashing cold water over his desires.

"You have been acting pissy lately, Fallon O'Callaghan, ever since I asked you about Rhiannon. I deserve to know what has been happening to my life."

Fallon ran a weary hand over his eyes. "I don't know what ye want to hear, what ye expect me to say."

"I want the truth. That's all I ever asked."

A war of emotions raged inside him at her pleading. The truth? What exactly was the truth?

"What aren't you telling me, Fallon? Are you saying I should have expected to find a handsome, sexy, *alive* man on my autopsy table? That I should have expected him to shift me home or that he moved into my home, all the while claiming to be my savior. From what, I've no clue. That this man has fangs, is stronger than the Berlin Wall, invades my thoughts—" She inhaled sharply as if to catch her breath before continuing, "—and oh gosh, let's not forget the most important part—that he died more than fifteen hundred years ago?"

By the end of her wild tirade, her tone had risen considerably higher than normal, and Fallon grimaced. He feared she tottered on the edge of hysteria, a nervous breakdown or perhaps a little bit of both.

He jumped to his feet when her face paled, and she wobbled. He grabbed her arm, led her to the front of the couch, and ordered her with a sharp, "Sit down before ye fall down!"

She flopped down on the cushions. The empty stare of her face alarmed him, sending his heart into a gallop. He rushed to the kitchen for water.

When he returned, her expression was one of dazed confusion. He wondered if she felt as he often did, on the threshold of plunging into a wild, endless void where the boundaries were comprised of walls built on a foundation of sheer emotions. Her emotions? His emotions? Their emotions?

In that moment, with fearful clarity, he realized he was responsible for this. His chest tightened, and his breath caught in his throat.

Sitting beside her, he forced the glass to her lips. "Drink, Lizzie. Come on, darlin'."

When her eyes met his, her expression blank, she shook her head. Liz brought her arm up and knocked the glass from his hands. She shot him a withering glance. "Leave me alone, Fallon."

She stood and stumbled. When he grabbed for her, she shoved his hand away.

A flash of panic coursed through him when her bedroom door slammed shut. He ran a frustrated hand through his hair.

Her way to protect herself, she had run away. From him. The thought shot despair through him. Would the truth bring her into his arms or send her further away?

Lizzie deserved to know the truth. His obsession with her was more than the need to keep her safe. It went deeper, not just under the skin, but in his heart and soul, those parts of him he had forsaken all those years ago.

But could she accept him?

He needed to know.

Chapter Twenty-Two

A kaleidoscope of bright colors surrounded her. Green meadows and blue skies, a variety of flowers lined the rolling hillside. The air so fresh, so clean, she drew a deep soothing breath into her lungs. It calmed her. Tears were gone, evaporated by the onrushing surge of tranquility this place always brought her.

Here, no one could touch or hurt her.

A coward for running and hiding, this place was her escape from the world, at least for a little while until reality pulled her back to the true world. It always did.

"Lizzie?" Fallon's whispered words broke through the silence.

Her serenity lost, everything turned sordid shades of black and white. A flash of wild grief ripped through her, and heaviness settled across her chest.

"Go away, Fallon," she cried, trying to flee further into her mind, to find harmony again.

He followed.

"Please, Lizzie, talk to me."

She shook her head, swallowing hard to bite back the tears.

"Why did ye run from me?"

"You wouldn't understand."

"Make me understand." He looked around. "What is this place?"

"It used to be my escape until you showed up."

"Come back with me?"

She choked on a sob. "Why? What's there for me? A job that's nothing more than an unpleasant chore now. A house, possessions...I'm not a materialistic person, Fallon. My house could burn to the ground today, and I wouldn't care. My life is no longer my own. I can't control what's happening in that world." She twirled in a circle, her arms spread wide around her. "Here, I have the power."

"Ye would stay in isolation?"

Her composure a fragile shell around her, she bit her lip and looked away.

"Would that be so bad?"

"Aye," Fallon's voice broke with huskiness.

"Why do you care, Fallon?"

His Adam's apple bobbed as he swallowed. He grew silent turning away from her. "I care, Lizzie, more than ye know." The intensity in his words startled her.

"Then why do you push me away?"

"Ye doona know my past, Lizzie. Ye doona know *me*."

"Because you won't let me," she said, in a suffocated whisper.

He turned to her. "Will ye come back with me?" Fallon muttered.

Shocked at the fierce sparkling in his eyes, she raised a hand, caressing his cheek. "Who are you, Fallon?"

Fallon caught her hand and pressed it to his cheek. "I'm death. All my life, death has surrounded me."

"You're not death. When I look at you, I see everything good. You try to hide that part of you, but I see it. This may be my escape, but your past is yours." Her gaze traveled over his face. "You don't want to feel again. You don't want to live again. Our pasts define us. Without it, we wouldn't be who we are."

"Lizzie…"

Covering his lips with one finger, she shushed him, then wrapped her arms around his neck and pulled him closer.

A growl rose from deep in his chest, a profound rumble that throbbed through her. The strength and heat of his body pressed against her, his hard chest grazed her breasts. A spark of excitement shivered up her spine, sizzled along every nerve, and fired her blood. She sucked in her breath, drawing the subtle spicy scent of his skin deep into her lungs.

His masculine scent enticed her, tempted her, until it took every shred of her will to keep from pressing her lips against his neck.

And then, his lips slanted over hers, and she closed her eyes in anticipation.

But nothing happened.

She opened her eyes only to find herself alone in the middle of her bed.

****

More confused than ever, the time had come for him to admit what he'd been denying since the day he met Elizabeth Forrester. Never before, even with Rhiannon, had he been this protective, this possessive of a woman. This obsessed. He wanted to tell her his story, but fear kept him silent. Fear she wouldn't accept him for what he'd done.

He didn't want to be alone anymore. He wanted Lizzie. A part of him needed to shove his entire life down her throat, force her to accept him. His older, wiser self warned against such callousness.

Wasn't that what he was? A cruel, heartless bastard?

In those few moments when he'd slipped into Lizzie's thoughts, he'd realized he craved not just her body in his bed, but all of her, given without doubts or reservations. He wanted to sanctify their union, to make her his.

He sought that as much as he ached to find liberation of the past that haunted him, freedom from the world he'd left behind.

Scotland.

The land of his birth. He missed her beauty and mystical powers with a passion that made him ache.

How long since he'd said good-bye to her? To his past? To Rhiannon?

More than a hundred lifetimes ago, but he'd never forgotten. His past sparked his existence, the way he'd lived for the past five hundred years.

Could he let go of that history after holding a tight rein on it for so long?

Another image flashed into his mind.

His uncle found him at the docks on the day he'd left his beloved country.

"And why would you run away from the home I gave you? I thank the good Lord your parents went to heaven before they saw what a disappointment their only child turned out to be."

Fallon refused to give voice to the grief and guilt his uncle's words brought him. He loved his parents and hoped they never saw him for the man he'd become.

Beaten down by his uncle's scorn and fists, Fallon turned away from faith and hadn't prayed since he'd been a child. He refused to embrace the religion his parents taught him. For all he had become, how could he bring himself to pay homage to anyone who could be so malicious?

He could no longer distinguish between heaven and hell, reward and damnation.

In his world, they were the same.

In spite of that, Fallon wanted Lizzie to be a part of his world. He needed her to be a part of him, but how could he condemn her to this?

Damn the gods.

****

She walked into this relationship with her eyes wide open, well, half open, but she'd understood from the beginning Fallon was more than a mere man.

Liz cursed, tossed, and cursed again until sleep overcame her.

Deidra Sidhe visited her again that night in her dreams. She apologized for her anger the previous night and begged Liz to help her.

Liz would never aid Deidra and constructed a mental white shield around her mind, blocking the woman from her dreams. She snuggled down in her bed, thinking what a nifty trick she'd just learned.

****

The glow of the sun rising high into the sky woke Liz. She stretched and rubbed her eyes.

She lay in bed for a few more moments before she threw off the covers and went in search of something to wear. After deciding on a pair of blue jeans and black tee, she dressed and left her room.

Fallon wasn't in his usual place on the couch, and Liz padded barefoot into the kitchen.

She came to a sudden stop to find him sitting at the table. He held a newspaper in front of his face. He must have sensed her presence, for he tipped down the corner. His tender eyes pierced her, sending shockwaves throughout her body.

The paper dropped to the table. He stood, walked over to her, and put his arms around her in an affectionate hug. The warmth of his fingers pressed into her back and tingled, sending goose bumps spilling up and down her spine. His arms flexed as they wrapped around her—undeniably masculine.

With his right hand snug in the arch of her back, his free hand cradled her cheek. He tilted her face upward so she couldn't avoid looking into his eyes.

Only then did he smile before his mouth lowered to hers. The caress of his lips on hers sent currents of desire racing through her limbs.

His lips parted and nudged hers open. The kiss deepened as his tongue delved into her mouth, hard and searching. Blood shot from her heart and pounded into her brain. Her knees trembled. If not for his hulking arms around her, they would have buckled.

Shocked by her own eager response to the touch of his lips, she returned his kiss with equal hunger. Her hands pressed into his back, pulling his body closer to hers. In his arms, safety and security enveloped her, and she never wanted to leave their refuge.

And then, reality set in.

A passionate good morning kiss was the last thing she expected when she walked into the room.

Over the past few weeks, he'd done everything to avoid her.

Why the sudden change? Maybe she'd gotten too close to the truth or maybe this hard, dominating kiss his way to mark her as his trophy.

Yet, this was the kiss of a lover, tender, sweet, sexual, not a kiss of domination.

Raising his lips from hers, he gazed into her eyes. Without saying a word, he led her to the table. After dropping a quick kiss to her forehead, he stepped away and tugged out a chair for her to sit.

She breathed lightly between parted lips.

Once seated, he gave the chair a slight push before he asked, "Did ye sleep well?"

His calm, we-do-this-every morning attitude penetrated her desire-saturated thoughts, and her temper flared.

Fury almost choked her.

"What's going on?" she demanded, then pressed her lips together.

His eyebrows raised, innocence written in his expression. "Have I done something to upset ye, lass?"

"Don't be cute," she snapped. "I can't sit across the breakfast table from you and chit-chat as if nothing's happening between us."

"Nothing has happened," he pointed out with maddening logic. "Believe me. I am achingly certain nothing happened. Lizzie, ye know as well as I do, I could do anything I want, and ye would love it."

Heat rushed to her cheeks. She ignored the warmth that spread across her cheeks and down her neck. She threw back her head and placed her hands on her hips. "Do you enjoy doing this to me?"

"What?"

"Fallon, I don't understand you. One minute, you draw me into your arms as if you want me there. You let me into your world. But in the next, you're pushing me away as if I have developed the plague."

"Lizzie, I want ye in my arms. I canna deny that anymore, but I'm afraid. There are things in my past I'm terrified ye wilna accept."

"I don't understand. The past is the past."

"Ye will, and when ye do, ye will understand why I canna let ye into my world. It's dangerous."

"I'm already in your world. Somewhere along the way, yours and mine have blended. Do you know what the amazing thing is? Here, in this room, I have never felt closer or more in tune to anyone in my life. Explain how that is possible."

Their bond deepened. It wouldn't be long before they both lost self-control.

"I canna."

She gave him a sad smile. "Let's get the terminology, right, okay? You can, but you won't."

"Lizzie…"

"No, Fallon, stop!" She lifted her hand, stopping him from speaking. "I'm tired of you telling me

161

what's in my best interest. I'm tired of you trying to influence my life. I used to have myself under control until you showed up."

A pensive shimmer appeared in his eyes and he leaned across the table. "Ye're no' going to freak out on me, are ye?"

Right. That did it! "You bastard." She jumped to her feet, the chair scraping against the linoleum floor. "I am a grown woman, and I can damn well do what I wish, when I wish, however I wish. I see the way you look at me. You and those damn sexy eyes of yours. You're saying I'm the one who's going to freak out? Let's see about that, shall we?"

His brows flickered a little, his expression one of pained tolerance. "Bloody hell, woman, get a grip. Ye canna help being the weaker sex. It is the way of nature."

"Me? Weak? I don't think so." As she spoke, she untied the sash around her robe. Her gaze never left his face.

Fallon stood, his eyes wide. "What are ye doing?"

Liz swept her robe apart, exposing a sheer off-white nightgown. She wore nothing beneath the skimpy piece of lingerie. Transparent, her body was completely revealed. Even though her face warmed, and her heart beat a lyrical melody against her breast, she refused to back down from him.

"Sweet mother of the gods," he murmured, his eyes widening, his tongue running over his lips. His legs gave in to his weight, and he slumped back into the chair.

The silence heavy, the air between them crackled.

"What's the matter, Fallon? Are you a *wee* bit weak in the knees, lad?" Liz dished out exactly what he had been giving to her.

Fallon didn't budge, his eyes fixed on her hardened nipples.

She pulled her robe back in place. With a smile, she sat down and poured cream in her coffee, attempting to maintain an air of detachment; although her insides churned.

Fallon remained silent, his eyes glued on her breasts, a bemused expression plastered upon his face.

All that blood must have rushed to his groin, she thought with an inner giggle.

She glanced across the table at him and whispered, "I have the right to know what the hell's going on. I've told you that before, but you don't care how I feel. I hate to break it to you, but this is not all about you."

Fallon stood and stretched out his hand to her. She looked at him, half in anticipation, and half in dread.

He nodded, clearing his throat. "After a show like that, I'll tell ye anything ye want to know. Come on. Let's go in the other room, and I'll tell ye all about Fallon O'Callaghan."

Chapter Twenty-Three

Without hesitation, Liz placed her hand in his and let him pull her to her feet. She thought he would guide her into the living room. Instead, he pulled her into his embrace and rested his chin on top of her head.

"I promised I would tell ye my secrets, lass. After I've told ye the sordid tale, I'll understand if ye wish me to go away." His breath ruffled her hair as he spoke. When he leaned back, there was an almost imperceptible note of pleading in his face. "But I'm telling ye up front, before I do this, I wilna leave ye until I'm sure ye're going be safe."

The uncertainty in his expression stirred her even before his lips covered hers in a featherlike kiss, and her heart jumped. He jerked away and led her to the living room where he sat her on the couch, claiming the chair opposite her. Head low, he clasped his hands together between his open knees.

Liz didn't say anything, allowing him the time he needed to gather his thoughts.

He drew a deep, agonized breath and whispered, "Here goes."

Fallon didn't look at her as he spoke.

"I was born August seventh, fifteen hundred and lived in a small Scottish village. At five, my parents died in a wagon accident while working the farm. I had only one living relative, Fergus McNevin. He lived in Edinburgh. I'd never met the man. Never knew he existed until I went to live with him and his wife. Once I got there, I understood why my parents dinna visit. Fergus hated my da, hated his Irish heritage and blamed him for taking my ma from her family. I was my father's bastard, no relation to him. My aunt, Matilda, took care of me. She made sure I stayed out from underfoot. So many times, I heard their arguing late at night. It dinna take long to realize he was talking about me. He called me the wee bastard boy. It dinna matter my parents were legally wed under the eyes of God."

He hesitated, raising his face to her. A new and unexpected tenderness surged over her at the glimmer of unshed tears in his eyes.

"Violent arguing forced me to cover my head with my pillow to block out the sounds. It dinna work. I heard. For days after their arguments, my aunt would be indisposed. One of the maids, Fiona, took over my care. She never told me what ailment plagued my aunt, but assured me that she would be better in a couple of days. No' to worry. I turned seventeen before I learned the truth." An inexplicable look of withdrawal came over his face. "My aunt took the lashes meant for me."

He swallowed hard.

"By this time, I was old enough to leave, but then, my aunt took ill. I couldna desert her to the likes of him, especially after all she'd suffered for me. One day, I walked into her room to find him standing over her, whip in hand. So frail, she could do no more than cower on the bed. I knocked him clean on his arse and told him if he ever touched her again, I'd kill him.

"Fergus never laid his hands on her again. His attentions turned to me. In the beginning, I tried to stay out of his way, but, by my interference, he vowed to make sure I lived a miserable existence. Believe me, he kept his promise. It took three of his men to hold me down while he whipped me. I gave up fighting and gave into the beatings. I was a coward, Lizzie, too spineless to leave."

He paused, his eyes filled with tortuous memories of the years of abuse he suffered at his uncle's hands.

"You stuck around to protect your aunt. That's not cowardice."

He smiled crookedly. "Whenever he had a bad day, mine ended with a whip on my back. And as I always did, I ran into the forest to lick my wounds. One day, Rhiannon was there picking berries. For a blueberry pie, she claimed." His voice trembled as though some emotion touched him. "Oh, she was a sight of beauty and innocence, inside and out."

An unconscious stab of jealousy pierced through Liz at the look of yearning she saw in his eyes when he spoke of this woman. Wanting to learn more, she kept silent.

"A Druid, Rhiannon, a magical maiden who gave me her time, her patience, and her love. She held me as I cried and listened when I ranted how much I wanted my uncle dead. She took away my pain, took me into her heart, and made me feel as though I belonged. Until I met her, I'd been only a shell of a person. No' a man. Nothing at all." He gazed at her, his mouth spread into a thin-lipped smile, and shrugged. "She brought out the best in me, made me feel worthy. We met every day for almost two years. The beatings didn't matter anymore. I suffered through them with a smile on my face because I knew Rhiannon would be waiting with open arms. I loved her, and I think she loved me. When my aunt passed of a lung infection, Rhiannon attended the funeral. Of course, having a Druid attend such a solemn gathering invoked my uncle's anger. He was infuriated that I had so little respect for my aunt...that I'd bring such filth to her interment. It was on that day, my life truly ended."

He drew a deep breath, reliving the painful

memories.

"I'd planned on leaving. I packed up my things and headed for the door when my uncle and his henchmen stormed in. By the time he finished with me, I swore the whip had a foot of my flesh wrapped around its leather strips. I couldna walk for a month. When I started to get around, he threatened me. If I ever saw Rhiannon again he'd torture her and make me watch. And then, he'd kill her, just for the fun of it. To him, the Druids were naught but heathens." He released his breath in a quick exhale, his hand massaging the base of his neck.

She swallowed hard and bit back tears. A soft moan slipped past her lips when he lifted his head. Tears trailed down his cheeks. He looked at her, and then blinked as if trying to bring her face into focus.

Pain and anguish ripped through her like jagged glass, holding her breath captive in her breast. No one should have to endure what this man had.

"By this time, I became a prisoner at Fergus' hands. Everywhere I went, his lackeys followed close behind. He even placed a guard at my door. I knew he wanted to kill me and waited for me to give him the reason."

"Oh, Fallon, how awful for you."

Fallon didn't acknowledge her, still lost in his memories. To him, she didn't exist, telling the story for himself, trying to work it out in his mind. Perhaps, to find out where it all went wrong.

"I let him command me like I was one of his servants, and I grew tired of it. Six months." He hesitated, pinching the bridge of his nose between two fingers before he looked at her. "It took six months before I could escape him. I snuck into a fishery and hid there until it got dark outside. When I left, the streets were empty, and I never looked back. I went to the Druid camp only to find the site empty. They'd already left the area. I never had the chance to tell her—." His voice broke, pain evident in his hunched posture and tense muscles. He held a tight rein on his emotions. "She never knew how much I loved her. I tried to find her. I searched for over two months. I got close a couple of times. Eventually, I found the Druid tribe, but Rhiannon's grandmother, Morfesa told me that-"

He stopped, and Liz's heart broke for him.

She reached across the coffee table and grabbed his hand in reassurance. "Fallon, no more—"

He shook his head. "I promised."

"I know about Rhiannon, Fallon. I'm sorry she died, and your child. You must have been devastated."

"What?"

"I'm sorry she died," Liz repeated.

"No, no' that. Ye mentioned a child. What child?"

Liz couldn't hide her astonishment. Seeing his blank expression, she gasped, "Oh, my God, I'm so sorry, Fallon. I thought you knew."

"How did Rhiannon die, Lizzie?"

"It happened a long time ago, Fallon. Let it go."

"No, I need to know. Tell me." His tone was urgent now.

"A story I read claimed Rhiannon died while giving birth to a child, a son."

Tears streamed down his cheeks, and he dropped his head into his hands. "Where did ye learn about that?"

"On the Internet. I thought you would have—"

He chuckled bitterly and shook his head. "I've relived my past in my head for so long I thought I knew everything I needed to." He shrugged, tears filling his eyes. "It was my life. I knew, or mayhap…I never imagined…a child. By the gods, a child."

She paused, unsure how he would react to the news his son died as well. "I'm sorry, Fallon."

"Please tell me it isna so, Lizzie. Tell me I dinna destroy both Rhiannon and my son because of my cowardice?"

"It was a story on the Internet, Fallon. Even if it is true, they died in childbirth. You couldn't prevent that."

"I should have been there for her." Tense lines creased his forehead. "I saw my uncle once more before I left Scotland. On the docks. He was right. I'm no' a man, I'm a coward. He told me he hoped my parents dinna see what I'd become."

"You weren't a coward back then, Fallon O'Callaghan, nor are you one now. You kept your aunt and Rhiannon safe from him. You were the one who sacrificed your life for them. You protected them from evil, and you did it the only way you knew how."

"Lizzie."

Liz walked over to him and knelt on the floor in front of him and covered his lips with one finger to keep him silent.

"Don't, Fallon. Please don't do this to yourself. You did nothing wrong. I don't think Rhiannon would blame you for what happened."

She removed her finger, replacing it with her lips. It was a soft, gentle kiss meant to console him. When she leaned back to look into his face, she shuddered at the look of pain in his expression. Leaning forward, she wrapped her arms around him, nuzzling against his neck.

He drew her close. His body shook with silent sobs and he cried for the woman and child he'd lost. She held him in silence, understanding that unless he released the pain and guilt he felt over Rhiannon's death, he would never feel worthy of love.

She held him for over an hour until his tears were spent.

Liz looked up at him, her eyes awash with his pain; though only a single tear trickled down her cheek.

"What happened to you, Fallon?"

Fallon cleared his throat. "I'm no' sure what transpired next. Morfesa told me I'd been chosen."

"Chosen?"

He gazed at her with a crooked smile and said, "I belong to a small militia of protectors known as the Síoraí's, although I doona embrace the legacy."

"What's a Síoraí?"

"A Síoraí is, in essence, the rarest form of immortal. In Celtic, Síoraí means eternal. There are four of us in existence. The gods of the Tuatha Dé Danann hold our spirits. Luna, the Moon Goddess, holds our soul. We survive by drawing on their supernatural power."

"It sounds like you've been blessed."

Fallon released a loud bark of bitter laughter. "Blessed? Are ye kidding? In order for us to achieve this grand blessing, we suffer, and we suffer dearly. They take everything that keeps us human. At the moment our last link to humanity is severed, immeasurable power becomes ours. To add insult to this grave injury, the gods give us fangs so we blend in with the creatures of the night. Sunlight is out of the question because if it touches us, it will destroy us."

"Is that why you don't accept your destiny?"

"I canna forget the past, Lizzie. To gain, I lost, and aye, I do blame the gods. It's with me every day, with every step I take. How can I protect an innocent stranger when I failed to protect the one I loved? Rhiannon died, and now, I find out I'm responsible for the death of my child, my own flesh and blood. I never even knew."

"That wasn't your fault."

"No? Well, that's a matter of opinion. Anyways, I

find it difficult to be loyal to anyone or anything knowing the pain they're capable of inflicting. They dinna give me the option to choose whether I wanted this life. It became mine. The gods are nothing but a group of spiritual beings on a power trip. They sit on their celestial arses, point their fingers, and expect us to do their bidding."

"If you don't want the power, why do you keep it?"

"Once received, the powers canna be taken away or given back. Only through death can they be returned. If needed, they'll be preserved for the next generation of Síoraí Guardians to be born."

"What if you decide to use your powers against the gods?"

"That wilna happen. They've created a failsafe, ye might say. Our powers are frozen when we stand in their presence."

"What do you hunt at night?"

"Half-breeds. Demons," he said with a significant lifting of his brows.

"Demons?"

"Aye. Vampires, werewolves, shape shifters."

Liz gasped. "I didn't think they really existed."

"They do, and they're deadly."

"Why do you call them half-breeds?" she asked.

"That's what they are. Over the centuries, their blood has been tainted. Some say, it's because they crossed breeds. They're no longer pure. They kill, hoping to find an innocent human who will cleanse them of disease and give them everlasting life as a human."

"Where do demons come from?"

"Centuries ago, a cabinet of the first evils, known as the Camarilla, ruled the demon world. They were the purest. An immortal vampire, Ághmach, claimed the high Vampryss, Deidra Sidhe, as his mate. Their offspring carried the purest blood lust and were considered absolute power. But they overstepped their boundaries, and the gods banished them."

Liz's heart stopped, and her stomach churned with anxiety at the name. The woman in her dreams.

She opened her mouth to tell Fallon, but the expression on his face stopped the words in her throat.

"Fallon?" she asked, tentatively.

She shivered as the color drained from his face; his eyes became icy and unresponsive.

"Are you okay?"

He shook his head.

"Fallon, talk to me. What is it?"

Fallon looked into her eyes and whispered hoarsely, "She's escaped. God help us if she walks among us."

"Who?" Liz asked, overcome with a dull ache of foreboding.

"The Vampryss, Deidra. The Queen of the Dead, the ultimate evil."

Chapter Twenty-Four

With a startled breath, her eyes shot wide open. They struggled to focus against sleep that lay heavy on her lids. In the haze of being half asleep and awake, Liz couldn't be sure what woke her. She rolled over, hugged her pillow beneath her cheek, and listened to the familiar soothing sounds that calmed her. Inside the house, not a sound, yet outside, the ocean waves swooshed on shore. Their gentle appeal lulled her back to sleep.

A week had gone by since Fallon shared his past. Seven days, seven nights, and yet their relationship remained taut with tension. She continued her ritual of heading off to work every day and left him brooding on the couch.

Only yesterday, she'd been standing over a corpse up to her elbows in bowel when she'd been struck by the realization that her life had become a mess, very much like the innards she held in her hands. The tattered remains of a once feasible life.

Liz thought Fallon's revelation of his past would bring them closer; instead their distance remained as wide as the Grand Canyon. He seemed possessed, more intent on destroying Deidra and her lair.

Liz fidgeted, drawing the comforter up around her neck, seeking that perfect position, the one that would send her back into a peaceful slumber. Just as she slipped into welcome oblivion, a feminine voice broke the silence.

She sat up and peered across the room. A shadow flitted in the corner of the room, and she called, "Who's there?"

And then, a woman dressed in a long black gown materialized from the darkness, her brows drawn together in an agonized expression. A grayish-colored haze surrounded her. The woman's mouth moved, emitting a jumbled mass of indistinguishable words.

An icy hand gripped her heart and squeezed, trapping her breath in her lungs. She bit her lip to stifle her outcry.

She drew a deep breath and forbade herself to tremble.

Fear turned to anger, which became a scalding fury that skittered up her spine and filled her vision with a red haze.

Liz stiffened—her neck knotted. She crawled from bed and stepped toward Deidra.

Before she reached Deidra, blue fire ringed the other woman, crackling flames that extended toward the ceiling.

Startled, Liz sprung back a step, but instead of heat, the blaze radiated arctic temperatures, wintry. She extended a hand in curiosity. Her fingers slipped into the iridescent flicker. The chill stroked her with an essence she didn't recognize.

"Deidra."

"You know my name?"

Liz nodded, clenching her teeth. "Of course. You do not belong here."

"I seek your help. I can ask no one else."

"I know what you are, Deidra, and I know what you want to do. There is no way in hell I'll ever help you." Liz turned away from the woman and closed her mind, refusing to let Deidra in. With a quick flick of her wrist, she ordered, "Now, leave my house."

Her insides trembled at her brave actions.

The malicious Vampryss snarled. Liz inhaled.

Hell would freeze over before she cowered before this creature.

Deidra's low shriek radiated, echoed, and then grew silent.

She glanced over her shoulder and released a shaky breath. Deidra gone, as were the insipid flames, but her departure left an evil residue within the room. It permeated the air with a stomach-turning stench that reminded Liz of death, the type that greeted her every day at work.

Fallon did not know of Deidra's visits, nor did she intend to inform him. Well, not right away anyway. At the moment, the woman posed nothing more than a nuisance.

She needed to see Fallon, to feel him next to her, safe in his arms. Liz walked to the door. She hesitated, her hand resting on the handle. He'd probably gone out. Disappointment stabbed through her.

A bright flash of light from the window drew her attention. She whipped open the window and shivered as the wind blew the red taffeta curtains against her. Clouds formed high above, and the water in the bay churned with white caps. A loud clap of thunder ricocheted across the sky, followed by a quick flash of lightning. Another storm brewed.

A frigid breeze brushed her face. She shuddered, closed the shutters and locked the window.

She crawled into bed. Warmth crept back into her body, but the heaviness that settled in the pit of her stomach kept her awake.

As she lay between the sheets, her breath tangled in her throat. Thoughts of Fallon sent her blood surging through her veins, strong, abundant, and vibrant.

Trapped in his own private hell, he hadn't asked for the life given to him. He was ashamed of his past, and wanted to keep her safe, to protect her from the evils of the world.

For how long? Days, weeks, months?

The notion of losing him pierced her heart. She swallowed hard.

"Crap." The word escaped on a soft stream of breath.

Sitting up, she grabbed the pillow and punched her fists in the center. She gripped the edges and twisted before she dropped the now fluffed pillow back on the bed.

She flopped down, curled into the covers and closed her eyes.

Behind closed eyelids, she envisioned images of a golden-eyed little boy growing up under such degrading circumstances. No wonder he exiled himself from everyone, spending his energies and anger on the gods. Weren't they responsible for his immortality? Didn't they wage a war on him? A war Fallon showed no intention of losing.

Stubborn man.

But how did Deidra Sidhe fit into the picture, and why did that woman haunt her? She wanted the Talisman, but why was the woman insistent she be the one to deliver it?

A lightning bolt flashed outside her window, followed by the deep rumble of thunder.

She whipped the covers over her head.

Sh…ugar.

****

He should be hunting.

Uneasiness seeped through Fallon like a mug of sour ale, making his stomach churn. With their bond growing stronger and stronger, his instincts refused to be ignored, and he would not leave Lizzie alone.

It had been awhile since Seth's last meal, and he happily took the night off. Fallon smiled, imagining his friend visiting the meat market for a well-deserved bite to eat.

Lying down, Fallon stretched his legs over the end of the sofa. With hands tucked behind his head, he stared at the ceiling from his horizontal position. He tapped a foot; his ankles crossed, and wondered what a person did in their free time.

Lizzie retired to her bed a little over an hour ago and was most likely asleep by now.

He thought of her, saw her face clearly, her eyes, heard the sound of her laughter, and then, visions of a completely naked Lizzie flashed into his mind.

Ample breasts, soft, their tips rose-colored and plump. Wide hips, creamy thighs, and the curly hair between her thighs the same color upon her head.

Fallon shivered with arousal and hunger.

One thin door separated them, and he planned to keep it that way. As much as he ached to walk through that door, he couldn't. The wood between them acted as a protective barrier around his heart.

He turned his attention to a topic much less desirable.

Deidra Sidhe.

Where could she be hiding?

He'd spent the last week searching for the Vampryss. The minions he caught refused to disclose her location despite his torture. What little information he managed to gather never panned out, ending in dead ends.

Bloody hell!

He feared he would be too late to stop her from releasing Ághmach. If the stories were true, no one in this world would be safe from their evil.

And because he couldn't shake this feeling, he did something he swore he never would. He called Devlin. Although the elder hadn't answered his cell, Fallon left him a message, letting him know his suspicions.

"No!"

At Lizzie's cry, spasms of alarm raced through

him, and panic welled in his throat. He vaulted from the couch to his feet and raced for her room. With his hand on the knob, he turned the handle and pushed the door open.

A crack of light from the doorway spilled across the bed. He released a deep breath at the sight of Lizzie in bed alone. A soft whimpering echoed in the room, and through the darkness. Lizzie thrashed about, moaning as though someone tormented her in her dreams.

He stepped across the threshold, scanning the room.

Empty.

From the side of the bed, he gazed at Lizzie. Sweat drenched her face, tears poured down her cheeks, and her head shook back and forth. She cried out, "No, go away! Leave me alone. Fallon."

Fallon's heart lurched. Her words hurt, as if a knife had been thrust into his chest and twisted. He couldn't blame her. What had he done for her? He'd brought her nothing but misery.

She wanted him to go away, and he turned to leave.

"Fallon."

At his name, he peered toward the bed. Her eyes were open, her arms stretched out to him.

"Don't leave me."

Fallon lay beside her and drew her into his arms. He brushed his hand across her hair and murmured, "Shh, I'm here, Lizzie. Ye're safe."

Nestled against his side, she fell back asleep. He gritted his teeth at the heat of her body melding with his.

It was going to be a long night.

****

She woke from a fitful sleep, one arm draped across a warm, rock-solid body. Still snuggled in the realms of half-sleep, she tightened her hold and pulled herself toward the warmth.

Soft, moist featherlike touches brushed against her closed eyelid. Warm, strong hands stroked her hair.

She smiled at the dream and yawned.

And then his masculine scent of musk, sandalwood and leather forced her eyes open wide.

Fallon.

She jolted up so fast she whacked her forehead against a hard, unmovable object.

A curse filtered through the room.

She collapsed onto the pillow and rubbed her forehead to ease the stinging pain. To her side, Fallon lay on the bed, his eyes closed.

"I'm sorry," she apologized, sitting up. "I didn't know you were there."

Fallon's eyes opened. He started to speak but snapped his mouth closed. He lifted a hand, and Liz watched as he wiggled his nose back and forth. His eyes watered, yet he still managed to glare at her with smoldering, accusing eyes.

"Is it broken?"

"I doona think so. I'm sure it'll be fine. In time," he said, with a grimace.

"Are you sure you're ok?" She knelt and bent over him. "Let me look."

His eyes traveled up the length of her body but never made it past the plunging neckline of her nightdress. Bent over him, she gave him an uninhibited view of her body. He received the full frontal.

She sat back, an unwelcome flush creeping into her cheeks. Her embarrassment changed to annoyance, and she asked, "What are you doing in my bed?"

The ferocious shining in his eyes shocked her, and she scooted backward on the bed.

Before her feet touched the floor, he grabbed her

and slid her across his body, claiming her mouth, forcing her lips open with his thrusting tongue.

Liz moaned her pleasure. Warmth spread through her limbs. Her head spun at the intense pleasure of his kiss as his hot breath mingled with hers.

His arms tightened around her. A thousand flames fanned over her body, burned her, incited her as they pooled into a molten zone between her thighs where she ached for him the most.

****

Fallon groaned at the intense heat swelling through his body. Blood surged through his groin, enflaming him, the involuntary tremors of arousal beginning.

Denial stabbed through his gut, and he jerked away, unable to continue. Not for lack of want. His need for her claimed him like no other. He did it to protect her. Her safety was more important than his lust.

"Nay, this isna happening," he murmured against her lips. "I canna let this happen. I'm so sorry, Lizzie."

He rolled to the edge of the bed where he stood, shaking with desire. He paused before looking down at her.

Pink stained her cheeks. The desire faded, replaced by raw hurt that glittered in her blue eyes.

"I don't understand, Fallon. What is wrong with me?"

Fallon flinched, fighting the need to drop back on the bed, yank her into his arms, and make love to her. Instead, he took a step back and shook his head.

"It isna ye, Lizzie. It's me. I am so sorry. Ye're like a fire in my blood, lass. Ye deserve more than a frolic in the hay."

"What if now...this moment...a frolic is all I want?"

"I canna do that to ye, lass. My life has been bonded to yers, and I need to find a way to set ye free…" He clamped his lips shut, refusing to utter another word.

Within him, the power of the blood bond grew. It pulled at him, begging him to consummate the union, to blend their bodies and unite as one. Lizzie touched him in ways that exceeded the false obsession influenced by their connection, but he wasn't selfish enough to subject her to his way of life.

His passion consumed him, hardening his body with a need so powerful he feared it. Lizzie's breasts heaved with a desire to be touched. His erection stiffened painfully. Damn the gods and their bloody crusade. He turned and left the room, his hands fisted and thrust deep into his pockets.

"Ye bastards," he muttered furiously under his breath, tired of being the pawn.

A red haze flared across his vision, his blood boiled a lava bed in his veins, and anger rippled along his spine.

And uncertainty.

How could he fight their control? Reclaim the free will they'd stolen from him?

When, and if, he and Liz made love, it had to be the right time for both of them.

Not influenced, not timed, and especially not forced by a blood bond created by the gods.

Lizzie deserved more than that.

They both did.

Didn't they?

Chapter Twenty-Five

Outside, the wind gathered force and drove the rain against the outer walls, battering it mercilessly, like the pitiful shack had been singled out for destruction. The same way the gods destroyed the temple in her Crimson Kingdom, they seemed intent on using the elements to demolish this place.

With still so much to do in this miserable world, it would take more than an elemental uprising to force her from this plane.

Although the Síoraí's woman emitted strength, Deidra found a way past her defenses, inside the barricades surrounding her. To her delight, her contact with the Princess became more frequent. In time, she would connect with her in the flesh but, for now, intruding in the Princess' dreams would suffice.

The emotional attachment the woman experienced toward her protector projected a repulsive sensation across the distance, which separated Deidra from her prey. And yet, their brief moments of anger stimulated Deidra's attacks. She fed upon the anger, fueled by it. The angrier the woman became, the stronger her essence.

And then, all Deidra had to do…follow the scent.

Soon, she would have the woman's location, and when she did, she would tear down her shield, infiltrate her mind, and control her.

Slow inch by slow inch.

****

The storm hovered over the lake, threatening to rise upon the beaches. The air, muggy and intense, spread a misty vapor across the land and created a sauna. It pulsed with warmth, electricity, and expectation.

Thunder rumbled, and lightning flared across the water, but the squall didn't drift toward shore.

The tension inside Fallon mirrored the pressures of the building tempest. He wanted to roar and run, punch anything in his path. He ran his fingers through his hair and continued to pace across Lizzie's living room.

When he could no longer stand the sounds of nature, he walked to the couch where he lay down and grabbed the pillow, shoving it over his head.

Lizzie would be home from work soon. He wondered if she was still angry with him. After their encounter this morning, she'd gotten up, dressed and left the house without so much as a word, leaving him with a colossal sense of loss. He deserved her anger but didn't know how to make it better.

The sounds of the storm faded along with the anxiety inside Fallon. Angry or not, he couldn't wait to see her.

****

Liz stood on the deck with a cup of coffee in her hands. She leaned forward against the railing. Her eyes scanned the horizon.

All that remained of the sun sent a last burst of brilliant red blush skimming across the water. The vibrancy danced across the surface of the lake, coloring the world in shades of bright orange and red.

She'd gotten home a couple of hours ago. After making a light supper, she grabbed a cup of coffee and headed outside to enjoy the sunset.

While at work, she came to a definitive conclusion. Although not pleased with Fallon, she wouldn't be angry. If he didn't want her, so be it. Her pride refused to allow her to force herself on him.

"Lizzie, it's time to come inside."

Lost in thought, Liz gasped in surprise at the sound of Fallon's voice.

"In a sec." She looked from the setting sun over her shoulder to see him leaning against the doorframe. "Should you be out here?"

"The sun's gone down. It only affects me when I stand in its direct rays. When it's like this, there's a slight tingling on my skin. Nothing more."

She turned back to the view.

The heat of the ceramic mug spread warmth across her palms. She brought the mug to her face and inhaled the fresh hazelnut aroma. Steam tickled her nose as she took a sip. The nutty flavor rolled around her tongue.

His footsteps crossed the deck. "It is a glorious sunset, isn't it?"

His breath brushed against her hair. "It isna as beautiful as ye."

Liz shivered at the sensual tone of his voice.

He shifted her so he could gaze down into her face. Mesmerized, she stared, her lips parted.

Fallon reached for the cup in her hands, setting it on the table. He held her hands in his. "I want to kiss ye, Lizzie," he whispered, his eyes probing hers, asking permission.

As much as she wanted to, she couldn't deny him, and caught her lower lip between her teeth. "I'd like that." She raised her hands to his neck and drew his mouth to hers.

His lips traveled over hers in a tender touching of flesh. His hand cupped her neck while his other caressed the side of her face and neck before sliding to stroke her shoulders. He turned her sideways to cradle her in his arms.

His mouth trailed her jaw, nibbling down her throat then back up to the skin beneath her chin. His lips traveled full circle until they returned to her mouth.

A soft groan escaped, fueled by her need for more.

Supported in his embrace, she shifted against the deep ache in her belly. Fire flowed through her veins and pooled between her legs.

Their breathing grew heavy. Soft moans and deep groans filled the air. When he pulled his mouth from hers, she traced the line of his firm jaw with her fingertip then kissed his neck below his chin until he tipped her face up and claimed her mouth again.

Fallon stiffened and pulled away, releasing his breath in a loud exhale. His forehead settled against hers. "I want ye, Lizzie, more than I've ever wanted any woman. Ye're no' a trophy to be won, lass. Ye deserve so much more than I can give ye."

Her hand brushed across his cheek. "I want you, too, Fallon, just you. If only you could see that." A sad smile tilted the corners of her lips. Her eyes caressed his face, her desire mirrored in his eyes. "Good night."

****

Surrounded by bramble brush and willow branches, Liz stood beside a rushing stream. Where was she? A jumble of confused emotions tore through her, and she looked up. A mountain stretched high into the sky, disappearing into a cloud of startling white mist.

To her right, she spotted a cave in the side of the mountain. From the cavity, a welcoming light glowed, calling to her, drawing her to its radiance.

She took three steps to the front of the mountain, held aside the limbs covering the opening and stared inside. A clear pool of water nestled on the opposite side of the cavern. The cerulean liquid spilled from its boundaries and disappeared over a rock ledge that separated her from the pool. The walls of the room were luminescent, shining of a silver fluorescent substance.

Nearby, a fire brightened the opposite side of the room. It flared with rolling flames, its light dancing upon the wall. An attractive sight, yet Liz remained reluctant to venture further into the cavern.

She didn't know who or what awaited her.

"Who's there? What...what do you want from me?" she asked, her voice catching in her throat. Her hands shook, and she clutched them in front of her in an attempt to still their trembling.

Her questions went unanswered.

Despite the fire, the chill of the cave penetrated her clothing. She wanted to leave, but a sixth sense warned her to remain.

Her nerves tensed. A spasmodic trembling swept over her limbs. She stepped into the cave and strolled toward the fire to warm herself. She clenched her hands until her nails entered her palms.

Except for the crackling of the fire, silence met her.

And then, a rustle of trees and a snapping twig drew her attention to the mouth of the cave.

Fallon.

He stepped across the threshold, his head brushing the top of the rock cavity.

His eyes narrowed in apparent suspicion when he saw her. "Lizzie? Is that ye, lass?" As he charged across the hard granite floor toward her, he glanced around. "Where are we?"

Nervous, she shifted from foot to foot and trembled with intensity. "I don't know."

The flames rose higher, dancing around them, enveloping them in warmth. The heat calmed her fears.

Liz shivered. His eyes were compelling, magnetic, and then he wrapped his arms around her. Their bodies blended, melded together by the heat from the fire.

Soft murmurings of encouragement surrounded them, voices just above the limits of hearing.

In the gaps where their bodies did not touch, a whitish hue intertwined around them, sealing the distance between them. Her body flowed against his, hungering and wanting. Time stretched. Liz didn't know how much time passed. Her hands moved over him in a soft caress, nurturing her growing hunger.

Liz had never touched anyone like this before.

Fallon lowered his head and kissed her. A thirst consumed her. His arms tightened around her, devouring all senses.

She wanted more, and oh, how she needed more. Of this, and of him.

Clinging to him, her head spun, and her points of orientation melted away.

Yes, oh god, yes.

So much energy in his touch, the magic left her aching for more. She caressed the strong tendons in the back of his neck, and the blood surged from her fingertips to her toes.

Their bodies swayed in a slow, fluid motion. Fallon lowered her to ground and lay beside her. Oblivious to the hard presence of the rocks beneath her back, Liz was only aware of the man looming above her. He closed the small gap between them and rubbed his body against hers. His erection, hard and hot, pressed against her hip. His face nestled her neck, his breath ragged in her ear.

"Fallon, stop!" she managed. Her voice sounded shaky even to her own ears. He hadn't wanted her before. What had changed?

"Stop what?" His tongue swirled around her ear lobe.

"This." She writhed beneath him, eager to touch his skin.

She hissed in pleasure. Desire shot over her like

red embers and scorched every inch of her body. Her breasts swelled even tighter against his chest.

"Or this?" His hand slid to the inside of her thigh, his thumb brushing against where she craved him the most.

Her toes curled in response to his touch, and she arched her back toward him.

"No!" A high-pitched, strangled voice echoed through the cave and bounced from the walls.

Ripped from her arms, Fallon flew backward into the shadows of the cave. Cold, empty and alone, a vital part of herself was torn away.

Liz sat up and searched the cave. Fallon?

She heard movement and turned toward the sound. Only shadows, nothing more, but something moved in the darkness, a black mass, and it headed toward her, its feet shuffling against the rocks. Eyes, a hellish red colored, illuminated the obscurity before the animal entered the light radiating from the fire.

She suppressed a gasp at the enormous, grotesque beast that came into sight. Walking on four feet, long silver-black fur covered its massive form. Pointed ears, a large snout and fangs, sharp and pointed, seeped from the corners of a twisted-shaped mouth.

She closed her eyes. Her heart pounded against her breast. Every nerve in her body screamed for Fallon. Scooting on her butt, she slid backward until she could go no further. Her back pressed against the granite walls.

A brief silence reigned in the cave before she opened her eyes. The creature now bent over her. She choked back a frightened cry and clenched her eyes shut again.

For the second time in her life, Liz knew true fear—not nervousness or apprehension, not the simple stress or nagging worries of everyday life, but true gut-wrenching terror.

Her erratic pulse nearly burst from her veins as panic rioted over her skin. Goosebumps formed on her legs beneath her pants sending chills spiraling up her back. Fear held her immobile. Gasping for breath and close to giving into blessed unconsciousness, she fought to remain lucid.

The creature made no sound, yet a parade of vivid images flashed in Liz's mind—vampires, werewolves, demons of various shape and sizes.

The creature's breath swept over her face, and she grimaced at the stench of decay that filled her nostrils. Its putrid scent grazed her neck where the scar of Fallon's bite marred her tissue. It snorted in disgust and transferred his attention to the other side of her neck, as though searching for an untainted area where its teeth could slice through her skin, into her jugular vein.

Liz willed the creature to leave.

A long moment passed until the creature slithered away. She opened her eyes a sliver to peer into the room.

To her surprise, it sat on its hunches, its breathing explosive in the darkness. Loud, the sound bounced off the walls.

It raised its head and cocked its ears as though it heard a sound Liz couldn't hear.

It rose and clambered to the entrance of the cave. When it reached the opening, it turned and looked at her. It smiled, baring rotten gray teeth before disappearing.

Liz's body went limp with relief, and she sagged against the wall. Closing her eyes, she whispered a soft prayer and released the breath she held.

A sudden burst of adrenalin rushed into her heart, and she sat up in panic.

Where was Fallon? Had the beast killed him?

Her eyes shot open to discover she no longer sat in the cave, but in the center of her bed.

Had it been a dream?

The door to her room flew open, and Fallon stormed in. His brows drawn in concern, alarm filled his eyes.

He rushed to her side. "Are ye all right, Lizzie?"

"What happened? What's going on?" She raised trembling hands to rub her eyes.

Fallon pulled her into his arm, resting his chin on the top of her head. "I doona know, lass. I doona know," he murmured in her hair.

Chapter Twenty-Six

Fallon glanced at his feet. The murky spray of water from the lake washed over them.

Where had the fog come from?

The pink hint of dawn stretched across the eastern horizon, but even the sun's rays couldn't penetrate the damp gloom. A gray mist swirled about the water and rolled across the dew-sprinkled sand in his direction.

He shivered with sudden cold and glanced up. A shrouded outline strode from the dense fog and lifted a lantern. The figure stepped closer and lowered the hood of his cloak to reveal his face.

Dagda.

Fallon sighed. "What the hell's going on around here, Dagda?"

"The arrival of the prophecy foretold many, many centuries ago. The destruction you see around you is the handiwork of the worst evil ever created."

"Deidra Sidhe. She has risen from her grave, hasna she?"

Dagda nodded. "Aye."

"I suspected as much. What does she want?"

"The Talisman you wear around your neck."

Fallon's jaw clenched. "She'll have to kill me to take the Talisman, and I'm no' ready to die."

A half smile crossed Dagda's face. He nodded as if pleased by his determination. "There is something else she needs to be successful in her plan."

"What's that?"

"The woman you protect."

Fallon's nerves tensed, his stomach churning with anxiety and frustration. "Lizzie? What does she want from her? Lizzie's done naught to her."

"Elizabeth Forrester is special…more special than you realize. The evil one does not see her for what she has done, but what the lass carries inside her. It is the key."

"The key to what?"

A warning cloud settled on Dagda's features. "To release Ághmach from the underworld."

There was a long brittle silence that grew tight with tension before Fallon asked, "Why Lizzie?"

"It is fated. Just as your life has been pre-ordained, so has Lizzie's. It is time for her to embrace her destiny."

"Are ye saying ye played a part is this? Ye did this to her?" Fallon's anger boiled and would have erupted if Dagda hadn't raised his hands in a sign of surrender.

"There is so much you don't comprehend."

"Then tell me," Fallon demanded.

"I cannot. Know that Lizzie is a vital piece in the battle we wage against Deidra."

"It is yer war. Why drag us into it?"

"Destiny."

"To hell with destiny. What could Lizzie possibly have that Deidra wants?"

"The power of the light. Protect them both well, my child."

"I doona under—" Fallon's voice broke off for the elder had already faded into the mist and disappeared.

Fallon ambled to the water's edge and stared across the misted sea, his anger bile that rose in his throat.

His eyes lifted, and he stared across the clouded skies. "Listen, gods, and listen well. When Deidra is gone, ye will all pay for what ye have done to Lizzie.

I hope ye rot in hell!"

****

By late afternoon, a layer of dark clouds swept across the sky, and a splattering of raindrops fell.

Hands behind his head, Fallon lay on the couch, mulling over Dagda's words, his thoughts saturated with confusion over the events that plagued this world. Regardless of where this situation headed, he vowed to protect Lizzie even if it meant forfeit of his own life. No matter how she became involved, Fallon would make sure she survived.

He drew a deep breath thinking of the strong-willed woman he'd come to know.

The patter of rain deepened to a steady drum pounding against the windowpane.

Damn, he loathed this weather! Inside Lizzie's home, sounds of wind and rain penetrated the walls around him. The squall raged with nerve-shattering fury. Thunder exploded at an ever-increasing rate as the rainstorm sought its full magnitude.

A loud bang sounded outside the veranda doors. He sprang to his feet and ran across the room. Dark storm clouds shielded the sun, and he opened the door a crack.

A lull in the wind preceded the gale as it gathered force again.

And then, the noise came.

Tap. Tap.

He opened the door and stepped outside, closing it behind him. Lizzie would kill him if he let the water soak her hardwood floors.

A sigh of relief escaped when he saw the table canopy bounce against the side of the house. Just the blustery weather. The wind caught the fabric, lifted it, and pushed it against the siding.

After lowering the awning, he headed back inside.

He lay down on the couch and closed his eyes.

Perhaps a little nap might make the afternoon go faster.

On the verge of oblivion, he woke and blinked in the lightest of light. A breeze of summer brushed his face. He smelled the sweet scent of heather, the fragrance reminding him of home in the hillsides of Scotland.

The soft, melodic singing of children floated across an unseen breeze, followed by their lyrical laughter. He smiled, his heart overflowing with the warmth of peace.

When his vision adjusted to the brightness, he looked up to see one of the tallest buildings he'd ever seen. Its top disappeared into puffy clouds, the color of which appeared synchronized to the white sheen of the gates. When he lowered his gaze, his eyes widened at the man who materialized in front of him. Tall, thin, with long whitish-gray hair and mild brown eyes, the man's flesh, unlined by wrinkles, appeared young, but his gaze held the wisdom of centuries.

"Who are ye?" Fallon asked, his voice soft.

"I am Camalus, God of Sky and War."

"Am I dead?"

Camalus smiled and shook his head. "No, my son, you are not dead. In fact, you are very much alive, if you would only let yourself live."

"I doona have time for riddles."

"You will understand the meaning of my words in time."

"Where am I?" Fallon asked.

"The Otherworld, a magical place where the gods reside."

"Why have you brought me here?"

"You are here to remember your past."

Fallon grimaced. "My past is branded in my memories. I doona need to reminisce about what's been a constant memento of my miserable existence.

I doona need yer pathetic reminders."

"You remember what you wish to. You let the pain of your past fuel you. It suffocates your senses and makes you afraid."

"I fear nothing."

"Even now, you deny it to yourself. You fear the greatest gift of life. You fear love."

Fallon grunted and scoffed. "There is a bitch running free itching to destroy the world. I doona have time for love."

"Do you hear the music, the songs around you? You were at peace when you first arrived. You gloried in it."

Fallon rubbed the back of his neck then shrugged at the God. "So? I fail to see what that has to do with anything."

"It has everything to do with it, Fallon O'Callaghan. Love is music, the songs that dwell in your heart. It surrounds you, yet you refuse to hear it. With your mind…see. With your ears…hear. With your heart…feel."

The words, a jab to his memory, rendered him speechless. Morfesa spoke those same words nearly five hundred years ago, and he'd never forgotten.

"Now, why are those words familiar?"

A loud sound, like the shot of a gun, raced through his body, and he jerked.

Camalus smiled. "Feel the love around you. Unlocking your heart will open more of your senses."

Fallon's eyes flared open, and he flew upward to find himself sitting on Lizzie's couch.

Frazzled, he ran a hand through his hair.

Why would a god of war speak to him of love?

What did it mean?

A door creaked opened then closed with a soft click. Seconds later, keys hit a wooden table, and he turned toward the sound.

Lizzie was home.

Chapter Twenty-Seven

Lizzie flopped on the sofa beside him and released a heavy sigh. Thick, black lashes covered her eyes, and she murmured, "Hi."

Surprised by the simple greeting, he returned it. "Hey, lass." He studied her features in concern. "Ye look exhausted."

Liz nodded. "Yeah. It was a tough day." Her eyes clouded. The fringe of her lashes cast shadows on the dark circles already imprinted beneath her eyes. "I just wish..." she started, but stopped and pinched the bridge of her nose between two fingers.

He leaned toward her, lazily picked up a strand of honey-colored hair, and watched as it slid through his fingers. So soft and feminine, she smelled of lilacs.

Her face turned in his direction, her eyes misty and wistful. He held her gaze for what seemed an eternity. A sensuous look passed between them. His skin prickled at the intimacy of that gaze, and a shiver of longing rushed him.

He framed her cheeks between his palms. When she did not shy from his advances, he lowered his hands, settling them beneath her arms and pulling her onto his lap. He pressed his lips to hers, caressing her mouth more than kissing it.

Bliss.

For so long, Fallon fought to avoid this. At the touch of her lips, all hesitation vanished. Every step taken, every path traveled led him to this point in time. His life brought him to her.

What stole his willpower and robbed him of common sense? To love? To feel? To free his emotions? Could this be what Camalus spoke of?

This woman succeeded in unlocking his heart and soul. She struck a vibrant cord in him, one he could no longer ignore.

Oh, gods, he shouldn't let this happen, but even as his body refused to obey, his heart nurtured the impulse.

He could no longer deny her touch nor could he ignore the truth. His heart hammered against his ribs. Lizzie belonged in his arms, and he wouldn't let her go. Not this time.

His fingers slid along the silkiness of her cheek and neck, her skin hot to his touch. He brushed his hand along the curve of her hip. Her soft release of breath fanned his face.

In a fiery haze, desire threatened to overwhelm him, and he held back lest he scare her with his passion.

"Fallon—" His name tumbled from her lips.

His gut clenched.

A change of heart at the last moment? Please, no.

He strained to steady his breathing and regain control. She'd destroyed his equilibrium, scrambled his senses.

He wouldn't force himself on her, but having freed his passion, it would cost him dearly to stop.

With arms around her, he appreciated her supple softness. "Aye?" he whispered into her ear, his breath stirring the tendrils of hair near her ear.

"Do you want me?"

"More than ye could ever know, lass." His fingertips traced the plane of her jaw, memorizing the curve there, the way her lips curled in a smile. He pushed stray tendrils of hair away from her face.

Teardrops glistened on her eyelashes and

slipped down her cheeks. He wiped them away with his thumbs. His fingertips drifted to her neck where the drum of her heart beat its life force.

He sensed Lizzie's acceptance in the way her body touched him, and yet, something held him back.

He pulled away, cupped her chin, searching her upturned face. "Are ye sure, Lizzie? Do you accept me as I am, and all that comes with it?"

She caressed his cheek. He gripped her slender hand in his, reading the answer in her eyes. He pressed his lips to her palm before he drew her closer, whispering in her ear, "Say the words, lass."

"I accept you, Fallon. Everything I am is yours."

Humbled by her tremendous generosity, her gift to him, he answered her the only way he could. His kiss tender and loving, he expressed with his body the deep emotions he couldn't describe with words.

Her arms circled his neck, her soft breasts pressed hard against his chest. She sat astride his lap and shifted her legs in invitation. Need engulfed him. He ached to bury himself deep inside her body, yearned for the safety she offered, warm and welcoming, his haven, a refuge, and a place of intimacy and ecstasy.

He groaned deep in his throat and took her mouth with savage intensity. Her mouth generous, opened for his kiss and the rapid thrusting of his tongue.

He pulled away to look into her eyes, eyes that sparkled with azure flame. She touched the cleft of his chin with her lips.

She murmured a protest when he lifted her off his lap. He stood, leaned down and swept her up in his arms. His eyes locked with hers and he carried her into her bedroom. With gentle urgency, he released her legs, her body sliding down the length of his, their arms locked around each other.

She stood on tiptoes, her hands caressing the soft creases of his face as though memorizing each feature. Her fingertips traced the scar along his temple while her other hand wrapped around his neck to draw his lips to hers.

Only the two of them existed in the room, the outside world forgotten.

Fallon never knew desire could be so intense, this overpowering, demanding, but also sweet and gentle. It pierced through his soul like a scorching poker.

He wanted her more than life itself.

Kissing her, and being kissed by her, stirred his body. Sirens sounded in his head. Had his existence been in preparation for this one sweet moment of union with her?

Always in the past, Fallon took control. He set the tempo of sex, but this pleasure journeyed well beyond the realms of physical unity...so much farther.

Here and now, neither one of them set the rhythm.

Lizzie not only received, she committed. She gave back more than he thought possible to give. Novice, she may be, but lovemaking became a new experience for him, too. An ambiance of inferiority and inexperience exhilarated him. He looked forward to learning the fine art of love with her.

Desire pounded the blood though his veins, raw and biting in his belly. He slid the shirt from her shoulders. Her skin gleamed alabaster white in the darkness of the room. He took a step back, needing to see her nakedness.

She unsnapped her bra and pulled the material away from her body. The swollen tips of her breasts clung to the fabric. When her rosy nipples sprung free, Fallon's breath caught in his chest. Blood sizzled through his loins, enflaming him until he strained against the front of his jeans.

She tossed the undergarment to the floor. Her skirt and panties followed.

He stood before her, their bodies separated by inches. They didn't touch. Fallon traced a finger along the velvety softness of her hips, gasping at her delicate texture. Her curves completed her slender body.

He glanced down at his trembling hands, too unsteady to touch such delicacy, but he couldn't stop now.

His gaze riveted to her face then raked over her body in admiration before gazing into her eyes.

"Ye are exquisite," he whispered.

Her eyes held him prisoner. She lowered her hands to the front of his jeans. She pressed her body, her flesh hot, demanding, against his while she fumbled with the zipper.

Covering her slender fingers with his, he helped her lower the zipper. Just as he watched her, she now watched him, and he took a step back to slide the jeans down past his hips until they dropped to the floor. His shorts followed.

The expression on her face fueled the torch burning in his body. Waves of ecstasy throbbed through him, and he stepped toward her and pressed her nakedness against his.

He wrapped his arms around her shoulders and under her knees to lift her in his arms. His mouth traveled over hers to reclaim her lips. Hypnotized by the touch of her lips, he moaned.

He walked to the bed where he laid her on the mattress. In the next instant, he lay beside her.

Supported by an elbow, he leaned over her. Her eyes followed his hands while they explored her soft ivory flesh, sliding across one velvety hip and thigh. When he fondled one small globe, its pink nipple marble hard, her body arched against his hand.

She raised her hands, pressed the palms against his chest, and pushed him away. "Fallon?"

The confusion he heard in her question gave Fallon pause. He looked at her face, his heart still, until he saw the longing in her eyes, and the timid smile curved her lips.

"I've never..."

A warm glow filled him, and he was, once again, a teenage lad on the shores of his beloved Scotland. Two bodies, one flesh, his home now resided within her. His life to be at her side for eternity. Lost in the fragrance of her body, everything else faded from sight.

"Me either," he whispered against her lips. He'd never experienced this before. "No' like this."

Intoxicated by her scent, he could almost believe goodness and purity existed on this plane.

And all because of her.

Fallon worshipped her, showing his appreciation for her and the precious moments she gave him. He explored the secret places of her body where he knew pleasure hid, memorizing her soft curves with his hands and lips until she trembled and became frenzied with wanting.

Her hoarse, dazed gasps brushed his ears. He continued his mouth's exploration of her skin, her erotic buttons which he teased with his teeth. Her breast surged at the intimacy of his touch. His hand traced a path over her skin until it arrived at the warmth between her legs. Her hips arched against his hand, and he suppressed a groan at the juices flowing from her like warm honey.

Her breath came in long, surrendering moans as his finger massaged her swollen bud. Easing a finger within, he thrust in and out, preparing her body to accept him.

As his finger nudged inside her, his lips covered hers, devouring their fullness. She moaned against his lips, her hands gripping his shoulders, and she writhed beneath him. His lips left hers to travel the length of her neck to her breast. When the warmth of his lips touched her aching nipple, her body curved upward, shuddering, her virginal muscles clenching around his finger.

He kissed the pulsing hollow at the base of her throat before his lips recaptured hers.

In a movement more agile than he thought her capable of, she reversed their positions until she sat atop him, cradling him between her thighs. When he tried to sit up, she pushed against his chest with the palms of her hands.

She pressed her lips across his neck and chest, pausing to trace her tongue about his pebble-hard nipple. Easing her body down his, he groaned when her breasts brushed against his shaft.

He growled and gritted his teeth. Her hands moved over his body, pausing at sensitive places, making his pulse leap. Only sheer self-control kept him from scaling upward when her palms circled his hardened manhood.

Clenching his teeth against her pleasurable, yet painful, exploration, he allowed her the freedom. She explored his body with her lips and her hands. When he could take no more, he reached for her.

"Come here, Lizzie," he rasped, his throat hoarse.

Pulling her up across his body, he rolled her to his side. He rose over her and kissed her with all the passion he harbored for her, settling his body between her thighs. He nestled, hard, pulsing, hot against her moist warmth.

Encouraged by the moan of ecstasy that slipped from her lips, he introduced himself by slow degrees until her virginal shield blocked his penetration. He eased in and out of her rhythmically, acquainting himself with the innermost mysteries of her femininity. So small, tight and creamy. A fantasy breathing life, milking him with her perfect body.

And those marvelous little spasms that rippled through her were answers to his prayers. He studied her face, and the brilliance of what she experienced shone across her skin, heating his own desires to unbearable heights.

He eased his hips forward. His eyes met hers, and he whispered, "There will be pain, lass, but I canna—"

He never finished his sentence. Lizzie gripped his hips and pulled him forward, taking him deep inside her. Her body came off the bed, her breasts hitting his chest. She gave a gasp of pain, and he started to draw away only to be stopped by hands that anchored him, her fingernails dug into his buttocks.

Concerned, he looked at her tender smile.

Sweet Jesus!

Her body teased him, encasing him in her warmth, hugging him. It took everything he possessed to go slow, to give her time to adjust to his size. Her thighs wrapped around his waist, forcing him deeper into her body. He shook with intensity.

She throbbed around him, squeezing him.

Fallon withdrew and then thrust inside her again. When he looked into her face, the passion in her eyes encouraged him and he quickened the pace. Her nails etched into his shoulders, her body keeping rhythm with his. Their bodies united in exquisite harmony. Lizzie met him stroke for stroke, the ecstasy mounting, exploding in a downpour of fiery sensations.

The pleasure she gave him intensified. She cried out as she peaked, and her body shuddered, spasms tightening around him. The force of her orgasm incited his own release, and he groaned, collapsing on top of her.

Sweet agony.

And in that moment, they united. Their minds, their bodies and their hearts.

Their ragged breathing echoed in the air. He lay motionless on top of her. His body weak, still tingled from his powerful release.

After a few moments while he regained control, he slid his weight off her. Rolling to his side, he pulled her against him, her head resting on his shoulder.

"I can feel your heart racing," she whispered.

She yawned, and he pressed a kiss to the top of her head. "Get some rest, lass."

Less than five minutes later, soft, even breaths hinted when she'd fallen asleep.

Lizzie belonged only to him, as if she'd been created solely for him. If he searched the world, Fallon would never find another who could ever fill the emptiness he'd lived with for so long. Whether he spent the rest of his life with her or was eternally doomed to live a life without her, he knew one thing—her body, her personality and her soul belonged to him just as his now belonged to her.

The thought barely left his mind before another followed.

This didn't change anything.

It couldn't change anything.

He had to let her go, but not tonight.

Tonight belonged to them.

Chapter Twenty-Eight

Fury choked Deidra at visions of the guardians and his mate's merged bodies that blazed behind her eyes.

"That bitch! She's lain with him." Her voice echoed off the walls of her tomb.

Her minions skulked into the shadows, and she scowled at their spinelessness. Perhaps in this era, they ruled, but in her time, they were no comparison to her fearless soldiers. Her army was trained, well disciplined and fiercely loyal to her and Ághmach.

She leaned back against her throne, closed her eyes, and sighed in remembrance. A proud race, the Camarilla were both respected and feared. They were the masters of darkness and phantoms who sparked horror in the corners of minds.

Boogiemen. She smiled and ran her tongue over the prick of her fang. Oh, to discover those wondrous days again...

A disgusting odor of feline penetrated her nostrils, and she opened her eyes. Dorian stood before her, his eyes a putrid shade of yellow. She shuddered at the nauseating color.

Clenching her teeth, she glared at him. "What the hell do you want?"

"My Queen, the Princess is within your grasp. Whether they have slept together or not, your connection with her is strong. Their relationship is volatile. If you bide your time, they will fight. Sustain your link during that time, and we can get a fix on her position."

205

Pure hatred shot through her like a hot poker, and she stretched out a clawed hand to grasp him around the throat. Lifting his feet off the floor, she smirked when his arms and legs flailed. He choked and gurgled as he gasped for deprived air. With a flick of her wrist, she tossed him to the floor where he slid across the concrete and smashed to a grinding halt against the brick wall. When he looked up at her, the tensing of his jaw betrayed his anger and disgust.

She quirked a questioning eyebrow at him, and he averted his face.

She would gladly kill the pathetic excuse of a creature if not for his knowledge of this world. Even now, the animals he called werewolves guarded her stronghold. They were crude, flea-ridden beasts, their powers weak and skills undeveloped, but their senses were sharp enough to raise an alarm if warranted.

Deidra snarled at him. "You're an idiot. Now that they have sanctified the union, her powers will grow stronger than before. It is imperative I find her *now*. We're running short of time."

Dorian rose to his feet and stepped hesitantly toward her. His brows drawn in an uncertain frown, but he continued in his attempt to reassure her. "The change will not happen at once. For the moment, she is still human. If your mind battles with hers long enough, she'll grow weary. That will give us the opportunity to strike."

Deidra waved her hand through the air. "Leave me," she shouted. The demon groveled before her, shielding his ears from her cry. The act of cowardice made her stomach twist and head ache. Disgusting. Her lip twisted and she dropped into her drab red chair.

After a few moments, she shot to her feet, a thirst filling her. Perhaps a speck of hunting might take the edge off her anger.

****

Meghan Crandall stepped from the late night coffee house. The streets vacant, most citizens abided the curfew established by the town.

If caught out after seven in the evening she'd be fined, but she didn't give a hoot. To hell with them. Since Todd moved out last week, she couldn't go home to their empty apartment. Too many memories confronted her there. Moving would be the best choice, but that took money. The small salary she received as a secretary didn't afford her much luxury.

Once across the street, she headed straight for the beach. The late night weather created a beautiful crisp evening, stars shining. A relaxing walk would do wonders. She pulled the collar of her jacket tight against her neck, shielding her skin from the cold breeze that whipped ashore from the sea.

After less than a dozen steps from the stairs leading onto the beach, sudden pain stabbed through her thigh.

"What the heck," she said, leaning down to rub the cramp from her muscle.

The pain came again. She flinched and grabbed the handrail to prevent her knees from buckling beneath her.

"Weakling," a voice said.

Meghan glanced up to find a woman standing over her, her lips pursed in disgust. Long black hair billowed in the breeze behind her. The moonlight played off the woman's ashen complexion.

"Who are you?"

Like a needle, the pain came again, probing all the way through to the bone, followed by heat. The burning radiated from the inside out. She dropped to the ground, writhing in pain.

"Betcha that hurts, doesn't it?"

Meghan pushed her feet deep into the sand in an effort to crawl away, horrified to see the sand give way under each thrust she made. She flipped onto her back and used her palms and arms to scurry backward, away from the monster that loomed above. "What do you want?"

The woman pointed a black fingernail to her head and smiled. Two-inch fangs bled from between her lips.

"God, oh God," Meghan cried, her stomach churning in panic. She spun onto her belly, rose to her knees and attempted to push herself to her feet. Pain blistered through her leg. She screamed and fell, rolling onto her back.

"Your gods cannot help you. I am the one responsible for your pain. Trust me, it will only get worse."

"Jesus, god, please!" Meghan swallowed a scream.

The sand beneath Meghan vibrated, and a swirl of the tiny particles blew into her face.

With one leg folded beneath her, the other straight, she tried to scoot away from the woman whose eyes now glowed red in the darkness.

The pain disappeared.

It took her a moment to realize the pain dissipated. When she did, relief rushed over her. Meghan coughed and attempted to swallow the dryness in her throat. Sweat dripped down her forehead to mix with the tears she shed. Moisture seeped along her backbone and between her breasts. A cool gust of wind drew a shiver from her.

She lifted her gaze. The place where the woman stood moments ago now a gaping black hole, but she remained nearby. Her deep, even breathing pulsed the night. She scanned the beach.

Where did that monster go? Would she return?

Meghan had to get out of this place and hauled herself to her feet, trembling. Motionless, she gripped the handrail and waited for a surge of dizziness to pass before propelling herself toward the pier and off the beach.

A residual ache remained from the strange attack, and she limped up the set of steps leading to the pier.

Shivering, the perspiration dried on her skin. Her hand rubbed her stomach in an attempt to calm it. She inhaled deeper breaths to slow down her heartbeat.

With each step, she gripped the railing tighter. About two steps from the top, the pain returned in triplicate, and she screamed in surprise. This time, the agony was so intense she dropped to her knees and struggled to breathe against its intensity. She ignored the sharp splinters piercing her skin as her fist tightened around the wooden railing. Her chest restricted, and she opened her mouth to scream.

From beneath the pier, a low voice called to her. "Come, child. I can feel your torture. Let me release you from it."

A small squeak escaped her lips when an invisible hand closed around her windpipe and squeezed. A solid object hit her behind her kneecaps. She screamed in pain as her knees buckled and she fell over the railing, landing with a solid thump on her back looking up into the star-studded night. The wind *whooshed* from her lungs.

The pressure around her throat eased. She released a strangled gasp. Meghan rolled onto her stomach, clawing at the sand. Inside her mind, a single prayer cried to God.

Her fingernails dug deep trenches into the beach and did nothing to prevent her from being pulled beneath the pier.

"Nnn…ooo!" Her voice stuttered out the stifled

cry, veiled by the sounds of the waves.

The tide rolled, the waves rushing in under the pier. Cold seeped into her skin. Her lips froze, numb from the arctic wind that blustered its way through the tunnel existing between land and pier.

Held down with a foot in the center of her back, Megan battled to be free. A cruel hand pushed her head under water. She choked on the liquid that surged into her mouth and nose as she struggled for air.

Something sharp jabbed into her shoulder and flipped her over onto her back.

Wheezing, she struggled for breath and coughed the pungent sea from her mouth. Her vision blurred by the water, she struggled to focus. With one hand, she swiped at her attacker. She glanced up. Through the cracks in the pier, a flicker of radiance from the stars filtered down upon her. Brilliant lights from the street lamps' glow haloed each side of the pier, like a smoky fog.

"Please," she begged.

A sudden explosion of decay whirled in the air. Acid rose in her throat, her eyes watered, and saliva dripped down her chin.

Whimpering, her teeth chattered, and her body trembled.

Two sharp-clawed hands grasped her shoulders, yanking her upward. Her feet no longer touched the sand, kicking and flaying inches above the ground. Closing her eyes, she waited for death.

And then, the throbbing pain began again, this time attacking her neck. Paralyzed by whatever forces gripped her, Meghan's body grew cold, weakening under the assault.

Shadows on a moonless night...slumber without dreams, and then blessed darkness. Her last thoughts were of Todd. She wondered if he'd miss her.

Chapter Twenty-Nine

Liz sighed in contentment, snuggling against Fallon's side. Her head rested on the crook of his shoulder. His arms tightened around her. She cherished each hard muscle against her naked body, and if possible, would willingly spend forever right here in his arms.

She ran her fingers through the hair on his chest, twirling the coarse black curls with her finger.

"Lizzie." Her name a whisper against her hair.

"Hmmm." She had little strength for more.

"Are ye ok, lass? I dinna hurt ye, did I?"

Liz lifted her head and looked at the uncertainty etched on his handsome face. A lump formed in her throat.

"You didn't hurt me, Fallon. You were so tender and caring. I never knew it could be like this," she whispered. Her eyes sought his. She caressed his tense jaw, hoping the small gesture might erase the concern in his expression. Dark eyebrows slanted in a frown, and she smiled, running a slim finger across them to smooth them away.

She pressed a soft kiss to his shoulder before snuggling back down, fanning her hands over his chest.

Hard ridges met her touch. A veritable rock.

She had his passion.

For tonight, it was enough.

She still sought his love, that part of his heart he seemed determined not to share with anyone. Maybe she'd wanted this from the beginning, but it hadn't been clear until right now in this moment.

What would happen tomorrow, when she wanted more than his passion?

The room darkened as a cloud passed over them. The air turned frigid, and a cold breeze drifted over her.

They were not alone. The hairs on her arm stood on end at the malevolent spirit that brushed an icy hand against Liz's cheek. The touch lasted only a second, but with evil so powerful and clear, Liz buried her face into Fallon's shoulder.

His arms tightened around her, his senses woke in tune to her. "Lizzie?" Hesitation filled his voice.

The vile essence dissolved and vanished. The weight of Fallon's hands on her shoulders ceased.

She released a shuddering breath and drew herself up on one elbow. Moonlight filtered through the window to bathe his handsome face. His brows creased in a scowl. God help her, she refused to tell him of Deidra's visions. She would deal with that creature herself in her own time but not tonight. It had taken them so long to get to this point she wasn't willing to sacrifice this time with him.

"It's all right, Fallon. They're gone."

"Who were they?"

She shrugged, in no mood to tell him the Vampryss bitch dared to intrude on their private time. "My ghosts. You know…those troublesome spirits? Sometimes they pop in at the most inopportune moments."

His muscles tensed beneath her hands, and he grunted. "Oh, and ye have had many moments like this, have ye?"

Her face flushed, and heat seeped into her cheeks. "You know what I mean."

He chuckled and pressed a kiss to her forehead. "I'm teasing, lass."

Raising her hands, she patted his cheek,

"Funny, ha ha!"

His eyes widened, and he chuckled again. "I thought so, if I say myself."

"Smartass!" The humor fled, her insides twisted, and she grew serious. Her fingers trailed down his neck to his chest where she traced the pattern of the tattoo. "Why a dragon?"

She lifted her eyes to his, waiting for his response.

"I spent some time in China before I came to the States. It represents the four elements. Air, fire, water, and earth. The elemental spirit rules the center as a balance."

"Balance?"

"Aye. It is believed the dragon possesses both form and force. They influence our personalities. Each element and its serpent have certain qualities, natures, moods, and magical purpose."

"And what is your purpose?"

Fallon turned on his side, one leg lying outside the covers. He pulled her close and whispered, "At the moment, ye are."

Bronzed perfection. Columns of polished muscles ran from his neck down, along his sides, thighs, calves. Fresh scars marred his flesh, a deep one just below his elbow. Lighter ones covered his upper arms and shoulder.

She peered into his eyes. Thousands of golden specks intertwined with other designs of yellow and black to ring his irises.

"Lass, I doona know what happens now. I wish—"

She stilled his words with a soft kiss, a tender kiss, and when she pulled away, she gazed into his face.

"Don't talk," she murmured.

"But—"

Covering his lips with her finger, she shook her

head. "Not tonight, Fallon."

She yawned, and he tugged her head back to the crook of his shoulder. She closed her eyes and drifted off, the scent of sandalwood and leather filling her nostrils. Fallon's scent.

Before she gave in to blessed sleep, Fallon kissed her forehead and whispered, "Rest well, Lizzie, my love."

****

Fallon rested his chin on the top of Lizzie's head. His gaze on the door, he exhaled. Tonight, no shadows eclipsed his heart. She gave him the sunshine.

A sudden movement near his feet sent his gaze shooting toward the bottom of the bed. He smiled at the sight of Liz's cat perched near his feet. There was something vaguely familiar about that damn cat, but what, he didn't know. Shaking his head, the cat jumped off the foot of the bed and disappeared from the room.

Wrapped in the silky cocoon of Lizzie's arms, sleep stole through his body.

He dreamed of a life with Lizzie, of children...their children in a world uninhabited by demons.

He was liberated, loved and blessed.

Fallon jerked awake, dazed and confused. His eyes searched the room.

A soft murmur drew his gaze to Lizzie, his beautiful, passionate, loving Lizzie. She snuggled against his side, her warmth comforting.

As he peered at her sleeping face, he couldn't stop the erratic beat of his heart. It swelled with a feeling he thought long dead.

Flawless.

A terrifying realization washed over him.

He couldn't allow this to change his decision, to deter his path. As much as he wanted to build a life with Lizzie, what kind of life could they have?

She'd never understand his world or the dangers he lived with. And even if she did, Fallon could never risk her life.

He pulled her against him and pressed a soft kiss to her forehead. When she cuddled even closer, he held her inhaling her sweet fragrance. Lilacs.

For tonight, he wouldn't let her go.

Tomorrow had to be different.

This had to end before someone got harmed, and he vowed it wouldn't be Lizzie.

He wouldn't leave her, but he would release her.

****

Liz crossed the threshold entering the kitchen. Fallon, with his back to her, pushed the buttons on the coffee pot.

He was barefoot, wearing only his jeans. As if sensing her presence, he glanced over his shoulder. He looked good enough to eat, with the exception of the scowl he wore on his face.

She scanned the room. Dried coffee grounds littered the beige Formica counter top, spilling onto the white linoleum floor. An open loaf of bread lay to the side of the sink, and she noted the toast in the toaster. She cringed at its charcoal appearance and imagined she might chip a tooth or two if she tried to eat it.

"Good morning," she greeted, in a soft voice.

His shoulders stiffened, and he swung around. "Morning," he replied, his voice gruff. He glanced over his shoulder and inclined his head to the coffee pot. "I was going to make ye breakfast, but I couldna figure out how to get that damn thing to work."

"It's not going to work by shouting at it," she muttered, brushing her tousled, unruly hair from her face, and stepped up to the counter beside him. "Here, let me. Have a seat. I'll make the coffee," she offered.

"Nay, I'll do it, or no' at all," he snapped.

"Fallon, don't be silly. You don't even drink the stuff," she said with amazing logic while she sidestepped around him to grab the pot from the hotplate.

His hand, quick as lightning, grabbed it away from her. "I'll make the damn coffee if it's the last thing I do. Now, sit down, and leave me be."

Seeing him acting this way sent a fierce stab of agony piercing her heart. Trapped in a vice grip, her chest throbbed, near to exploding from the pain. She'd expected, oh, she didn't know what she expected. Definitely not the treatment she was getting.

Perhaps she expected a mellowing, actions that said they'd overcome one obstacle in their otherwise unorthodox relationship. Her stomach flip-flopped, and she folded her hands at her waist, the heels of her palms pressed tightly against her housecoat. He'd rebuild the boundaries that had separated their worlds and shut her out again.

She bit her bottom lip. Crying would be stupid, but so would beating him upside the head with the frying pan sitting in the dish strainer. Of the two options, the frying pan looked to be the outright winner. "Do you want something to eat?"

"I doona eat, or have ye forgotten?" He asked his eyes averted, his voice heavy with sarcasm.

She flinched at the hardness in his tone.

Without the control she clung to, her resolve would have shattered. "Fallon, about last night—" Her voice did break then, and she clamped her mouth shut, her teeth gnawing on her bottom lip.

"Last night—" He hesitated, his eyes fixed on the pot in his hands before he completed with, "— was verra nice."

"Nice?" she echoed in disbelief. Her temper flared, and she shot around the table. When she stood in front of him, she poked a finger into his chest…hard, and felt a brief stab of satisfaction at the grimace crossing his features. "Nice? Just nice?" Her voice rose. "I don't believe you." She stopped when she recognized the hysterics in her voice, determined not to travel down that road.

He grabbed her hand, stilling her jabs. "What are you trying to say, Lizzie?"

She yanked her hand away. Furious, she replied through stiff lips, "Nothing, Fallon. I'm saying absolutely nothing."

"Lizzie, last night, things got out of hand."

"Why? Because you caved and let someone inside the wall you've placed around your heart?"

He made her so mad she wanted to scream. What did it take to make him open up to her? Last night, she'd caught a glimpse of his soul. Why did he insist on burying it?

"I'm a man. What we did last night doesna have to involve emotion."

The cynicism of the remark grated on her, igniting the already burning blaze inside her.

How dare he?

With both hands on her hips, she confronted him.

"If you're the man you claim you are then act like one and stop running." Liz ran a hand through her hair, her fingers catching the tangles. She winched. What was she doing, tossing out insults like that? She drew in a deep breath and blew it out in a puff. "I'm sorry."

"Don't be. I deserved it."

"What you deserve is a frying pan cracked upside your head to knock sense into your ass, but I'm too much a lady to do that."

He grabbed her arms, forcing her to look at him. "Lizzie, I am sorry things turned out like this. I dinna mean to hurt ye."

"You didn't hurt me, Fallon." She jerked away, unable to look at him anymore, and muttered under her breath, "Not last night." She blinked back the tears, reached into the refrigerator, and cleared her throat before she asked, "Would you like some orange juice?"

Carton in hand, she turned, only to discover he'd left the room. Her eyes shot to the cafe doors leading to living room. They swayed to and fro in the wake of his exit.

She sighed and shook her head.

After grabbing a glass from the cabinet, she poured herself a small amount of juice and wondered if it were too early to mix in a little vodka. She picked up the glass and swirled its contents before downing it in one gulp.

Hot blazing fury raged over her. Her vision blurred in anger. With the glass clutched in her fist, she swung around, raised her hand and chucked it at the door. The sound of shattering glass pierced the silence of the room. It struck the wall six inches to the left of the doorway and shattered into a thousand sparkling diamonds that rained to the floor.

After a brief sense of satisfaction, irritation settled in. Now, she'd have to clean up the damn mess.

She dropped into the chair, rested her elbows on the table, and ran her hands over her tired eyes.

When did Fallon intend to stop running?

Chapter Thirty

Liz cradled the phone between her shoulder and cheek. She set the kettle on the stove and flicked on the burner.

"You have got to be kidding me?"

"Liz, I shit you not. There are five more bodies at the morgue. Four were found at the River Bay campsite, the other one under the pier."

"Same M.O."

"Yeah. Ripped to pieces, if that's what you call an M.O. All together, we got three adults and two teenagers."

Her stomach lurched. She struggled to keep her dinner down. Swallowing hard, she shut her eyes and visualized the scene: ghastly murders, blood-soaked carcasses, scattered skin fragments, and unidentifiable body pieces littering the ground.

Her legs trembled. She swallowed hard again, pushing past the sour taste in her mouth.

"Liz, are you still there?"

"I'm here." Her voice croaked. The bitter bile lingered in her throat, making each breath a conscious effort.

"I wanted—"

"Murray, I'll be there in the morning."

Murray groaned on the other end of the phone. "Why not tonight? Is it because of that stupid prank? That was months ago. I don't know what happened and did some checking at the precinct. No one would do that to you."

A quick flash of heat flared into her cheeks at

the memory of Fallon popping off her table naked. She took a deep breath, held it, and waited for her insides to stop churning.

"I'll see you in the morning. Good night, Murray."

She hung up the phone to Murray's frustrated "Liz—"

The kettle squealed. She jumped.

Pouring the boiling water into her mug, she dropped a tablespoon of honey into it. The water darkened. She wrapped her hands around the cup, absorbing its heat and raised it to her face. The hot steam warmed her face and the smell of her honey lemon tea calmed her nerves.

She peered out the window. Beams of light from the full moon splayed across the water's surface, illuminating the entire area. Almost nine o'clock, and it looked as if it were four in the afternoon.

A loud crash from the porch shattered the silence of the house. Caught off guard, she jumped. Turning to the window above the kitchen sink, she stared out.

Sudden movement in the corner of her eye drew her attention. Bending over the sink, she pressed her face against the glass. She scanned the beach and surrounding areas.

Three dark figures, partially hidden in the tree lining her drive, skulked in the shadows. They kept pointing at her house, and she came to the quick conclusion that they were discussing her home.

She jerked away from the window, shut off the light and dropped to the floor, sitting on her haunches. Her eyes wide, her gaze shot around the room in search of a weapon. Remembering the large butcher knife in the dish strainer, she turned and stretched an arm to grab the blade, which she clasped between both hands.

Her stomach knotted, the fear so tangible, she

gagged on it. She fought for self-control. Adrenalin rushed through her veins even as tears slipped down her cheek.

Where the hell was Fallon?

****

Fallon hiked the ridge. So windswept. So open, as if the very land itself, the soil and stones reached up on tiptoes to lift themselves and touch the sky.

Free in the intimacy of the wild, he wished this great crest might convey a little bit of itself to him, a persona he could wrap around himself and hide from the rest of the world.

When it grew dark, he'd left Lizzie's house. He needed to put space between them.

Their bond, intensified by their lovemaking, gripped him. She was here, inside him, beside him, in everything he did.

What the hell had he done?

He'd made love to her, consummated their union, and then he'd walked away. The look of anguish on her face would forever be branded in his memory.

Damn the bloody gods!

Better to hurt her a little now than to hurt her later when he walked out of her life. And he would. That was imprinted in stone. How exactly he planned to do that, he didn't know. Not yet. Elizabeth Forrester was his mate...his true mate.

He'd fucked up good this time.

He walked until he reached the ultimate point of the ridge where steep, high cliffs plunged down toward the lake. Cliffs hugged the lake like a mother nestling her young to her breast.

The summit itself lay bare of trees, except for the few that survived the harsh winter. Clustered in a group of three, they found protection in a secluded area of the bank. Little foliage grew here, and Fallon kicked at the tuff of dirt, sending a spray of dust

221

flying around his face.

He stood at the edge where he had a perfect view of Lizzie's home. The lights shining from her window visible even at this distance. What was she doing now?

He knew he'd hurt her, but how could he go back and explain his reaction to their lovemaking? She'd think him a fool.

His self defense mechanism kicked into high gear forcing him to lash out at her. He regretted his angry words, an attribute that kept him sane. His self-preservation. For centuries, he'd survived by that.

But what of their bond?

As a Síoraí Guardian, Fallon had never chosen a mate before and didn't know what to expect from this point forward.

He suspected it couldn't be good.

Movement near Lizzie's house caught his eye, and a sudden rush of fear coursed through him.

Dark shadows scurried around the boundaries of her property.

The light from Lizzie's windows snapped off.

His heart pounded, and he took a deep breath.

Demons!

Thrown off balance, he'd forgotten to call Seth, but he hadn't planned to go far. Alone, defenseless, and unsuspecting, Lizzie would be killed.

How had they found her?

The demons snuck around the garage. A flutter of alarm raced through him, and he closed his eyes. Blood surged through his veins, and he shifted to the destination in his mind. When he arrived, his eyes shot open.

He stood on the opposite side of the house, out of sight.

The moon cast dim shadows around the building. He slipped deeper into the darkness, stalking his prey. With his head bent low, he skimmed the area, his eyes narrowed to slits. The vampires' blood-tinged scent filtered across the breeze, granting him the knowledge of their exact location.

He inched across the grounds, his brows drawn together in concentration.

The sounds of muffled voices echoed from around the corner, and he stopped, cocking his head in that direction.

A slight shadow to the left of the door drew his attention. In one fluid motion, he reached into his jacket, grabbed a stake, and flung himself through the air. He tossed the piece of wood and hit his mark, dead center in his chest. The blue-skinned, pale-faced vampire exploded before Fallon landed in the grass.

One down, two to go.

Just as he rose to his feet, something flew at his head. He ducked an instant before it connected, and the piece of plant pottery shattered against the ground. Fallon shifted, reappearing beside the second vamp, whose drooling mouth dropped open in surprise. With a quick flick of his wrist, he stabbed the vampire in the chest, destroying him.

One to go.

Fallon swung around as the final bloodsucker rushed from the darkness. Fallon knelt down and sent him flying over his back. In a smooth, fluid motion, he pulled another stake from his boot and sliced.

He missed.

The vamp caught his arm and knocked the stake to the ground. Fallon kneed the parasite in the stomach and watched in satisfaction as he doubled over.

Before he regained his balance, Fallon grabbed him around the throat and squeezed.

"Who sent ye?" he demanded.

A choked gurgle met his question, forcing him to release a bit of the tension in his hands.

"Answer me!" His voice, though quiet, held an ominous quality, threatening.

"No one." The man's guttural voice held a hint of apprehension.

A satanic smile ruffled Fallon's mouth.

Keeping one hand planted around the demon's neck, Fallon reached for the knife resting against his hip. After releasing it from the sheath, he lifted it to the parasites thin-skinned blue veined neck where he applied just enough pressure to pierce the flesh. Blood trickled down the vamp's neck.

The demon shrieked a high-pitched scream that would make even the strongest cringe.

"Ye're naught but an insect, and I'll squash ye beneath my foot. If ye wish to live another day, ye will tell me the answers I seek."

He sliced a bit more, drawing another howl. This time, he'd hit an artery, for blood gushed from the wound.

"The Queen. She is looking for you and your woman."

"How did ye find us?"

"Luck." The demon's voice rose higher as Fallon pressed. "She has granted all demons your scent. We recognized it as soon as we approached."

"Does she know where we are?"

The vampire shook his head, his yellow eyes wide in alarm. "We only stumbled upon you by accident. You haven't given us time to send her your location."

"And I wilna allow it now."

The blade sliced deeper, and the creature screamed, "But you said…"

With a quick swipe of his blade, Fallon cut the demon's throat, the sharp edge easily sliced through the muscles, tendons and bones. The vampire's eyes widened, spewing blood from its mouth, until it dropped limp in Fallon's grip.

"I lied," he muttered and twisted the vampire's neck until the remaining bones snapped and the head separated from its body. The demon disintegrated in his hands. He sheathed his knife before brushing the demon's ashes from his hands.

"Lizzie," he whispered aloud, rushing into the house.

She sat on the kitchen floor, knees pulled up to her chest, arms wrapped around them, clutching a knife between her palms.

"Lizzie."

Her body jerked, and she flashed the knife out in front of her. Her hands trembled, and her eyes widened.

He knelt in front of her and eased the knife from her stiff fingers. "It's okay, love. They're gone."

She gazed into his eyes, and he read the uncertainty in her expression. "They're gone. All of them." Her voice trembled. "Are you sure?"

He nodded. "I'm sure, Lizzie. Ye're safe." He stretched out his arms to wrap around her.

She shot to her feet, sending him falling on his ass in surprise. With accusation in her eyes, she stared at him. "You left me, you bastard."

Pushing himself to his feet, he said, "I'm sorry, lass."

"Leave me alone, Fallon. You did this. You're responsible for all of this. Stay the hell away from me."

And with that, she ran from the kitchen into the living room, leaving him staring after her. A moment later, her bedroom door slammed. Shock coursed through him. An arctic bitterness followed by emptiness engulfed him.

Perhaps his plan worked well after all.

Chapter Thirty-One

The days crept by, hazed over by a precarious calm that surrounded Liz and Fallon. Their relationship strained, much more cordial than before.

Since the day of the attack, Fallon watched a change cross over Lizzie. Subtle at first, the episodes came more frequently. She was edgy, absentminded, and sometimes incoherent in their conversations. She would stop in the middle of a sentence and gaze out with her head inclined to one side as if listening to something that failed to reach his ears.

He made numerous attempts to get her to open up to him, but she clamped her lips tight each time.

Stubborn.

She refused to talk to him, claiming the voices inside her were dead.

She lied. He heard the small waver in her voice and indecision in normally confident steps.

And then, one evening, he returned to Lizzie's house empty-handed again. Seth met him at the door, wearing a mask of apprehension that heightened Fallon's own concern.

"What's the matter?" Fallon asked, hard put to keep the anxiety out of his voice.

"Liz woke up about a half an hour ago, screaming and calling for you."

Fallon didn't hesitate and headed toward the bedroom.

"She's calmed down now," Seth said, moving to stand behind him.

Despite Seth's reassurance, Fallon needed to check for himself. He cracked the bedroom door and glanced inside. Lizzie slept on her stomach, her face turned in the opposite direction.

He faced Seth. "Did she say anything when she woke up?"

Seth shook his head. "Not a word. She seemed relieved to see me there, rolled over and went back to sleep."

Her strange behavior and now her nightmares concerned him. He vowed if she needed him, he would be there. A warning snaked its way from Fallon's stomach, up to his chest, constricting his breathing. What secrets did she keep from him? Did she see his demise? Dear god, did she see her own death? He looked down at his hand. It shook. A life without Lizzie? No!

The hunting would cease, at least until Liz explained her secrets to him. This decision didn't alter his plans. He'd sworn there would be no relationship between them, but he wouldn't let her face the darkness alone.

The following night, the stillness inside the house was disquieting until Lizzie's screams shattered the silence.

Her cries were born of sheer terror, and Fallon rushed to her side. Her eyes wide with fear, she sat straight up in bed, her hands raised in front of her as if to ward off an unseen attacker.

Fallon soothed her in his arms, whispering soft words until she calmed down. She begged him not to leave, her arms wrapped so tightly around him he struggled to breathe.

She collapsed against him and fell back to sleep.

He spent the night in hell. His body roared to life with her curves against him, and he fought the hunger that flared through him. What he felt for Lizzie beyond simple desire. It was an aching, an anxious, endless need that threatened to suffocate him.

Clenching his teeth, he vowed to stay. He couldn't leave her to face her terrorizing dreams alone.

When morning came, she acted like nothing happened. He confronted her about her dreams, but once again, she pulled away from him.

To Fallon, she never acted quite right.

Fallon ached to probe her thoughts. Privacy be damned, but he couldn't do it without her sensing him. Their union sanctioned, they were so in tune to each other, she would know in an instant if he broke his promise.

He sat at the kitchen table. Lizzie stood at the sink washing dishes. She stiffened and turned to stare at him.

She opened her mouth to say something but snapped it shut again, lowering her eyes as she turned away.

To hell with blood bonds, manners, and his promise! He tried to reach into her thoughts.

Liz swung around and threw him a disproving look that would have frozen even the strongest of men in their tracks. He tossed her a sheepish grin in return.

"Don't do that."

"I wanted yer attention."

"Why?"

"Damn it, Lizzie. What's the matter with ye lately? Ye doona even know I exist."

"I thought that's what you wanted?"

"Lizzie."

"Look, Fallon, I'm not in the mood for childish games. You've told me how you feel. There's no need to act as if you're concerned now."

"That's no' fair."

Her brows rose high on her forehead and her

mouth opened. "Not fair? You're kidding, right?"

"It appears ye're no' in the mood for conversation, either."

"No, I'm not." She sighed. "Don't you feel them? Can't you sense...?" She faltered, her attention drawn to the door. When she turned away from him, he read dread in her eyes.

"You haven't a clue what I'm talking about, do you?"

Fallon shook his head, keeping his questions on hold as she rambled.

"The evil in the air smothers me. Deidra is here, on this plane. She's been in my mind."

At the mention of Deidra's name, heat prickled his neck. Fear knotted his stomach. Nerves tensed, he jumped to his feet, knocking over the chair in his haste to get to her side.

Deidra in Lizzie's mind? Nay, that wasna possible, was it?

And then, Dagda's words echoed in his thoughts. Lizzie was the key Deidra needed to release Ághmach from the Underworld.

"What do you mean?" He grabbed her arms in his hands and gave her a little shake.

She managed a casual shrug that didn't quite work. "Never mind. You wouldn't understand."

Fallon increased his grip and pulled her near, urging her to look at him.

"Make me understand, Lizzie. Let me see what ye see."

Tears welled in her eyes. She swiped them away before they fell.

She shook her head. "I can't. It's too frightening."

"I canna protect ye if ye wilna let me in."

"You can't protect me from what's in my mind, Fallon. No one can."

"Let me try. Please, Lizzie, let me try," he

pleaded as his hands caressed her cheeks.

His lips dipped toward hers, but before their lips met, she covered his hands with her own, pulling away. "No."

"Talk to me, lass. Will ye no' tell me what's going on?"

"I can't talk to you. I can't talk to anyone."

"About what, darling? What do ye want to say to me?"

"The voices in my head…" She closed her eyes. "There's so much noise."

"Shut them out. Ye shut me out. Use yer powers."

"I can't. I've tried."

"Aye, ye can." He gripped her shoulders. "Damn it, ye must."

Her eyes snapped open, staring into his. "Fallon, I'm afraid."

The floodgates of her mind opened, swamping him in her fears. And what horror she held!

Fallon tuned into her thoughts and exhaled, his breath burning the lining from his lungs. He looked at her, failing to keep the astonishment from his expression.

One thought pierced his heart. How could she be too afraid to let him hold her right now?

"For the love of the gods, lass, why do ye think one touch from me, one embrace, would shatter ye into pieces?"

Barely holding onto her own strength of mind, she turned her head away.

"Lizzie, ye doona need to bear this alone, no' anymore. I'll help ye get through it. Whatever happens, it'll happen to both of us."

Before he uttered another word, darkness filled his mind. Alone once again, Fallon knew she'd withdrawn from him mentally.

Outside the moon rose high into the sky, and

Fallon's muscles tensed with the urge to hunt, to release his anger by killing, destroying, annihilating. The only way he could free Lizzie would be to destroy Deidra, and he couldn't do that sitting around here.

Perhaps some time away, a separation might do them both good. He needed to get out, and he turned and reached for the telephone.

Time to call in the babysitter.

****

Liz woke to find herself on the floor; a fierce shaking rattled her body, her nightgown soaked with perspiration. She glanced at the blue digits of her alarm clock on the bedside table.

Midnight.

Confused and disorientated, she swallowed down her dry mouth. Groggy with sleep, images of Deidra flashed in her mind. At first, a stunning woman stood in front of a bonfire. Then, she changed and turned into a creature with long painted fingernails, fangs and ruby red lipstick that stood out against her pasty white flesh. She lifted one clawed finger into a curled gesture of irresistible power, beckoning, calling to Liz, and ordering her to open the door. The gesture, although slight, did not allow refusal.

And yet, Liz refused, just like the last time, and the time before that, and before...How much more could she take? Not again, she thought, wringing her hands together. She fixed her gaze at the window where the moonlight drifted through. When the mental image faded and she gained some control over her trembling muscles, she rose and made her way to the bathroom. As she passed through the living room, the picture from the TV illuminated the room. Seth occupied her couch, not Fallon.

She groaned. Would it never end? Would she ever find a peaceful life again?

Steady, Liz, she told herself, turning the faucet on. She cupped the running water and splashed it on her face. Reaching for the towel on the rack, she swiped the droplets from her skin and stared at herself in the mirror. She tried to convince herself she would return to the land of the healthy, to the world of normal people. If only she remembered what that was like.

She walked to the bedroom and slid beneath the sheets, the smooth linen a cool caress to her skin.

Liz pulled the comforter around herself, silently berating herself for her cowardice. She'd slipped when she'd mentioned Deidra's name to Fallon. Thank god she had enough sense to stop before she told him of the woman's torturous whining.

How could she tell Fallon about the voices she heard every day? She kept hoping they would grow tired and go away, but her gut told her different. They were continents apart from the usual voices. These were compelling, almost as if the owners of the voices wanted to control her, to lead her to do what they wanted. Fallon couldn't help her anymore than she could help herself.

Fatigue overshadowed her thoughts, and she drifted into a state between waking and sleeping, her mind playing with dreams and rearranging reality.

"Come to me, my pet. It is time for us to meet."

Liz ached to tell the hoarse feminine voice to shut up and leave her alone. She closed her mind, but the voice broke through, slow at first, then louder, and stronger.

Shaking her head in denial, Liz struggled against the command. "No," she whispered, grabbing the pillow from beneath her head and slamming it over her ears. "Go away!"

"I cannot! Open the door for me. Invite me into your home."

The pleading drew her from inside, calling to her, until there could be only one answer.

"Come now. Open the door." The urgency of the words swirled through her mind. She fought the demands, fought for control, but the hypnotic voice twisted her thoughts into a jumbled mass of confusion. Her limbs stiffened, rigid, but she floated upon a silvery cloud, her body as light as a wafer.

She thought of Fallon, her last coherent reflection before she slid from reality and sped along the persuasive current toward agreement. Her body moved of its own accord, one step after another from one room to the next. The voice, insistent, demanding, and she had no choice but to answer. "Yes."

****

"Hey, Liz, where you going?" Seth sat up from the couch. His eyes followed her as she came out of the bedroom and headed for the front door, a strange empty look on her face. Her eyes glowed with an odd inner light.

Before Seth had time to react, she flung the front door open in invitation and said, her expression blank, "Come."

"Liz...*No!*" Seth shouted, shooting up from his position on the couch.

A large black cat shot over the threshold, across the room, and pounced on him. Both of them collided onto the coffee table with a loud *crash*. The wood splintered beneath their combined weight.

Pain numbed Seth's skull, and his vision darkened. With an inward push, he mustered enough strength to toss the cat through the air. It collided with the desk, bringing the computer to the floor. The monitor flew through the air and smashed against the bricks in the fireplace. The screen exploded in a flare of blue glass that sprayed around the room.

Seth gasped, his breath returning to his lungs. The cat growled exposing pointed fangs. It charged toward him again.

Lizzie screamed.

Seconds later, sharp teeth sank into his neck. Pain soared white hot through his body.

Then everything went black.

Chapter Thirty-Two

Seth's bellow equivalent to a bucket of ice-cold water poured over her head. Liz jerked from her trance, but not in time to slam the door shut.

The scene before her unfolded in slow motion— the large jaguar leapt on Seth and sunk its teeth into his neck.

A scream bubbled up her throat. Spinning around, she grabbed a heavy brass candlestick from the shelf and rushed to Seth's aide. She swung the candlestick across the animal's spine and breathed a sigh of relief when the cat released its hold.

Her eyes widened when the sleek black creature turned on her, growling in outrage. She waited for it to pounce.

Instead, it stood on its hindquarters, its paws flailing at the air. Her stomach clenched when its face distorted, its nose and fur sucked into its skin. Four padded paws became hands and feet. Hair became flesh. That cat's visage was no longer feline but that of a man. He towered over six foot and had sable black hair and obsidian-colored eyes. His nose, hooked, stood out prominent in his pale face.

A flash of terror curled around her spine.

"Hi." His quiet voice held a hint of bitter hatred.

Liz's stomach churned, the nauseating bile burning a hole in her throat.

When he lunged for her, she scrambled backward. Adrenalin flooded her veins, and she ran into the kitchen. She turned when the kitchen table lay between her and her attacker.

He strutted through the cafe doors, leaving them swinging in his wake. He prowled until he stood on the opposite side of the table facing her.

He held out his hand. "Come, there is no need to fight."

"Then get out of my house."

"I cannot. At least, not until I have what I came for."

"And what is that?"

"Why you, my dear."

Liz backed up until her butt rested against the counter, her hands slipping into the drawer behind her. Her fingers wrapped across the handle of a carving knife.

She pulled it free and held it before her, threatening. "Stay the hell away from me."

"Or what? You'll kill me?"

"Yes." The knife wobbled in her hands. "Please don't make me do it."

He chuckled. "I do not believe you have quite mastered your skills to kill." He shook his head. "Although I must say, I am impressed with your strength and fortitude. You are a fitting woman for a mate." His expression changed, serious, deadly. "It is a shame you are mated to a Síoraí."

Before Liz blinked, the man leapt across the top of table, landing at her side. He snatched the knife from her hand and tossed the blade to the floor where it landed with a loud *clink* against the tiles.

When he turned back to face her, he stretched out a hand to seize her wrist. She jumped out of reach, and he cursed.

Liz grabbed the cups and saucers from the dish strainer in the sink and flung them at his head. He ducked the incoming missiles, and her glassware shattered against the cabinets behind him. Shards of glass rained to the floor in a mix of clear and beige colors.

He tilted his head to the side and roared with laughter at her attempts to escape.

Liz gasped for breath, close to hyperventilating. In desperation, she snatched the glass casserole bowl from the counter, took two steps toward him and slammed it across the side of his head.

His laughter broke off, his eyes smoldered. He hissed with fury and advanced. Glass crunched beneath his shoes. Fear, stark and vivid, raced through her veins as she receded, her breathing erratic gasps in her lungs.

When he stood less than a foot away, he raised a hand, slamming his fist against the side of her head. The impact knocked her to the floor, and stars floated in front of her eyes.

He towered over her. A triumphant smile curved his lips.

The silence lengthened between them. No match for his strength and power, she needed to think. In a last ditch effort, she forced herself to stop and lay still as he advanced.

When he stood over her, she brought her foot up and smashed it into his groin.

He groaned and dropped to the floor holding his genitals. Good to know these creatures suffered the same afflictions as normal men.

Liz scrambled to her feet, sidestepped the writhing man and ran for the door.

He grabbed her ankle, catching her off guard. She lost her balance and fell face first to the floor. Pieces of her broken saucers jabbed into her forearms, and slivers of glass flew into her face. Trickles of blood cascaded down her cheeks as the serrated shards pierced the skin.

She snatched up a two-inch piece of glass, oblivious to the sharp edges pricking her palm, and slashed at the hand on her ankle. He howled at the pain, releasing her.

While her attacker lay on the floor, one hand thrust between his legs, the other waved wildly through the air, blood spraying everywhere. His blood.

Jumping to her feet, she took a final look at the fallen man and pushed through the kitchen door into the living room.

She stopped.

Deidra.

The Vampryss held an unconscious Seth by the cuff of his collar. Blood poured from a cut above his left eye. Crimson rivulets streamed from the jagged tear on his shoulder, inches from his carotid artery.

Liz looked at Seth's pale face then to the rise and fall of his chest before releasing a sigh of relief.

She muttered a quick prayer of thanks.

The woman's lips curved in satisfaction. With an easy flick of her wrist, she tossed Seth to a short, dumpy man who stood at her side. He grunted at the unexpected weight.

Liz couldn't hide her stunned surprise at the picture of the coroner from Rapid Rivers, Jack Stannard, holding a knife to Seth's throat, a crooked smile on his face. "Jack?"

"Little Lizzie Forrester." He glanced sideways at Deidra and asked, "Are you certain she's the one?"

Deidra's eyes never wavered. "Aye, but I need the Talisman before the world will belong to us."

"What do you want of me?"

"The world, my dear." She peered at Jack. "Didn't I just say that? Is she dense?"

"I won't help you," Liz declared, squaring her shoulders and refusing to back down from this bitch. "I won't!"

Deidra smiled, and Liz flinched at the sight of two-inch long fangs slipping from the corners of her mouth.

With eyebrows raised in question, Deidra

queried, "What makes you imagine you have a choice in this?"

"There is always a choice, Deidra. Haven't you ever heard of free will?"

"Nothing is ever free, human!" The words spat out, and Liz wiped the woman's spit from her arm.

Gross!

Liz spun around at the crash of the kitchen door swinging open and banging against the wall. Half-cat man limped over to where she stood.

"You bitch!" he growled, raising his hand.

Her mind screamed, *"Fallon!"* before he brought his fist down across her cheek. She held onto consciousness for only a moment before blessed darkness seeped in.

Fallon was the last person on her mind before she fell to the floor unconscious.

Chapter Thirty-Three

Halfway down the alley, a hard object slammed into Fallon, striking him dead center in the back, knocking him to his knees.

In the next instant, something equivalent to a meat cleaver sliced into his shoulder, piercing his flesh. He roared at the searing hot pain that rippled through him. Warm fluid oozed from his shoulder and spilled down his chest.

He growled deep in his throat, and with a force bred of anger, shot to his feet. His attacker, surprised by the swift action, released his hold and fell to the ground.

Hands clenched at his sides, Fallon swung around. He smirked at the flicker of fear in the eyes of the four demons, three vampires and a werewolf, who snuck up on him.

The werewolf who'd sunk his teeth into Fallon's shoulder picked himself off the pavement. Half-man, half beast, he reminded Fallon of a rabid dog with a bad case of alopecia. Fallon's blood dribbled from his six-inch fangs.

As Fallon stepped forward to retaliate, Lizzie's cry echoed in his mind, and he froze. A sensation of intense sickness and desolation swamped him at the panic in her tone.

All of a sudden, three of the vampire disintegrated. Fallon stared, motionless, as Devlin strode from the settling vampire dust. At his side, the youngest of the Síoraí Guardians appeared. Cameron stood an inch shorter than Devlin, but just as powerful in stature. He rushed forward, and with a series of quick punches and jabs cornered the werewolf against the brick building.

Devlin hurried to Fallon's side. "Liz needs ye, Fallon. *Go now!*" The magnitude of urgency in his voice filled Fallon with fear.

A pulsing knot filled Fallon's stomach. His eyes widened, and he shot a surprised look at Devlin who had erupted back into the fight. Over his shoulder, Devlin shouted, "Go! We'll take care of this guy."

Needing no further encouragement, Fallon visualized Lizzie's living room.

His heart stopped, and his stomach knotted at the destruction. The room lay in shambles. Furniture overturned, damaged, some destroyed. The computer smashed beside a pile of kindling that was once, he supposed, her desk.

Silence met his ears.

He rushed from room to room, flinging each door open with a resounding crash. First he checked her bedroom, spare room and then the bathroom.

Empty!

In the kitchen, shattered dishes littered the floor. In the midst of glass shards, a perfect handprint of blood added color to the devastation. He backed out of the room, nausea rising like acidic bile in his throat.

"Lizzie," he called, his voice choked. "Where are ye, lass?"

A deep groan rang out in the room.

Fallon's gut twisted and he hollered, "Seth?" Another groan. "Where are ye?"

"Over here, under the sofa," came the muffled reply.

Fallon rushed to where the sofa lay overturned, kicking the broken end table from his path. With one sweep of his arm, he lifted the piece of furniture and tossed it aside. Fallon stretched out his hand and helped Seth to his feet.

He grimaced at the blood coating Seth's face and chest. "Are ye all right?"

"I'm fine." His lips quirked into a humorless grin. "It's all a façade, remember? Besides, what's a little blood, give or take?"

"What the hell happened here?"

"I don't know. One minute, the house was quiet. Then, Liz walked from her room. I never gave it a thought. She wanders around a lot at night, but damn it, Fallon, she walked to the door, opened it, and invited the fucking bastards in." Seth's gaze searched the room before returning to Fallon's face. "Where is she?"

"She isna here. Who did she let in?"

Seth shook his head. "I'm not sure, but I'd swear Deidra Sidhe led the pack. She had Liz under some kind of mind control. I hollered out, but I was too late."

"No' as late as I," Fallon whispered. Fear gnawed a whole in his heart, and a bitter cold despair seeped into the caves of his soul.

Seth clapped Fallon on the shoulder. "We'll find her, Fallon. We will."

Fallon wished he felt as positive as Seth sounded and didn't mention the blood painting the kitchen floor. Aye, they would find her, but would they find her alive?

Seth stood, groaned, and held his head. "Damn, I'm going to kill that cat."

Lizzie's cat sat on the overturned couch, but at Seth's words, she sat up on her hunches. The line of hairs on the back of her neck and along her spine rose. She hissed before disappearing down the hallway.

Seth laughed then grimaced, "Smart cat."

"Aye," Fallon agreed, although his thoughts were with Lizzie, and he cared nothing for the cat or its strange behaviors.

Fallon stood and flipped over the couch for Seth to sit.

"Fallon," Seth whispered.

Fallon caught the undertone of importance in Seth's voice and turned to look at the other man's pale face.

"What is it, Seth?"

"Look," Seth said as he raised a bloodied finger.

Fallon's gaze followed in the direction Seth pointed. He walked over, tossed aside the broken pieces of desk, and pulled a wooden box from beneath the debris.

He carried the box to the couch where Seth sat, not certain why it carried any meaning for his friend.

"Turn it over," Seth whispered.

Fallon flipped the wooden box right side up, and nearly lost his grip at the image painted on top.

Seth cocked his head, brow raised. "What does it mean?"

"I doona know," Fallon whispered.

"It's hand carved, and bears the same design as the Talisman you wear. Its intricacy is amazing. What language do you suppose it's written in?" Seth's finger traced the singed scripture.

"It's ancient Celt. It says...*Lia Fail, the Stone of Destiny, the stone who knows the heart of man.*"

"How did Liz get it?"

Fallon shook his head, overcome with a sudden sense of urgency. "This is a sign. I doona know what it means, but I've got to find her." A stabbing need ripped through his gut.

Barely-controlled power coiled in his body...a mix of fear and determination. Already responsible for one woman's death, he'd be damned if he'd be the cause of another.

Chapter Thirty-Four

"Get moving!" the man growled, giving her a not too gentle shove from behind.

Liz stumbled. Fear and anger knotted inside her. The back of her neck prickled. Her rebellious nature took over, and she shot the man a nasty look.

"Go," he said, with a nod. He stretched up his hand and shoved her again.

Her legs wobbled, but she refused to budge, her gaze sweeping the hallway. Every ten feet, doors were closed, except one on her left, which stood wide open. Situated at the end of the corridor sat a large plate-glassed window that stretched from floor to ceiling, smudged with filth and grime. Light slipped through the cloudiness and emphasized the thick dirt on the floor. She considered making a run for it but didn't know what would greet her on the other side of the glass.

She grimaced. Her eyes shot to the guard. He looked at her with a mocking expression as if he read her thoughts.

Her temper soared. "Keep your hands to yourself," she insisted, with deceptive calm.

Liz shivered as he smiled, a grin with half-rotten, half-missing teeth, yet his two fangs stood out without distinction.

"I've heard gingivitis can lead to bad breath and other health issues. You really should see a dentist," she remarked, before turning away.

He chuckled, the sound malevolent, and pushed her again.

After a few more steps, her escort gripped her arm and pulled her to a jerking halt.

"Stop!"

Liz jerked her arm away and faced him. "Stop! Go! Make up your damn mind, will you?"

"You've got a smart mouth, don't you?" With a jerk of his hand, he pointed to the open doorway. "In there."

She walked forward but hesitated, her hand resting on the doorframe.

"Move your ass."

His hand slammed between her shoulder blades, propelling her into the room. She stumbled from the force and fell, smashing her kneecap on the cement floor. Liz bit her lip to keep from crying out.

Tears stung her eyes as she raised her chin sending a cool stare in his direction.

With a triumphant wink, then a grin, the man closed the door. Jovial laughter followed him down the hall.

"Bastard," she murmured under her breath.

Standing, she straightened her shoulders. She rubbed her palms together to ease the sting of her fall before brushing the dirt from her pants. The dust flared around her face. It entered her nose and irritated her nasal passages.

"Ah—" A sneeze threatened. Using her thumb and forefinger, she pinched the bridge of her nose and rubbed at the offending tickle.

Still holding her nose, she tugged on the doorknob with her other hand.

Locked.

Swirling around, she dropped back against the thick steel door. Her gaze assessed her surroundings...a room approximately ten by ten, dingy white walls with spider webs decorating each of the four corners. She shivered as a chill ran up her spine. She hated spiders. The furniture consisted of an old hospital bed and a laminated nightstand with three drawers. An ancient rusty metal tray table, pre-stainless steel sat on the opposite side of the room beneath a clear block twelve by twelve window.

Window!

She rushed to the windowpane, stood up on tippy toes to peer over the sill. A steep, rocky cliff dropped straight down, and she was assaulted by a dull ache of foreboding. Below, the waters of Lake Michigan splashed against the boulders lining the shore.

She was trapped.

Her attention returned to her prison, and she released a sigh of defeat. She wrinkled her nose at the musty odor that seeped from the air ducts.

Her location was no longer a secret, at least, not to her. She'd known where she was when she woke from her fist-induced unconsciousness. Lying on a cold white tile floor, the area reminded her of her exam room at the morgue. The difference, this place was filthy and definitely lacked the sterility of a traditional medical facility.

Closed a long time ago, The Bradford Institution would be in such a state of disrepair. It was the only logical choice.

White sheets lined the mattress of the bed. After testing the rusty springs, she slumped down and curled her knees to her chest in a fetal position.

What was going to happen to her?

The draw of sleep beckoned to her, and she closed her eyes and dreamed.

The sun bled through the clouds, casting light on the world. Fallon and Liz made their way to the beach below her house. When they reached the sharp boulder pile, Fallon lifted her into his strong arms with ease.

Her eyes were tired. Her muscles ached; their

heaviness weighed her down. She laid her head on his shoulder and closed her eyes, comforted by his nearness.

When he stopped, she lifted her head. They'd traveled half the distance across the rocks. She peeked at Fallon to ask why he'd stopped, but the words stuck in her throat.

His golden eyes darkened, filled with pain. Her heart contracted as she slid one hand up his chest, over his tattoo to his neck, her fingertips trailing along his jaw to his lips. Her hand brushed across his scar where she traced the pale mark.

A startling burst of honesty filled her. She was not immune to Fallon O'Callaghan or his hidden charms. He possessed fire, strength, goodness, and he accepted her for who she was and what she could do. He hadn't laughed at her when she told him she spoke to ghosts.

And she loved him with all of her heart.

He leaned toward her, their faces mere inches apart.

"Fallon," she whispered, against his lips.

He set her on her feet and took a step away. Her hand remained clasped in his.

The skies grew dark. A black cloud shaded the sunlight.

Lightning struck the beach less than ten yards away, illuminating Fallon's face. He jerked his head up as the incoming storm created a luminous lightning show against the backdrop of the night. His hands slipped away from her until only their fingertips touched. Below, the water hit the rocks and splashed around his ankles.

"Fallon?" she began again, but stopped when he held up a hand to still her words.

"I saw it, Lizzie." He turned to face her. "I saw the truth. I'm sorry, but I have to leave." Then he disappeared over the edge.

"Fallon, no!"

Lizzie woke with a start, her heart beating against her breast. "No!" she whispered. Her words bounced off the small expanse of her prison.

Closing her eyes, she murmured aloud, "Fallon, hear me, oh please, hear me!"

A slight pressure, a sound, brushed against her mind.

"Lizzie, where are ye, love?"

For a fraction of a second, relief flooded through her, quickly replaced by terror as she fixed her eyes on the door.

"Where are ye?"

His voice, low and soothing, calmed her fears, and she answered, this time using only her mind. *"The old abandoned Bradford Institution."*

"I'm on my way."

Before she lost her connection, she sent him a calming *"Don't worry"* message and hoped he understood.

****

Fallon opened his eyes to Seth's furrowed brows. A reassuring smile lit up his face as he looked at his friend. "I know where to find her."

Seth released a thankful sigh. "Where?"

"The Bradford Institution." Standing, he cleared his throat. "Call the other Guardians and tell them where I've gone. Let them know that Deidra is holding Lizzie prisoner."

Seth shot to his feet and placed his hand on Fallon's forearm. "You can't think to go rushing in there. You don't know anything about that place. You need to wait for the others."

Fallon glanced down at Seth's arm and weighed it with a critical squint before looking into the other man's eyes. "Seth, let go, or ye will be going with me. I'm no' going to wait for them."

"I know you want to rush in there on your white

horse and save the day, but you can't. They won't hurt Lizzie. She's a pawn to get you there so they can capture the Talisman. Your heart is speaking, not your brain."

Fallon swallowed and drew a deep brisk breath before muttering a curse. Seth spoke the truth.

How paradoxical! His life hinged on sacrifice, even now.

Bitterly amused by the irony of the situation, he clenched his teeth. Long purposeful strides carried him across the room where he pulled Devlin's card from his jacket pocket. With nimble fingers, he punched in the numbers.

The Guardian answered on the first ring. "Aye."

"Dev, it's me."

"Fallon?" Fallon heard surprise in the elder's voice.

"Aye. Look, I've got a situation here. The bitch Vampryss has Lizzie."

Devlin muttered a curse. "Where are ye?"

"Forty-three Bayshore Drive. Tell me where ye are. I'll come get ye."

The air stirred behind him. "I'm already here." Fallon jumped at the sound of Devlin's voice behind him.

"I dinna know ye had the power as well."

"Aye, there's a lot ye doona know about us." Devlin's eyebrows rose, but he quickly changed the subject. "Do ye know where she is?"

Fallon nodded. "Aye, she's being held at the Bradford Institution."

"Let's go! Cameron and Cara are traveling by automobile. They're in Rapid Rivers, so it might be a while before they arrive."

"So, it's just the two of us?"

Devlin inclined his head in a deep gesture, which Fallon took as an affirmation. "Flash in outside the building, Fallon. I doona think it's a good idea to shift inside the walls. I doona know the floor plans so it's best to start on the outside and work our way in."

A quick nod of agreement and Fallon closed his eyes.

From the outside, the Bradford Institution might have presented a large, intimidating place to anyone except him.

The crescent moon provided enough light to discern silhouettes and shapes. That was all he needed. His stealth—marksmanship would do the rest.

He turned to Devlin who appeared at his side. "In case we doona have time later, thanks for yer help."

Devlin nodded. "Come on! Let's go get yer woman."

Inside, their backs against the wall, they made their way down the long hallway. Broken glass cluttered the walkway and crunched beneath their feet.

At the end of the corridor, they entered a room. The shades were drawn, and blackness swallowed the room. Fallon made out a motionless body lying across a bed on the opposite side of the room, pale, white legs stuck out from beneath the sheet. His gaze pierced the darkness, gauging the body's breathing.

There was none.

His heart leapt into his throat and, in two steps, he towered over the body. He lowered a trembling hand, gripped the covers in his fist and whipped it away. It wasn't Lizzie. He let out a harsh breath he hadn't known he held.

Dark crimson splotches of blood stained the mattress. Someone spent a lot of time on him, slicing him, dicing him, and then bleeding him dry. They used a knife with a small blade to make two-inch slices on his arms and legs. Teeth marks marred his chest and stomach. They fed from the cuts for about a week before the man succumbed to death. Fallon shuddered at how much the man must have suffered.

Fallon picked up a torn, beige shirt from the floor. A Sheriff's badge on the pocket caught a moonbeam and glimmered. Fallon read an article in the newspapers just last week about this man. His family had posted a reward for any information about his disappearance.

"It would appear Deidra and her crowd are no' particular in their choice of meal. Everyone has been looking for this man for over a week."

Devlin shook his head. "If a body bleeds, demons feed."

Fallon inspected the room. Black powder burns of a gun blast stained the wall, splattered with bits of fur and gore, a tell tale sign that werewolves were involved in the man's murder. The officer's revolver, broken open, lay on the floor, its barrel and stock matted with bloody fur. It appeared that the man ran out of time to reload and used the revolver as a club to beat at his attacker.

Fallon's eyes searched the darkness at the base of the corner wall. A trail of blood seeped into the cracks where the rotted floorboards split from the wall.

The hair rose along his shoulders and forearms, an electrifying sensation that something powerful and dangerous lurked nearby. A strange fear pricked his chest.

Fallon and Devlin traveled deeper into the building.

"They know we're here," Fallon sneered as he witnessed the shapes of large fur-covered animals backing into the shadows. Werewolves...and they granted them clear passage.

The instant Fallon crossed the threshold of an open doorway an evil energy prickled his mind. His skin crawled, but he refused to yield to the force. He drew on inner strength to fight the power of its malevolence.

At the same time, he glanced at Devlin whose face twisted in his own private agony. His eyes were closed.

Fallon reached out and grasped Devlin's shoulder. He squeezed while he continued to fight the tentacles burrowing in his mind.

After several seconds, Devlin's eyes opened, and he exhaled slowly. He nodded to Fallon and raised his hand, exerting a slight reassuring pressure on Fallon's hand.

An instant later, the energy disappeared, as if it never existed.

"What happened?" Devlin whispered.

"Who was it, is more the question," Fallon replied, and stepped forward. "She's waiting for us."

Fallon and Devlin traveled further into Deidra's living quarters. With every step he took, Fallon reached out to Liz with his heart but received no response.

In the basement, they peered into each room they passed. The first two doors revealed darkened, empty rooms.

Fallon motioned Devlin on, but Devlin grasped Fallon's arm and leaned close to his ear. "Have ye reached her yet?"

When Fallon shook his head, Devlin urged, "Find her and quickly."

Again, Fallon projected his thoughts. This time his head reeled as the thought was not only blocked by an impenetrable black wall but pushed back at him with such tremendous force that electric prickles of fire sprinted across his skin.

Fallon leaned against the wall and gulped in air.

Acid swirled in his stomach. Nausea forced bile into his throat.

He pushed himself away from the wall.

"Lizzie!" he yelled, a single shout that broke the suffocating silence of the hall.

He started forward again with Devlin close on his heels. Fear added speed to his legs. Fallon willed himself to ignore the evil force bearing down on him.

He glanced through two more doors. Empty, he raced past them.

"Lizzie!" Fallon shouted again.

A moment later, he froze at the faraway echo of her voice.

Fallon and Devlin sprinted toward the sound. They turned another corner and reached yet another door where Fallon stared through the small-windowed opening. Lizzie, her eyes closed, stood in the center of the cell motionless, her back stiff.

She wasn't alone.

As though she sensed his presence, her eyes shot open. Frantic thoughts reached out to him. *"No, Fallon, go back. It's a trap!"* Even as her scream faded in his mind, he crashed through the door, his need to get to her overriding all else.

He stopped short. His breath caught in his throat at the bruise visible on her pale face. He gritted his teeth in fury, but at the anguish on her face, he released his breath in a slow puff and sent her a reassuring smile.

Her hands clenched together at her middle, and she twisted them together as though wringing out a wet rag. She shook her head when he took a step forward.

They stood in a room, the size of a small parking lot, but they weren't alone. Goosebumps alerted him to the presence of demons before they slithered from behind concrete pillars and came into view.

Ambush.

An object, bright and shiny, near Lizzie's throat attracted his attention. The feline scent of cat drifted across the space that separated them. The stench familiar, it filled his nostrils.

Dorian!

Now he understood why she stood perfectly still.

Rage engulfed him, and he fought back the urge to leap across the room and destroy the bastard who held the blade to Lizzie's neck.

Chapter Thirty-Five

"Do ye always hide behind women, shape shifter? Why doona ye come out and fight like a man?" One corner of Fallon's lip twisted upright. "Oh, I forgot…cat…ye're a pussy, right?"

Dorian's face appeared over Lizzie's shoulder followed by a maniacal laugh. His eyes locked on Fallon's, and a satanic smile spread across his thin lips as he pressed the knife to Lizzie's neck. She gasped, and a trickle of blood fell beneath the blade.

His anger became a scalding fury that suffocated Fallon. He glowered at the man. "Ye're a dead man." A thin chill hung on the edge of his words.

Dorian laughed, the emotion humorless. He glared at Fallon. "I almost believe you." He pressed the knife to Lizzie's neck and grinned when she whimpered. "But I don't think you'll take chances with her life."

Fallon stepped forward, but Devlin placed his hand on Fallon's shoulder and whispered, "No, Fallon, he will kill her."

Fallon and Devlin tensed as demons slithered from the shadows of the room. Vampires with pale white flesh riddled with bluish veins, longhaired werewolves with two-inch long fangs flaring from large muzzles surrounded them. Their numbers more than tripled the two guardians. The air thickened with the bitter stench of rotting flesh.

The circle opened, and a woman with black hair that hung to her waist, and a lithe, muscular body, stepped forward. Her black eyes narrowed into two dark slits as they fastened on Dorian. She raised one pointed finger to the tip of Dorian's blade and lowered the sharp point. "I need her, you fool."

Dorian's hand dropped, and with a low growl, he skulked into the shadows.

Deidra turned eyes of contempt to Fallon. "It is good to see you, my gallant knight. Have you come to save your precious mate?" She flicked Liz's blonde curls; although her eyes never wavered from Fallon's face.

"Deidra Sidhe. I've been looking for ye," Fallon said with a sneer.

Deidra smiled. Her yellow fangs slid out over her bottom lip.

"As I you. You have been quite elusive, my fine guardian. Now, give me the Talisman." She quirked an eyebrow in question holding her hand out. "You did bring it with you, didn't you?"

"Let her go, and I'll turn it over to ye."

"Hand it over first then we'll talk." She grabbed Liz by the hair, yanking her head backward. Liz cringed but clamped her lips closed.

Fallon's jaw clenched, his gums burned until his fangs erupted from the soft tissue.

Deidra yanked again.

This time, Liz cried out in pain.

Fallon roared with outrage. His body propelled forward by the force of his rage. When a dagger appeared in Deidra's hands, the blade pressed against Lizzie's neck, he hesitated.

"Let her go, bitch, or ye'll rot in hell."

"You are in no position to make demands. Hand over the amulet, or I will slit her throat. Princess or not, I swear I will."

"Princess?"

Deidra's eyebrows rose, an indication of her confusion. "Are you telling me you don't know your woman is the Princess of Light?" She laughed, raising her eyes to the ceiling before she hollered, "And you believe I'm evil. You never told him. Hmm, what is that saying I've heard, oh aye, aye, I have it, that's the black calling the kettle pot?"

Fallon turned accusing eyes to Devlin and whispered, "Do ye know what she's talking about?"

Then Fallon remembered Dagda's word. Lizzie had a light inside her. It was a light Deidra craved.

Bloody hell!

"Who is that behind you? Why does he need to hide from me? Is he afraid to show his face?" Deidra asked, tilting her head to the side trying to peer around Fallon.

Devlin stepped from the shadows. "Hello, Dee. It's been a long time. And for the record, it's the pot calling the kettle black. If ye want to live in this world, get it right, will ye?"

If possible, Deidra's already alabaster complexion turned a paler shade of ashen at the sight of Devlin.

"Devlin? It's not possible. I saw you—"

"But it is, Dee, and all of this stops immediately."

"I'm surprised you are here with this one."

"Why is that?"

"If I recall correctly, the gods have done nothing to gain your favors. I am shaken to see you stand with them after what your mo—"

"I am the first of the Síoraí. I witnessed what ye did to the people of Kale, innocent women and children. When ye destroyed the village, I vowed to stop ye then, as I will now. I wilna let ye hurt her."

"You, of all people, know how stubborn I am. Don't you remember, love?" she said with sarcasm, her eyes flashing. "I'll have Ághmach beside me, where he belongs. Only he truly understands me."

"I canna let that happen."

"You can't stop me."

Fallon's mind reeled with confusion, attempting to understand the exchange between Devlin and Deidra.

"I take it ye know her?" he asked Devlin.

Devlin never took his eyes from Deidra when he said, "Aye. Dee and I go way back, doona we, love?" His voice ended on a note of pure sarcasm.

Her eyes turned red and glowed of molten blood. Over her shoulders, she screeched at her minions, "Kill them, and bring me the amulet."

Devlin drew his sword. The extended blade glinted in the corner of Fallon's eye. He spun around and pulled two retractable swords from the inside of his own jacket. A quick flick of his wrist extended the sharp blades.

The demons attacked, surrounding the two warriors.

A blue-tinged vampire charged. Fallon sidestepped him. When the creature passed, he stuck his foot out, tripping the bloodsucker. The vamp dropped to his knees. As he rose, Fallon brought one of his swords down and severed its head. The demon disintegrated into a pile of grayish dust.

Fallon whirled to face two more as they rushed him. He moved his hand, deflecting the dagger aimed at his heart and kicked up his foot. The glint of a razor blade protruded from the tip of his boot, slicing the vampire's neck even as he tossed one of his swords into the chest of another.

Demon after demon exploded into masses of powder that sifted across the air.

Fallon chanced to glance toward Lizzie. She stood beside Deidra, head down, chewing her bottom lip. As if sensing his eyes on her, she raised her gaze to his. Their eyes met, and his breath caught in his lungs.

Instead of being frightened, a scowl furrowed her brows. Her lips thinned with anger. The smooth skin of her cheeks colored a vibrant red, a glowering mask of rage.

****

Liz's muscles tensed in disbelief and anger at the scene unfolding in front of her. She took a step toward Fallon, but the sharp prick of a sword pressed into her chest, halting her. The stench of decay filled Liz's nostrils, and she winched at the vulgar smell.

"So, do you love him?" Deidra asked in a mild, interested voice.

"Who?" Liz clamped her jaw tight and stared straight ahead.

Deidra snorted in her ear. "That one. The one you bedded."

"His name is Fallon, not *that one*."

The Vampryss grunted.

"Why don't you let them go?" Liz asked, her voice neutral; although anger singed the corners of her control. "You have me. Isn't that all you need?"

"You would beg for their lives?"

She laughed to cover her annoyance. Instead she shook her head. "Beg? I don't have to. They're handling themselves pretty well, don't you think?"

"Only for the moment."

Liz shrugged and chuckled. "You've lost more than half your army, and there are only two of them."

The point of the blade dug deeper into her ribcage. It tore through her clothing, pricked her skin, and she grimaced. Without thought, she brought her palm down on the top of the blade and shoved it away. "Get that thing away from me."

Deidra chortled and stepped to her side, maintaining her grip on the weapon, which she held six inches from Liz's side. Liz turned, eyed the

259

weapon, and then shot the Vampryss a look of annoyance. She was done playing games.

"You know, once, Devlin belonged to me. I gave him my heart, but he loved another." A shadow of pain filled her eyes. "His mother…she turned him against me. She encouraged his marriage to Valeria." Suddenly, Deidra's expression turned to happiness. She grinned and tossed Liz a look of satisfaction. "On the day of his marriage, Åghmach helped me. We made him pay. They all paid for his deception."

Liz jerked in surprise. "Kale…you destroyed the entire village because of Devlin."

Deidra's eyebrow flashed up, and she giggled. "Aye, but then I realized it didn't matter. I didn't love Devlin. Åghmach was my man, and that night, he made me forever his."

"Oh my god." Deidra's words slammed into her like a brick wall, knocking the breath from her. Lizzie swallowed hard. The pictures on the Internet…the dead children and babies, charred bodies, dead animals, burning buildings…everything she'd read about Deidra was true. Damn it all, she had to help. She had to stop this vicious beast. She had no choice but to resist, to fight until the very end, even if it meant her own death. "I'm not going to help you." She sucked in a shallow breath and clutched her hands together in an attempt to still their trembling, while she waited the Vampryss' reply.

"You have no choice."

She inhaled sharply as, in the next instant, Aunt Rea's voice resounded in her ear…in a language she'd never heard before, and yet, she understood every word.

"Elizabeth, fight, you are the Princess of Destiny. Use the power of the light. It is yours to control."

Those ancient words opened the floodgates to

Liz's psyche. The reasoning for her mystical visits of the dead and her physic powers all became apparent. It prepared her for this instant in time, the moment her body would be released from its dormancy.

She knew what she had to do.

Possessed by strength and power, she raised her hands, facing her palms outward.

****

Fallon watched in amazement as Lizzie's body sparkled white diamonds, radiating a potent luminosity in the room. She raised her arms with palms pointed outward, her fingers spread open. Her eyes glazed. Electricity crackled in the air, and the atmosphere thickened with tension.

Words of a foreign language spilled from her lips. Lightning bolts shot from her fingertips. Currents of energy hissed and sizzled around them. One by one, the demons in the room exploded in a bright flash.

"No!" Deidra screamed and hurdled herself at Liz. She wrapped her arms around Lizzie's body, trying to smother the power surging from her body.

Lizzie jerked from Deidra's arms and spun around surrounded by a whitish hue, Deidra embossed in a glittering, blood-red mist.

Liz stood tall, her hands rested on her hips. Her face pinched, concentration furrowed her brow. Her eyes fixed on the Vampryss. The corner of Deidra's lip curved upward into a snarl and revealed her fangs. A growl thundered in the room, and then Deidra raised her hands.

Fallon started forward, but stopped, squinting against the flashes of light that suddenly flared across Lizzie's body. Zigzag bolts of lightning sparked from her body, jetting in all directions around her.

The power inside Lizzie grew, and bolts of electricity pierced her body. His eyes squinted against the bright light.

And then, nothing, just the shadows of the room.

Deidra wrenched back. Her shoulders drooped in exhaustion. Her eyes dull, she stared at Lizzie with an emotion close to admiration.

"You win this time, but it is a war that's not over yet." With those final words, Deidra's body faded, shimmered into a red mist, which rose and disappeared through the cracks in the ceiling.

Once again, the room filled with a total of twenty or less demons that had been waiting outside the door for the light to vanish. Vampires and werewolves surrounded them.

Fallon rose to his feet, ready to fight.

"Yer leader has deserted ye. Why do ye continue to fight?" Devlin asked in a breathless voice.

"Because they wish to die," Fallon answered for them.

A click of teeth snapped behind him, and instinctively, Fallon stepped sideways. He swept his foot out as the werewolf passed, tripping the six-foot black furry mass into the wall. Fallon dropped into a defensive crouch as adrenaline pumped through his veins. His hand gripped a rusted metal pipe from the floor. As the animal charged, he lifted the conduit. The werewolf landed on the corroded tip. Fallon gave it a sharp twist embedding it deeper into its heart. The creature howled before it dropped dead at his feet.

The remaining werewolves, witnessing this demise, glanced at each other. Their ears flapped back, and they shook their long snouts. They turned on their heels and left, apparently deciding this was not their battle to die for.

For ten minutes, Fallon and Devlin vanquished vampire after vampire. The room filled with gray powered dust.

When it settled, the two men shared a half-hearted grin.

"I knew ye were guardian material." Devlin grinned.

Fallon didn't comment. Instead, he turned to Lizzie and opened his arms wide. "Come here, love."

Lizzie flew into his arms. He leaned back to drink in her face. His hand caressed the bruise on her cheek. "Are ye ok?"

Her arms tightened, and she smiled. "Now that you're here, I'm fine."

"How touching."

Dorian's voice ricocheted and bounced off the walls.

Fallon released Lizzie pushing her behind him. He growled deep in his throat. "Ye're mine, bastard."

As Fallon stepped forward, Dorian swerved to the right and shot his dagger toward Fallon who threw out his hand to deflect its path. Just as he would have wrapped his hand around the handle, a rat scampered out from behind a pillar near the doorway, startling him.

As the rodent rushed Fallon, its small body extended a full six inches and grew in length the closer it got. Its long muzzle flattened and shrunk to a smaller version. Prickly black fur disappeared, replaced by human flesh. By the time it reached Fallon, the rat had turned into a man with brownish red hair.

Devlin reacted first, tossing his dagger deep into the shifter's heart sending the man to his knees at Fallon's feet. Fallon gripped the man's neck and twisted in until the bones broke. He tossed him to the ground and turned.

Fallon couldn't breathe for a full heartbeat as he saw the dagger protruding from Lizzie's chest.

No! Fallon's mind screamed in denial.

It couldn't be…

"You should have backed off," Dorian said,

between clenched teeth. "But that's all right. The best way to kill someone is to always aim for their heart. She dies because of you."

The demon smiled, withdrew another dagger from the sleeve of a black, leather coat that hung to his knees. The dagger zinged through the air toward Fallon's heart.

Fallon's powers surged, eyes narrowed in hatred. He caught the dagger in his fingers and sent it back in the direction from which it came. Dorian never had time to react before the blade embedded itself deep in his chest. The half vampire, half shape shifter collapsed and dropped to his knees. Instead of disintegrating into a pile of dust, Dorian's body burst into a puff of flames before it evaporated.

Fallon spun around, the center of his attention now focused on the slight woman who'd fallen to the floor, writhing in pain.

He rushed to her side, dropped to his knees and drew her across his lap into his arms.

His entire being screamed out in pain.

"Come on, love," he whispered, gently rocking her in his arms. "Doona die on me."

Fallon peered up as an outline overshadowed them. Devlin stood there, and he read the sympathy in the elder's eyes even before he said, "I'm so sorry, Fallon."

Fallon shook his head. Nothing mattered except the woman who lay in his arms. She choked, struggling to breath. Her eyes opened, and she reached up and touched his cheek with a cold hand.

"I never knew what love was until I met you, Fallon." She coughed. Blood trickled from the corner of her mouth. "I love you," she whispered. Her gaze traveled over his handsome face as if struggling to memorize every inch.

Her breathing grew shallow, each breath a conscious effort. The warm stickiness of her blood coated his hands and slipped through his fingers to cover the cold, hard floor with dark crimson.

Tears fell down his cheeks, and he shook his head and begged, "Doona leave me, Lizzie."

He grabbed her hand and pressed her palm to his lips.

Then he felt it, that last expulsion of breath from her body. She went limp in his arms. Her hand dropped away from his face.

"No!" his tortured bellow echoed in the room. Cradling her head, Fallon rocked back and forth. Grief and despair tore at his heart, and compulsive sobs shook his body. Tears spilled down his face.

Fallon threw his head back and cried out as the pain of loss tore through him. He'd lost the one woman who had shown him how to live again. She'd released his tortured heart, reached inside, and jumpstarted it for the first time in five hundred years.

Now she was gone.

No! His heart screamed in denial.

She had believed in him, and he let her die.

How could she be dead?

How could he have allowed this to happen?

Fallon finally understood sacrifice.

Chapter Thirty-Six

Her spirit slipped from her body. Peace warmed her like the golden sun, and she never wanted to go back. She floated upward, elevated far above the ground.

Below her, Fallon's shoulders shook with grief over her motionless body.

Sadness over what might have been filled her.

Hovering higher, she left the building and whirled into the air. Fallon disappeared from sight, and she turned her attention to the panorama around her, the air filled by mystical presences.

Suspended in the heavens, they drifted through the night, unhurried and content, just like her.

The moon cast white light upon beams that illuminated the darkened backdrop. Four or five stars orbited around them, moving in slow motion as if guiding them to their destination.

Below, a river rushed through a mirage of bright lights. The dark water glowed with inner luminosity.

The temperature of the air dropped five degrees as she moved toward a cluster of fluffy white clouds. A cool mist vapor touched her cheeks, and she released a sigh of pleasure.

Exiting the other side, she came to a stop. For a moment, her gaze studied her surroundings until the haze separated.

Three figures stepped toward her, their faces indistinguishable. The closer they came, the brighter the light surrounding them grew.

A woman with long raven hair stepped into

view. High, exotic cheekbones accentuated green eyes of polished jade set in a delicate face. Two men, one with curling black hair, the other light brown, flanked her on each side. All of them wore silken white robes tied at their waists by a braided golden cord.

The woman smiled and stretched out her hand. Liz put her hand in hers. "I am Danu." With a slight tilt of her head, she indicated the two men beside her. "And this is Dagda and Lugh."

"Gods of the Tuatha Dé Danann?"

"Aye."

"Then I am in heaven?"

"In our heaven, child, known as the Otherworld, but here you cannot stay."

"But it's so peaceful here. Why can't I stay?"

"One day you will join us, but not this day. Your place is beside your mate."

"Fallon?"

"Aye, the Rebel Guardian. Fallon O'Callaghan is your soul mate, your life mate, and you are his life. You were born to be together."

"I don't understand."

"He has suffered. His pain so great he has shunned us."

"Can you blame him?"

Danu smiled with soft eyes. "We do not blame our guardians for their actions. As gods, it is often difficult to appreciate human emotions. We wish to ease their pain if they allow. Fallon feels he deserves the pain and has chosen to live with it."

"No one deserves that kind of pain."

"Fallon's pain is self-inflicted. He believes he is responsible for Rhiannon's death."

"Why did Rhiannon and their child have to die?"

"Fate. Her destiny was decided long before her birth. Rhiannon's death severed Fallon's link to humanity."

"What about his uncle?"

"There were no emotional ties to his uncle. Fallon despised him. They shared no bond. At least, none that would impair Fallon's emotions."

"Why would you allow a child to be conceived if this was meant to happen?"

"Call it a failsafe. Fallon's internal fire is strong. His defiance was foreseen. It was also destined that you would become a part of his life, his mate. He has yet to accept what he is, but we believe that will come in time. You will be the one who gives him the strength to accept who he is."

"Why me?"

"You were born to become the savior of a great man, a guardian, and the protector of mankind." That voice...Liz recognized that voice.

"Aunt Rea?" Liz's eyes locked onto the clouds behind the gods.

Her mouth dropped open.

Aunt Rea floated from the mist toward her.

"Yes, my darling, it is I."

Liz ran into her aunt's outstretched arms, tears of joy spilling down her cheeks. "But how can you be here? How is this possible?"

Her aunt offered a gentle smile. "Anything is possible if you believe."

"Your aunt has been with us for a long time, my dear. She is the Goddess Branwen," Danu announced, stepping forward.

Liz gasped. "Goddess?"

Danu nodded. "Aye, your aunt is the true goddess of love and beauty. Both of those traits have been passed onto you. It was time for her to come home to us, just as the time came for you to receive your gifts."

"Gifts?"

Aunt Rea's arms tightened around her. "I know there were times you didn't understand nor want them, but aye, child, they are gifts."

"Her gifts were passed to you, yet she retained a strong bond with them. It has been this connection that allowed us to keep a protective hand on you," Danu reinforced.

Liz turned in her aunt's arms and grinned at the goddess. "Protective, huh? Then why am I dead?"

Danu grimaced. "An unfortunate necessity, I'm afraid."

"Necessity?"

"I always said you were destined for greater things, Liz. This is your time to shine through the darkness."

"I still don't understand what's happening, Aunt Rea. Why me? Why now?"

"You are the keeper of the light. A princess. While the guardians are chosen for their passions, their fires, and even their brawn, you were chosen for the flame of destiny you carry inside you. For you to receive the absolute power you've been destined for, you must die and be reborn into your new role as the Princess of Light."

"Wow, and I thought a trade-off meant giving up a candy bar for a rice cake."

"You will become immortal and live forever."

"And you knew this about me, and them, before we were born?" Liz couldn't hide the astonishment in her voice.

Danu laughed. "We did."

"I still don't understand why you've chosen me."

"Because of who you are."

Hopeful, Liz's gaze darted around the golden plateau, searching. "What of my parents? Are they here?"

Rea shook her head in apparent sadness. "No, Liz. They're not here. They are in their own special place."

Tears filled Liz's eyes as she thought of the two

people who, even after their death, remained spiritually close in her heart. "Are they happy?"

"Aye, they are very happy, and they will be together throughout eternity."

Chapter Thirty-Seven

He took deep breaths until he was strong enough to raise his head. His throat ached.

With fingers light against her face, he smoothed her hair from her brow, her skin still warm against his hand.

How could she be dead?

He closed his eyes, pain piercing his soul.

Lizzie's death was his fault. It happened again. Just like Rhiannon.

Seconds passed. Flashes of every precious moment he spent with her replayed in his mind and stabbed at his heart.

The darkness behind his eyelids brightened, and he shifted, with no control over the destination. When he opened his eyes, a dazzling, celestial chamber surrounded him, and he stood on a golden plateau.

With Devlin beside him, a smile lit up the elder's face.

Fallon looked around. Whispering trees and swaying blades of grass surrounded them. Above him, silver clouds floated in a lavender sky.

He took a step forward. "Are we dead?"

"Nay, we're very much alive."

He thought about Lizzie, picturing her long, blonde hair blowing behind her.

And then, she stood before him. Not in solid form, but a mist of her former self. Her eyes, luminescent and warm, emphasized the alabaster confines of her face.

She gave him a smile full of love.

"Lizzie, lass? Is that ye?" He sent the question outward, using his mind to search the truth, to search for her.

Something gentle brushed warm against his cheeks. A soft caress. He knew that touch. Within it, he felt love…Lizzie's love.

"Yes, Fallon, I'm here."

The skies darkened, and the moon appeared from behind a cloud. The wind whipped up.

A shiver slithered up his spine.

He gazed at Lizzie. She bore no fear in her eyes, and a smile remained fixed on her lips.

Numb, Fallon stared down at the scene he'd left moments ago. Her pale, deathly still body lay against the cold concrete. A chill pricked his skin at the blood spilling the life from her. Pain stabbed his heart, and his stomach knotted.

Reality struck like a blow to his gut, and he hurtled back to the present.

Lizzie, his Lizzie, dead, yet she stood before him? How is that possible?

He lifted his eyes in confusion. "How?"

She shrugged. "I'm still learning a bit about that, but as soon as I understand the gist of it, I'll be sure to let you in on the secret."

"A ghost? Are ye a ghost then, lassie?"

"She's a princess, Fallon." The voice echoed from the mist behind Lizzie, and a surge of anger flared from him as Danu came into view.

"Ye're the one responsible for her death."

"It was her destiny."

"Her destiny should include a long life, a family and babies." Tears filled Fallon's eyes as he thought of everything she had lost. "I canna place all the blame on ye. I'm just as guilty for taking that away from her."

"Fallon, no one has taken anything from me."

"Look at ye, lass." His eyebrow rose, and he waved his hand before her. "Ye have no body." His voice broke, fighting back the rush of emotions.

Danu laughed. "Her body will be restored, my Rebel Guardian."

"I'm no' yer anything. What of her life?"

"That will be returned as well."

Uncertainly gripped him while he waited for the catch. He rubbed the back of his neck, all the while keeping his eyes fixed on the goddess. "What will it cost her?"

"She is the Princess of Light, Fallon."

Fallon's knees buckled when Seth stepped from the mist. Overcome with an anger so overpowering, he shook with it. "Seth, doona tell me ye're a part of this fiasco?" Without giving Seth time to answers, Fallon continued on in outrage. "I trusted ye. How could ye, of all of them, betray me like this?"

Seth grimaced. "You don't understand what's happening here. I am your friend. I have always been your friend, but I have also been your protector. It was my place to protect you and make sure you found your way to Liz. She is where your destiny lies. Together, you will spend eternity together protecting those who cannot protect themselves."

"So, she will always be in danger, and I am forced to live with the fear that those bastards will find her."

Seth smiled. "Eternity, Fallon. Your Lizzie will live as an immortal beside you. Those babies are your future. There will always be danger, but she will now become just as difficult to kill as you, probably even more so. You will protect each other."

"Eternity? Are ye serious? And what of Deidra?"

From out of the mist, Camalus strode into the circle of gods, goddesses and guardians.

"Deidra Sidhe has secured a place on the earthly plane for a short while which makes your jobs more difficult. There will be more innocent people to protect and a more vigilant watch to be taken. You must accept your true destiny, son, and become the guardian we have always known you could be."

"It will never end. How can ye expect any of us to live happily ever after? To raise children in a world full of chaos and violence?"

Camalus smiled. "You cannot live your life in fear. Deidra Sidhe's time is short. A little patience is all that is needed. The pieces are not in place to send her back to where she belongs, but that too, will come to pass. Trust in that knowledge."

Danu walked to stand beside Liz who watched Fallon.

Inside him, his disbelief changed to anger, then shock until partial acceptance swept over him.

"It is time." Danu murmured. With a brief wave of her hand, Liz's body was returned to her.

He glanced into her eyes. "I'm sorry, lass. I never would have—I dinna want this for ye."

Liz covered his mouth with the tip of her index finger, shushing his words. "When will you understand, Fallon, this isn't about you. It isn't even about me."

"But—"

She shook her head. "No buts. It is time to let go of the past and look toward the future."

"I doona know if I can."

"To accept the past is to accept me."

She leaned up and pressed her lips against his in a soft, gentle kiss. He closed his eyes.

After a moment, he cleared his throat, and stepped away.

When he opened his eyes, they were standing in her living room.

****

A fire beckoned to Liz, a deep, powerful heat that vibrated through her body. She wrapped the bathrobe around her, left her room and padded into the living room.

She paused and tried to focus in the darkness.

Panic shot through her; then Fallon's form became clear. She pressed a hand to her chest and let out a relieved breath.

When they'd returned from the Otherworld, he insisted that he needed time to digest the information he received. To do that, he needed space.

He must have sensed her standing above him for he sat up and asked, "Is everything all right?"

Liz held out her hand.

"No."

He placed his hand into hers and stood. "What's the matter?"

"I'm cold, Fallon."

"Lizzie?"

"I need you. I'm cold. Warm me."

The heat flickered in his eyes. "Ye doona know what ye ask."

"I do. Make love to me, Fallon. Please."

His eyes widened and he murmured, "Lass, I doona think—"

She buried her hands in his thick hair and pulled his head toward her. He took a deep, shuddering breath and returned her kiss. With a soft groan, he lifted her in his arms and carried her to the bedroom.

He stopped when they reached the foot of her bed where he released her legs. Her body slid down the length of his, and she stood before him.

Cradling her face between his hands, he kissed her mouth, like the dusting of a feather. Then his lips brushed across her throat and collarbone where he nibbled, leaving a damp trail of ecstasy.

"Ye smell so good, Lizzie, and ye taste so delicious. Yer skin is as soft as silk." His mouth melded into the cleavage at the V of her robe. He straightened, looked into her eyes, and reached for the sash that tied her robe about her waist.

He slipped his hands inside her robe and moving them across her chest, shoulders and down her arms, peeled the garment from her body. She pulled her arms from the sleeves and waited for him to settle his hands on her and ease her nightgown off. Placing one hand on his shoulders, she stepped out of it.

Fallon's breath hissed through his teeth. "Ye're beautiful, lass."

He took a step away. The heat drained from her. She shivered. Without taking his eyes off her, he shed his own clothing. Moonlight filtered through the window, highlighting the sheer male beauty of his face. Her breath caught at the shimmer of his masculine body, his broad shoulders and hard chest.

He slid his hand to the gentle swell of her hip and then to the lace of her panties, tapered to a fetching V, bordering her thighs. He slipped his fingers into the waistband and tugged them down.

His hands trembled. He kissed her again, hard and quick then pulled away. She gripped his shoulders and whispered, "Make love to me, Fallon. Love me."

The warm glint in his eyes made her shiver. His thumb swept across her lower lip. "Lizzie." His voice was a rough whisper.

He left a chain of scalding kisses across her throat and chest. As she watched, spellbound by the magic powers of his lips, he pressed his mouth against the tip of her breast and suckled the pointed tip into its warm depths.

With a shuddering cry, she fell back. His caresses went on and on, and with each flexing of his lips, desire coiled in her belly like a tight spring.

"Lizzie," he whispered raggedly in her ear. "My darlin' love."

She fought to breathe. Fallon plunged inside her, filling her. Her legs took their cue from him and fluttered in rhythm.

A delicious frisson of pleasure crept up the skin of her inner thighs, belly, and breasts, responding to his lovemaking.

He thrust with long, luxurious, pounding strokes. A milky stream rolled inside her. She searched for his mouth, found only his shoulder, and bit, with renewed pleasure and total selfishness and no concern whatsoever of his pain.

"Fallon!" she gasped his name. Every nerve in her body clambered for release. She lifted her knees to take him deeper. The tension built within her until wave after wave of intense pleasure poured over her and jolted every nerve.

A shudder seized him and his body stiffened. He buried his face in the crook of her neck, slow to recover. "By the gods," he whispered.

He rolled to the side, pulling her against him. The minutes ticked away, and she fell asleep wrapped in his arms.

****

Fallon kissed Lizzie's forehead, inching away from her. He settled her against her pillow and tucked the comforter across her shoulders. Assured she remained asleep, he slid to the edge of the bed, where he stood, turned and stared at her.

Exquisite, inside and out, Lizzie continued to amaze him.

He'd come so close to losing her, the memory a sick and fiery gnawing that stabbed his insides. A suffocating sensation tightened his throat.

Fallon slipped from the room. In the living area, he settled down on the couch, his hands rested behind his head. He chuckled at his feet dangling over the end of the short couch.

His eyes toured the room, which appeared as if

nothing happened. Lizzie's furniture mended, everything stood where it belonged, thanks to the gods' magic touch. The ancient box had been placed back in hiding behind Lizzie's computer desk.

Aunt Rea told her the box held the power of the centuries, and only Lizzie possessed the knowledge and patience needed to release it when the time came.

Fallon planned to search for Jack Stannard tomorrow evening, but instinct warned him the man wouldn't be found. Fallon suspected good ole Jack followed Deidra wherever she'd gone, but he would meet up with the coroner again.

Next time, he wouldn't be the body in the bag.

Seth remained behind in the Otherworld concluding their friendship in this world. Fallon would miss the man, but things between them were different, changed. Seth's betrayal hit Fallon hard. It would take time, but Fallon wouldn't forget the friendship they shared.

Meow.

Fallon shot upward as Lizzie's cat jumped on the couch and mewed in his ear.

"Damn cat." He chuckled, reached for the shorthaired black and white cat and settled the animal across his chest. The feline reminded him of a woman; therefore he'd dubbed her Ms. Kitty. For some reason, Fallon found himself attached to the soft, furry bag of bones. He petted her ears, drawing a soothing purr from her throat.

Without warning, Ms. Kitty jumped from his lap and pranced across the floor. She spun in circles several times as if dancing for him.

Fallon sat up. "What's the matter with ye, cat?"

And then, she stood on her hind legs. Her paws flailed at the air. He shook his head and blinked. By the time he opened his eyes, the cat had grown six inches in size.

A moment of panic seized Fallon. He gripped his thigh and cursed, "Bloody hell."

His eyes shot to the mantel where his sword sat, out of reach. He wore only jeans and had no way to defend himself against a shape shifter. His eyes shifted to Lizzie's bedroom door, thankful it remained closed. He turned back to the cat, now the size of a small child. Her fur sucked into flesh, human flesh, and the shape of a woman took form.

With the transformation complete, she turned to face him.

He jumped to his feet and froze in stunned surprise. The heat drained from his face, and he nearly choked on his whispered, "Rhiannon?"

A smile of enchantment touched her face, and she nodded. "Hello, my love."

Chapter Thirty-Eight

He stared at the face he'd committed to memory a lifetime ago. In all this time, she hadn't changed, still as lovely as ever.

Thick black hair hung in long graceful curves over her shoulders. The loose tendrils framed a quiet, oval face. The delicacy and strength he fell in love with radiated over her features.

The corners of her mouth turned upward into a smile. She walked, her steps slow and graceful, to stand in front of him. "Fallon, it is good to see you again."

"Rhiannon? Is it really ye?"

She smiled. "It's me, dearest."

Fallon stood still as shock raced through him. "How is it that ye are here?"

Rhiannon held out her hand to him. Without hesitation, he slipped his hand into hers, lacing his fingers through hers, and pulled her into his arms. He closed his eyes and lost himself in her smell...the brisk floral scent of roses.

Oh god, so long ago.

She pulled away. "Come. It is time for us to talk."

He opened his eyes, and Rhiannon tugged him toward the veranda doors. He hesitated and shook his head, his eyes moving to Lizzie's bedroom door. "Nay, Rhiannon, I canna go. I canna leave Lizzie unprotected."

Rhiannon smiled in understanding. "We will not be gone long. I ask for a short walk on the beach.

She will be fine."

With a glance toward Lizzie's bedroom door again, he nodded.

Together, he and Rhiannon stepped onto the beach, nearing the water. When they stopped, he released her hand and turned to face her. He stared, his heart pounding.

"Rhiannon," he said, wonder in his voice.

"It's me, Fallon. You're not crazy."

"No? Why doona I feel as confident as ye sound?"

"I'm here to release you."

"Release me?"

"Aye. For so long, you have refused to let go of a past that was meant to occur. You blame yourself for what happened to me, but it wasn't your fault."

Fallon ran a frustrated hand through his hair. "Why does everyone keep insisting I had nothing to do with it? I was a coward. If I stood up to my uncle when I became an adult, none of this would have happened."

"Shhh! You were no coward. You tried to protect me the only way you knew how. I never doubted your love. I never doubted you. I always knew you would come for me."

"But I was too late."

"You weren't. Everything occurred as it should have."

"It dinna have to be like that, Rhiannon."

"Why are you so stubborn?" She folded her arms across her chest, her brows drawn. "You cannot change the past."

"What of our child?"

Rhiannon smiled gently. "Our child is hale and hearty with me. His name is Kreigh. He has your face and your eyes."

"I was never given the chance to see him grow. What they did wasna fair. The gods took ye and my child from me."

"They gave you reason to fight."

"You were both pawns to get me to do what they wanted."

"You and I were never meant to be."

Fallon shook his head. "We were never given the chance to find out if we could make a life together."

"If you want to blame anyone, blame me, Fallon, for I refused to let you go. In order for the gods to satisfy me, they gave me Kreigh, my ultimate link to you, a gift to make it easier for me to let you go. The gods marked you as a Síoraí. I couldn't interfere with that. I knew what a great warrior you would be."

"I could have done both."

She shook her head. "No, you couldn't. You have refused Lizzie's love because of the danger in your life. You would have done the same with me, especially knowing I carried your child."

She was right, and he knew it.

She continued. "Fallon, you bear the mark of the moon. That makes you a very powerful man. You also bear another mark. My grandmother told you that you were twice marked."

"How do ye know that?"

"I've been allowed to watch. I have seen the paths you have walked, paths that kept you alone."

"My choice to make."

She shook her head and smiled. "A choice you were allowed to make."

"No one controls me."

Rhiannon laughed. "No one has power over their own destinies, Fallon. Not even you. Do you know what the other mark you bear stands for?"

He tilted his brow, looking at her uncertainly.

"Inside that mark lies the face of a woman."

"I've always believed it was yer face I carried."

Her mouth curved with tenderness. "It is the face of Elizabeth Forrester. As I said before, we were meant to be together only for that brief time. Without the loss of our love, you would never have been able to move forward in your predetermined destiny."

"I never wanted anything but ye."

"And now?"

"What?"

"What do you want, Fallon O'Callaghan?"

Fallon thought of the woman standing before him and then of the woman sleeping in the house not thirty feet away. His sweet Lizzie who had the patience of a saint, the determination of a bull, and most importantly of all, she was the keeper of his heart. When he had given up on life, she pulled him from his shell and made him feel things he never thought he'd experience again.

When he turned his attention to Rhiannon, an understanding smile spread wide on her lovely face, and in that next moment, without doubt, he knew what he wanted.

He wanted Lizzie, forever and always by his side. He wanted to build a new life for them, and yes, he wanted children with her, whatever the future brought. The gods gave her to him, and as Seth said, it was time for him to make the right choices.

"Tell our son I would have wanted him." He choked on the words.

"He already knows." Rhiannon caressed his cheek. "Live, love, and be happy. That is all I ever wanted for you."

"I'm sorry," Fallon whispered.

Rhiannon giggled and held a hand against her breast. "For what? For living? Kreigh and I have created a new life, a new home for ourselves in the spiritual world. The gods have granted us solace against pain. We're happy, truly we are. What would make me happier is for you to let go of the past."

Fallon glanced toward the house and smiled, feeling a sense of genuine happiness for the first time in centuries.

"Thank you."

"There is no need to thank me. Now go and tell that woman you love her."

Rhiannon's final words, "Be happy," echoed as she faded into a shimmering white mist and floated toward the moon.

"I'll never forget ye," Fallon whispered. His eyes followed her essence until it disappeared.

For the first time in his long life, a great burden lifted from his shoulders.

Morfesa's words from so long ago echoed in his thoughts.

With your mind…see.

Lizzie's inner beauty released him from his prison. Blood coursed through his veins like an awakened river.

With your ears…hear.

Lizzie's breath, her every word, her dreams whispered across his heart. His heartbeat, vibrant and full of life, throbbed in his ears.

With your heart…feel.

Lizzie's heart beat in tune to his. Her love encircled him, enveloping him in her warmth.

He couldn't deny the truth any longer, nor did he want to. He loved her with all of his heart and soul. With her in his life, he'd never be empty again. A warm glow flowed through him, his heart sang, and he exhaled a long sigh of contentment.

Seek forgiveness, for only then will you find release from your pain.

Rhiannon granted him that final gift.

He lifted his head to the heavens and nodded, finally accepting the destiny granted to him so long ago.

The stars twinkled in acknowledgement.

"Fallon."

He turned. Lizzie stood on the deck, her bathrobe wrapped around her slender frame. Her arms clutched the fabric to her waist.

She offered him a small, shy smile, her fingers knotted and twisted at her waist, belying her calm façade.

His mouth curved into a welcoming smile. "Hi."

"Are you all right?"

He stared at her and chuckled. "I'm fine. Ye might say I've been cleansing my soul."

"Cleansing your soul?"

He strolled up the steps onto the veranda, his eyes never leaving her face. When he reached her side, he pulled her into his arms and pressed a kiss to her forehead.

Into her hair, he whispered, "I've been freeing myself for ye, letting go of the past."

Lizzie leaned back and peered into his eyes. "And are you free?"

He grinned. "It wasna easy." When she would have spoken, he gripped her hands in his and shook his head. "Lizzie, I know I've been a bastard. I canna excuse my behavior, and as much as I want to, I canna change it. There's something ye need to know. I love ye. I want to spend the rest of my life with ye, and only ye."

Moisture sparkled in her eyes, and she reached up to caress his cheek. "It's about time you came around. I was afraid I'd have to take my frying pan to you."

"Will ye marry me?"

She gulped hard. Tears rolled down her cheeks. She stared into his face, and promised, "Yes, Fallon, I will marry you, my gallant knight. I love you with all my heart and soul...forever."

Standing on tiptoe, she touched her lips to his, lingering. He moved his mouth over hers, devouring her softness. His tongue traced the fullness of her mouth. They held each other, and both of their worlds flooded with light.

But what would happen when the time came to live up to the Síoraí crusade, to lay his, and perhaps her life, on the line against evil again?

Fallon vowed to be there. Wherever Deidra was, he would be ready for her the next time she came around. When she tried to kill Lizzie, the situation became personal, deadly serious, and that bitch out there had made an enemy.

But that was tomorrow.

Today, it was time to live and lay his echoes of darkness to rest.

No longer would he live in the shadows of his past, for Lizzie's love gave him light to see the future. Theirs was a love that would burn bright for all eternity and beyond.

With their arms wrapped around each other, they strolled toward the door. Before they entered the house, Fallon turned and looked across the beach as another thought struck.

"What's the matter?" Lizzie asked. Concern etched her face.

He gazed down into her eyes. "I think yer cat ran away. I'm no' certain if she will return."

Lizzie frowned, puzzled. "Ummm, Fallon."

"Aye?"

"I don't have a cat."

"Of course no'." He threw back his head and burst out laughing. His arms tightened around her and with sincerity, he started, "Lizzie—"

"Shh." Lizzie placed a finger over his lips. "Just tell me you love me. That's all I ever need to hear."

His eyes darkened. He covered her hand with his, sucked her forefinger into the warmth of his mouth, sliding his tongue around her fingertip before he released it.

Sighing, she reached up and drew his head down to her. A soft and loving curve touched her lips, and her eyes sparkled with a sensuous flame.

"Better yet...show me," she whispered, before she kissed him, long and deep, passionate.

Without breaking their kiss, he swept her into his arms. She squealed in stunned surprise and leaned back.

"I love ye, lass, and it will be my pleasure to show ye how much...over and over again."

And he did, true to the Síoraí way, eternally.

A word about the author...

Victoria Noxon is a hopeless romantic. Her passion for reading began at an early age so it seemed quite natural when this obsession transformed into a love for writing. She writes contemporary, historical and dark paranormal stories about strong, sexy heroes and the beautiful, intelligent heroines who rule their hearts during the day and their bodies at night.

A mother of four, she resides with her husband of twenty-five years in Upstate New York where the number of cows far outweighs the number of high-rises. When she's not reading or writing, she works full-time at a local area hospital.

For more information, please visit her website at:
www.victorianoxon.com